PRAISE FOR *Woman of Light*

"*Woman of Light* is a Western novel—it cares deeply about the land-scape. The terrain of the Lost Territory teems with life, even as settling pioneers call it empty. The cold mountains and expansive plains of Colorado serve as stand-ins for the harsh realities Luz endures. No land can be truly conquered. No people can be truly conquered either. Not as long as their stories, and their memories, endure."

—*The Boston Globe*

"Absolutely engrossing."

—*Shondaland*

"A lush, gorgeously realized work of historical fiction, a thrilling and intimate family saga, and a powerful indictment of white violence that deformed the American West."

—*Lit Hub*

"A novel with vast reach."

—*Electric Lit*

"Magnificently imagined . . . a testament to the power of story."

—*The Rumpus*

"An intricate, magical read that carefully balances hope with the sad-ness and rage of living in a time and place where racism happens in a thousand ways every day."

—*BuzzFeed*

"Impressive . . . It's clear [Kali Fajardo-Anstine] has talent to spare."

—*Publishers Weekly*

"Sensory-rich details . . . a lush, immersive historical novel."

"Following her gorgeous story collection . . . Kali Fajardo-Anstine's first novel opens with a scene of fairy-tale resonance: An abandoned infant of unknown parentage is taken in and raised by a village elder. From that moment on, *Woman of Light* retains a mythic quality while following the stories of five generations of an Indigenous North American family, from their origins, border crossings, accomplishments and traumas to their descendants' confrontation and acceptance of their family history."

"Fajardo-Anstine's first novel reaches back into the late 1800s to render an extraordinary, many-threaded tapestry of multiple lives and complex origin stories. . . . Combining extensive research with a propulsive narrative that spans decades, Fajardo-Anstine delivers a historical novel that never feels like a history lesson. She does so in in prose often joyous and warm but unsparing in its depiction of oppression based on race, gender and class. Mysterious and vivid, *Woman of Light* is an extraordinary painting of a vibrant world both old and new."

"[*Woman of Light* is] impossible to put down. Fajardo-Anstine's compelling writing paints a convincing portrait of a city in flux, haunted by white violence, and portrays a complex female friendship, a vivid love story (or three), and a story of family and memory in the American West."

"[Fajardo-Anstine] is taking a big gulp and shouting herself far and wide with *Woman of Light*."

"Generational grief and love as well as a strong sense of place are the backbones of Kali Fajardo-Anstine's novel, *Woman of Light*. . . . This is a searing look at the racist history of the West, Denver in particular, a past that is often elided."

—*Napa Valley Register*

"Transporting . . . luminescent."

—*Good Housekeeping*

"Real history is what makes the cast of characters in the book impossible to forget. . . . *Woman of Light* is not merely a novel set in the Southwest. It centers the communities that Colorado and other western states like it have long attempted to erase and ignore. That Fajardo-Anstine writes Western literature is undeniable. She completely shatters the expectations that have been set around the genre—namely that it be white and male, often dehumanizing to Indigenous people, and featuring reductive portrayals of the land and animals of the Southwest. . . . At its core, *Woman of Light* is, in many ways, a gift to Fajardo-Anstine's family. A mirror, pages of immortality that will live on because their stories have been written."

—*Sweet July*

"Luminous and hopeful."

—Fredricksburg *Free Lance-Star*

"Effortlessly stunning . . . This book is about Luz and Diego and Denver and the Lost Territory; ultimately, though, it is about stories—who gets to tell them and which ones survive. . . . *Woman of Light* proves the past is the prologue, insisting we map the Lost Territory onto our stories even when search engines don't recognize the term. It is a sprawling and gorgeous exploration of the land we have come from, the past we have failed to acknowledge and the persistence of stories through time and space."

—*Chapter 16*

"An unparalleled generational saga [from] one of the most potent voices in contemporary Latino and Native American literature."

—*BeLatina*

"A classic legendary Latinx story and a punch that says she can square up with any contemporary writer. Quite literally—Fajardo-Anstine can do both, she can do it all."

—Lupita Reads

"A rich and ambitious book that reminds us of the importance of preserving our family histories."

—ROXANE GAY

"*Woman of Light*, Kali Fajardo-Anstine's dazzling debut novel, is a direct embodiment of . . . tradition and a gift to every reader enthralled by a good family saga. . . . Fajardo-Anstine is quickly establishing herself as one of our modern masters. Her sentences sing and her grasp of character and atmosphere is vividly cinematic."

—PHILLIPA SOO, award-winning Broadway singer and actor, for *Book of the Month*

"*Woman of Light*'s scope called Willa Cather to mind—but Fajardo-Anstine shines a spotlight on characters whose stories often fall into the shadows."

—CELESTE NG, author of *Little Fires Everywhere* and *Everything I Never Told You*

"*Woman Of Light* is an intimate and intensely moving story of a Latinx and Indigenous family in the American West. . . . Kali Fajardo-Anstine's lyrical, unpretentious prose renders the generations of women of this story in all of their complexity, offering a nuanced perspective on how the past can inform the future. Fajardo-Anstine proves she is a formidable, necessary voice in fiction."

—TAYLOR JENKINS REID, author of *Malibu Rising*

"With a single phrase, a single line of dialogue, a single description, Fajardo-Anstine has the power to accurately express the joy and sadness in a person's life, their history, how the world comes into contact with us, and how we come into contact with the world. The combination of composed style and passionate world-view underlying all of her work is truly wonderful. It's captivating. Fajardo-Anstine is a special author to me."

—MIEKO KAWAKAMI, author of *Heaven* and *Breasts and Eggs*

"This novel is indelible, shining its big light on the Lopez family so brightly that I could draw a map of their breath. . . . An absolutely glorious novel."

—EMMA STRAUB, author of *All Adults Here*

"A rare and wondrous kind of novel that assembles the universe from mere words, whose unforgettable characters haunt like long shadows in the southwestern light."

—GARY SHTEYNGART, author of *Lake Success*

"Pure, simple, and luminescent. There are no other words to describe Kali Fajardo-Anstine's *Woman of Light*; a brilliant conflagration of a story that opens the eyes and inflames the heart."

—CRAIG JOHNSON, author of the Longmire series

"A cinematic, epic story . . . Kali Fajardo-Anstine brings her keen understanding of desire, vulnerability, and destiny to this gorgeous reclaiming of lost history."

—MIRA JACOB, author of *Good Talk* and
The Sleepwalker's Guide to Dancing

ALSO BY KALI FAJARDO-ANSTINE

Sabrina & Corina

WOMAN
OF
LIGHT

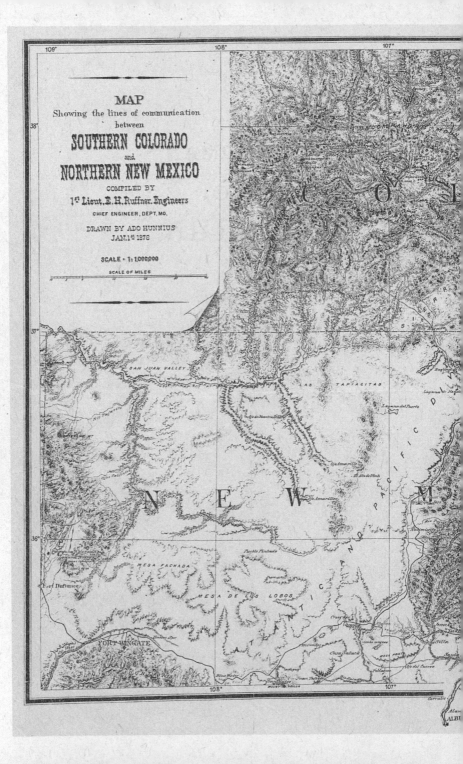

MAP

Showing the lines of communication

between

SOUTHERN COLORADO

and

NORTHERN NEW MEXICO

COMPILED BY

1st Lieut. E. H. Ruffner. Engineers

CHIEF ENGINEER, DEPT. MO.

DRAWN BY ADO HUNNIUS
JAN. 1st 1876

SCALE · 1: 1,000,000

SCALE OF MILES

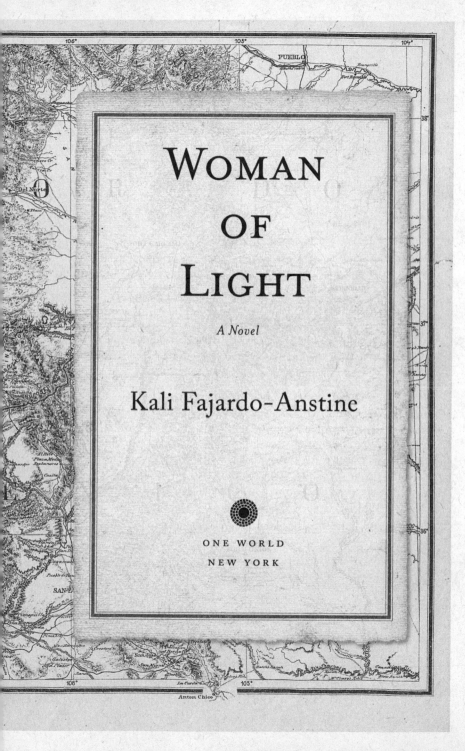

WOMAN

OF

LIGHT

A Novel

Kali Fajardo-Anstine

ONE WORLD

NEW YORK

2023 One World Trade Paperback Edition

Published in the United States by One World, an imprint of Random House, a division of Penguin Random House LLC, New York.

ONE WORLD and colophon are registered trademarks of Penguin Random House LLC.

Originally published in hardcover in the United States by One World, an imprint of Random House, a division of Penguin Random House LLC, in 2022.

LIBRARY OF CONGRESS CATALOGING-IN-PUBLICATION DATA
Names: Fajardo-Anstine, Kali, author.Title: Woman of Light : a novel / by Kali Fajardo-Anstine.Description: First Edition. | New York : One World, [2023]
Identifiers: LCCN 2021027959 (print) | LCCN 2021027960 (ebook) |
ISBN 9780525511335 (trade paperback) | ISBN 9780525511342 (ebook)
Classification: LCC PS3606.A396 W66 2022 (print) |
LCC PS3606.A396 (ebook)| DDC 813/.6—dc23
LC record available at https://lcc.loc.gov/2021027959
LC ebook record available at https://lcc.loc.gov/2021027960

Printed in the United States of America on acid-free paper

oneworldlit.com

2 4 6 8 9 7 5 3 1

Book design by Caroline Cunningham

Title page: Map: Colorado and New Mexico Oversize Subject File, American Heritage Center, University of Wyoming; antique paper: freeimages.com/Davide Guglielmo

For my familia

(In memory of Grandma Esther & Auntie Lucy)

And to the people of Denver

What is past is prologue.

—*statue, National Archives, Washington, D.C., based on
William Shakespeare,* The Tempest, *act 2, scene 1*

Outside is the big world, and sometimes the little

world succeeds in reflecting the big one so

that we understand it better.

—*from Ingmar Bergman's* Fanny and Alexander

FIRST GENERATION (PARDONA PUEBLO)

Desiderya Lopez, the Sleepy Prophet of Pardona Pueblo

SECOND GENERATION (PARDONA PUEBLO
AND THE LOST TERRITORY)

Pidre Lopez and his wife, Simodecea Saluzar-Smith

THIRD GENERATION (THE LOST TERRITORY
AND DENVER, COLORADO)

*The Split Sisters, Sara and Maria Josefina,
the children of Pidre and Simodecea*

FOURTH GENERATION (DENVER, COLORADO)

Sara's children, Luz and Diego

Maria Josie's son, Bobby Leonor (stillborn)

FIFTH GENERATION (DENVER, COLORADO)

—Herein lies

CONTENTS

CONTENTS

CONTENTS

PART 4

The Sleepy Prophet
and the Child from Nowhere

The Lost Territory, 1868

The night Fertudez Marisol Ortiz rode on horseback to the northern pueblo Pardona, a secluded and modest village, the sky was so filled with stars it seemed they hummed. Thinking this good luck, Fertudez didn't cry as she left her newborn on the banks of an arroyo, turkey down wrapped around his body, a bear claw fastened to his chest.

"Remember your line," she whispered, before she mounted her horse and galloped away.

In Pardona, Land of Early Sky, the elder Desiderya Lopez dreamt of stories in her sleep. The fireplace glowed in her clay home as she whistled snores through dirt walls, her breath dissipating into frozen night. She would have slept soundly until daybreak, but the old woman was pulled awake by the sounds of plodding hooves and chirping crickets, the crackling of burnt cedar, an interruption between dawn and day.

"Enough is enough," Desiderya muttered and cursed as she slow-rolled from bed onto her balled feet, the noises maddening as she stood. Her back was permanently bent in a slight L, and her long, woven skirt brushed the floor matted in sheepskin. She wrapped herself in a white shawl, and slid her hands into fox-fur mittens, fingerless to easily handle her tobacco. Her pipe was formed of mica clay, and the sparkling burn illuminated Desiderya's grooved face as she hobbled toward the door, soon fastening a red handkerchief beneath her broad chin. The warmth of her breath tried to linger inside the home, but Desiderya hacked into a phlegmy cough and wrangled the air back into her lungs. *You're coming with me,* she spoke and walked outside.

Known as the Sleepy Prophet, she was an important woman in Pardona. During ceremony, she went into trance, recollecting a thousand years' worth of visions, but her output was unsteady. Many years later when radios had come into fashion and everyone had a massive box near their altars beneath the vigas, the few who still remembered Pardona recalled Desiderya Lopez and how her spirit antenna was often broken. But, sometimes, many times, it worked just fine.

Desiderya stood at the arroyo's uneven banks, smoking her pipe and considering the sloping way blue darkness layered the nearby mountains. The arroyo gurgled beneath slender ice. The Spanish had named the stream Lucero because starlight shimmered over the water's trickling back, as if the earth had been saddled with sky. The galloping sounds in her dreams had vanished, and the sacred mountains looked upon Desiderya with what felt like amusement in their grouped trees and rock veins. She squinted and turned over her pipe, removing the mouthpiece with her right hand. She stepped over hardened snow toward a rattling among dormant thistle and chokecherry trees, snagging her left thumb until Desiderya bled darkly about her fingerless mittens.

"Who's making that racket?" she called out in Tiwa. When

there was no answer, Desiderya tried her various dialects, and finally, after waiting several heartbeats, she turned away from the water and brush and said in Spanish, "Freeze then, baby."

Pidre cried. Loud as a drum.

Desiderya pulled at the thistle and chokecherry branches, their stems flickering like the souls of the newly dead. She gasped at the sight of all the trouble.

There, an infant with wet gray eyes, a baby boy who reached toward the Sleepy Prophet, his face striped in shrubbery shadows.

Desiderya grunted as she lifted the baby from the weeds. He was cold, the bear claw around his neck dusted in snow. "We'll get you warmed up," she said with a calm urgency, carrying the baby to the water's edge, his face cradled to her low breasts. She dipped her left hand into the thinly frozen creek and rinsed the dried blood from her fingertips before smearing a droplet onto the baby's cheek. He did not cry at the coolness—instead he locked eyes with the Sleepy Prophet, his brow furrowed, serious in his demeanor. Desiderya chuckled at his angry baby face. "It will only be a moment," she explained. "I am looking for a message." Over the baby's face, the water reflected the sky, those reddish and winged planets.

"You were left," Desiderya said after some time. "Left to be found."

The baby surprised her then, gathering his lips and attempting to suckle her spacious chest. The Sleepy Prophet laughed. "Been dry for some time, little one."

Dawn now, orange and lavender lines appeared beyond the eastern mountains. The world warmed as Desiderya carried the baby through the desert, her fur slippers cracking through iced snow. She hummed prayers to the baby as she walked, songs about heat, greetings of light, the blessings of the sun and moon. She

brought the baby to the center of Pardona, past the adobe homes
with their blue doorways to deflect drifting spirits. In the distance
a cemetery of wooden crosses was scattered about the hillside, as
if the Spanish had once spilled a bucket of Catholicism over the
land. At the old mission church in the plaza, a white cross leaned
left and the air sounded with the squawking of sparrows and
wrens. Desiderya left the pink-hued morning and entered the
church, blessing herself and the baby with holy water at the door.
As was tradition, beneath the floorboards, four dead priests were
buried. Their spirit voices greeted Desiderya as she stepped over
the ground above their coffins. They told her in Spanish that they
knew of a secret, and the Sleepy Prophet groaned with annoyance
before she asked them to *go on, spill it.*

"Tell me," she said.

"Can't," they said.

Desiderya stomped the floorboards. She rattled the walls.

"Ouch," they said.

"Out with it," she said, and stomped once more.

"Fine," they said. "The baby has a name. Would you like to
know?"

When the dead priests relented, Desiderya repeated the name,
her voice echoing throughout the dirt-walled sanctuary. She
looked at the baby, who had scratched a faint purple line into his
cheek with his translucent fingernails. Desiderya noted to cut
them later. "Pidre," she said and smiled at the baby. "Like stone."

Deeper inside the chapel, several young women were on their
hands and knees sweeping the floor with horsetail brushes. Dried
rose petals were piled around them, and at the altar was a clay
statue of La Virgen de Guadalupe, dressed in red silk. The young
women were preparing for her Feast Day, and the church smelled
of incense and blue sage and the copal traded and carried from

1,400 miles south in Mexico City. They gazed at the Sleepy Prophet as she stepped before them with the baby in her arms.

"Who is that?" asked a young woman.

"Pidre," she said, thumbing the baby's bear claw.

"From where?"

"Seems he's mixed blood," said Desiderya. "Maybe Spanish. Probably not French. I'd say from his blanket he comes from the southern villages."

"Who abandons their own?" another young woman asked with disdain.

Desiderya thought of why babies are sometimes left. She saw images in her mind that she'd rather not see, felt profound hunger, witnessed a village perched high on a hill, horses slaughtered for food, a church crumbling back into the earth from which it was built. The Sleepy Prophet studied Pidre then. He gazed upon her face with recognition. His spirit felt complementary, an old friend, a grandson she had fished from the weeds.

"We cannot know the depths of another's sacrifice," Desiderya said, easing the baby into the young woman's arms. "For now, find him a breast. One that works."

As a child, Pidre was a great hunter with a stern expression over his cloudy eyes. Often haughty, he was disciplined by the men of Pardona with a grass lash. He giggled his way through beatings, a spirit, the people said, that couldn't be tempered. When the other boys threw stones at his back or smacked his ankles with broken cornstalks and called him names like Snow Blood and Sky Eyes, he didn't meet them with violence. And over time they relented, for Pidre had the gift of storytelling and a strong ability to tell jokes. Once, as the women prepared meals for All Souls' Day,

Pidre, a runt of a boy with spidery arms and twig legs, hid beneath fat loaves of horno bread. He lay on the table covered in dozens of steaming loaves, inhaling the yeasty scent until the other boys entered the kitchen for their afternoon snack. At that moment, he raised his arms as if climbing from a shallow grave. The women screamed and beat the bread flat with their brooms and handkerchiefs. Later when Desiderya heard about what Pidre had done, she told him it would have been much funnier if he'd been naked. "Like a real demon."

Within eleven years, Desiderya Lopez lay dying of old age on the sheepskin rugs in her clay home. The earthen smell of her bedroom had been replaced with the stale stench of sickness, a body soon to erode. On her altar, she had placed dried apricots and biscuits for the journey. The air sounded with music, a distant lullaby prayer. Pidre rested his face in the nook between her neck and shoulder, her silver hair plaited around her distinguished face. He kissed her sectioned braids. He listened to her shallow breaths, the sounds of her spirit slipping away.

"You're only little now," said the Sleepy Prophet, "but I saw you as a man."

Between tears, Pidre asked, "What am I like, Grandma? Who do you see?"

"You live near a large village on the other side of the Lost Territory, along a river, surrounded by their mines."

"Mines?"

"Their gutting," she said. "You'll have a fierce wife and daughters. Do not be vengeful people."

"Grandma," he said. "I don't understand."

"Oh, my baby. You will."

"I miss you," Pidre cried. "I already feel it. I am missing you now."

"But I am still here," Desiderya closed her eyes and winced at a pain that seemed lodged within her heart. "Pidre," she said.

"Yes?"

"You gave me such joy," she wheezed into the ghost of a laugh. "You are my grandson, and you are my friend. Thank you for coming into my life."

She let out her final exhale, her breath circling the room. At that, Desiderya Lopez, the Sleepy Prophet of Pardona Pueblo, moved from the temperature of the living into the temperature of the dead.

As Pidre grew up, he was well liked and respected among his people. Mexicano, French Canadian, and American traders often traveled through Pardona, bringing their weapons and furs, metal trinkets and fancy candies. Pidre had an eye for these things, and an ear for languages. He bartered with the traders and stored their impressive items beneath his sheepskin. In exchange for small tasks, Pidre would dole out candies to the children of Pardona. At seventeen, he announced to the elders that he was interested in leaving the Land of Early Sky. He was a businessman, well suited for the white world. There were many objections among the elders, who had so graciously taken in the child from nowhere. "We are your people now."

Pidre said, "I know where I come from, but I'd like to see the other side, too. The Sleepy Prophet predicted it."

After much deliberation, the elders agreed that it was time and sent the boy off with many beautiful pots, furs, and handcrafts to trade for the white man's money in town. There were several nights of dancing, the clowns came out in their black and white paint, the women gave offerings of Winter and Summer food, and the men presented their advice: "Be wary of their currency, for it is marked with blood." Pidre said he understood and embraced his elders with gratitude.

On the morning he left, Pidre headed north from Pardona, steadily walking a dirt path lined with sapphire mountains and the winding stream of Rio Lucero. He carried a kidney-colored satchel given to him by the Sleepy Prophet, worn straps knocking against his hip. The sky was endless and overcast in simmering clouds, and the pungent sagebrush reached for Pidre every step of the way. He felt small against the vastness of world until he felt struck, somewhere deep inside his heart, with the enormity of his Grandma Desiderya's invisible air.

PART 1

ONE

Little Light

Denver, 1933

Luz Lopez sat with her auntie Maria Josie near the banks where the creek and the river met, the city's liquid center illuminated in green and blue lights, a Ferris wheel churning above them. The crowds of Denver's chile harvest festival walked the bottomlands with their faces hidden behind masks of turkey legs and bundles of buttered corn. The dusk air smelled of horse manure and gear grease and the sweet sting of green chilies roasting in metal drums. Through the smog of sawdust and food smoke, Luz was brightened by the flame of her kerosene burner, black hair curled around her noteworthy face, dark eyes staring into a porcelain cup. She wore a brown satin dress dulled from many washes—but still she shined.

"Tell me," said an old man in Spanish, fiddling with the white-brimmed Stetson across his lap. His eyes murky, faraway. "I can take it."

Luz searched inside the cup, tea leaves at the bottom. Along the edges, she saw a pig's snout, and deeper into the mug, far into the future, she glimpsed a running wolf. Luz placed the cup on the velvet cloth over her booth's wide table, which was really an old Spanish door, the rusted knob exposed like a pointed thorn.

"Gout," she said. "A bad case."

The old man lifted his hat to his sweat-salted head. "The goddamn beans, the lard Ma uses."

"Can't always blame a woman," Maria Josie interrupted with reserved confidence. She was thickset with deep brown hair cut close to her face, and she wore workmen's trousers and a heathery flannel with wide chest pockets, her dark eyes peering through round glasses. She told the old man that almost no one she knew could afford lard anymore. "Especially not in an abundance, señor."

"You'll have to give it up," Luz said sweetly. "For your health, more time at life."

The old man swore and tossed a nickel into Luz's tackle box, leaving the booth with the hunkered posture of a man bickering with himself.

It was an annual festival, a grouping of white tents and a lighted main stage. Denver's skyline around them, pointed and gray, a city canyon beneath the moon. Rail yards and coal smelters coughed exhaust, their soot raining into the South Platte River. Young people had unlaced their boots and removed their stockings, wading into the moon's reflection. Bats swooped low and quick.

"Can I interest you ladies in a reading?" Luz asked. Two younger girls had slowed their pace, dissolving cotton candy onto their tongues. They gawked at Luz's teakettle and leaves, her tackle box of coins.

The taller of the two girls said, "Bruja stuff?"

The shorter one giggled through blue teeth and licked the last of her candy. "We don't mess around with that," she said and reached across the booth. She pushed aside a mossy stone, snatching one of Diego's handbills. The girls locked arms and skipped down the aisle between tents, bouncing to the main stage where the Greeks were hosting their annual contest, "Win Your Woman's Weight in Flour."

Maria Josie whispered, "The young ones are no good."

Luz asked why, and said at least she was trying.

"Focus on the viejos—they're steady."

"Sure they are," Luz said. "Until Doña Sebastiana comes."

Maria Josie laughed. "You're right, jita. Never met a dead man with a future."

Onstage, Pete Tikas was at the microphone in a maroon suit with a red carnation pinned to his lapel. "Calling all homegrown Denver gals," he shouted, tapping the platform with his wooden cane, the sound booming. He owned the Tikas Market, and folks from all over, nearly every neighborhood, called him Papa Tikas. They brought him gifts from their gardens—rosemary and cilantro, bootleg mezcal. They named their babies Pete and carried them into the market, wrapped in white blankets. While many Anglo-owned stores turned them away, Papa Tikas welcomed all. *Money is money*, was his motto, though it went beyond that. He cared about his city, about the people his store fed.

"I kinda like these big ol' gals," said Maria Josie, motioning through the night toward the main stage. "Maybe we'll get customers from all this ruckus."

Luz and her older brother, Diego, had lived with their auntie for nearly a decade. When Luz was eight years old, her mother, Sara, decided she could no longer care for her children, sending them north to live with her younger sister, Maria Josie, in the city. Whenever Luz thought of her mother, she felt like a stone was lodged into her throat, and so she didn't think of her often.

"Doubtful," said Luz, sliding lower behind her booth. "They're just causing a scene."

Maria Josie flashed an ornery smile. She had an elegant gap between her front teeth. "Hell, some of those girls are pretty cute." She pointed to the dozen or so women ascending the stage. Tall ones. Short ones. Those with the heft of their railroad worker men. Big-boned gals from the Martinez clan who didn't have a chance against the chubby Gallegos. *Pick us. Weigh me. I'm the winner, winner.*

The first woman took to the scale and Papa Tikas hollered, "One ninety! You can do better, ladies." A regal woman in an orange shawl was next. She had a dazed look, as if she'd walked into her own birthday party expecting a wake. The crowd trembled with applause.

Maria Josie shook her head and pushed back in her chair, the front two legs lifting from the silty earth. She motioned with a kissy mouth to the bleachers, stage left, where Diego twirled beneath the metal slits in barred light. "Look at that boy now," she said.

He was on in twenty minutes. Dirt coughed beneath his feet, his mouth as open as a third eye socket. He moved in patterned steps, a dancer beating an invisible flame. Although she couldn't make them out through the harvest light, Luz knew that her brother's snakes, Reina and Corporal, were nearby in their wicker basket. The breezeless weather was good for a festival, even better for the snakes. Within a month, Reina and Corporal, six-foot-long rattlers, would curl beneath a heat lamp in Diego's bedroom. They could die if left under an open window, a wintry draft freezing their bodies in an instant. Cold-blooded, Luz had learned, meant something.

"If I told you I killed it myself, would you believe it?" It was

Lizette, who had approached the booth in a secondhand fur coat, rabbit or fox, most likely stolen or pawned by her fiancé, Alfonso. "Real eye-catching, huh?"

Maria Josie slammed her chair back onto four legs. She leaned over the booth, rubbing with her index finger and thumb at Lizette's disintegrating jacket. Flecks of powdery fur floated in the dark. "Skinned it yourself, too?"

Lizette frowned and flicked her right hand, as though she smoked a cigarette that didn't exist. She plopped down in the chair across from Luz, sliding open her green mermaid clutch, rows of loosened beads across the siren's face. "Read for me, prima? Same as usual," she said, "but more on Al. I think he's cheating. That son of a bitch."

"Only a fool would do such a thing," said Maria Josie sarcastically. "Unimaginable."

Lizette blushed. Her ridged cheekbones gave her an ornamental look, and her eyes were a galaxy of greens and golds and black. The cousins had been inseparable since Luz first arrived in Denver. "Thank you, Tía," said Lizette.

Luz reached for her brass kettle, the water kept at a low boil over the kerosene burner, her fingers scented with fuel. She lifted the kettle and poured tea into a white cup. It was always the same when she read for Lizette. Usually she saw a doll and a rattle, and in recent years, as her sight grew stronger, Luz glimpsed a sunny apartment with a yellow kitchen, white French doors, brick walls.

"Think of your question," said Luz, handing the cup to Lizette. "Don't get sidetracked like usual."

Lizette held the cup to her mouth, puffed as if blowing out birthday candles. "Me?"

"Yes, you," Maria Josie said.

Lizette stared coolly at Maria Josie before finishing her tea and handing the cup to Luz. "What's the damage?"

Delicately, Luz placed the cup brim down, draining leftover tea on a cloth napkin, the brown water bleeding onto the fabric. She turned the cup counterclockwise three times before flipping it over and gazing inside, the leaves darkly drenched like ground liver. A star, a boot, stray images along the ridge. Luz focused until the symbols blurred, giving way to another view, a moment caught like trout from a river. Black hair rising and falling over white sheets, Lizette's curls perfumed with rose water. A long, airy moan. Teeth against floral pillows, a curved toe hitting a metal bed frame. Luz closed her eyes, she turned away from the cup.

"Wow, Lizette," Luz said, flatly. "You aren't even married yet."

Lizette removed a penny from her clutch and dropped it onto the table. "Stop looking!"

"You asked me to!"

"Better not be," said Maria Josie, with seriousness. "Who can afford a baby right now?"

Lizette stuck out her tongue. She stood and smacked her own ass draped in the decaying fur coat and walked off toward a hat booth, her pockets holey without change.

"That girl," Maria Josie said, "is unscrupulous."

Through a sound like falling ice, the Ferris wheel shifted its gears. Maria Josie stood from her seat. She placed both hands firmly in her pockets and told Luz that she was going in search of atole, but her gaze drifted, her attention clearly on Mrs. Dolores Reyes, the young widow kicked up against a steel pigpen in a peach polka dot dress, her beige pumps covered in mud. She smiled as Maria Josie headed her way.

—

The festival was packed, and from somewhere among the tents, a man whistled at Luz, then another hissed and clicked his tongue. She hunched forward, hoping to make herself small, unnoticeable. Luz hated to be left alone. But she kept it to herself. Maria Josie had taught Luz that showing fear drew more of it. And there was a lot to be afraid of. Luz glanced toward her knife, slipped gently into her boot, a comfort just to keep it there. On the main stage, the woman in the orange shawl waved as she carted away her flour. Neighborhood children then scrambled onto the platform. Diego paid them in licorice and baseball cards to stack fruit crates, his stagehands of twig arms and legs. One of the boys hollered into a red bullhorn. "Arriba, mira, you'll see him soon. Diego Lopez," the boy shouted. "Snake Charmer."

Diego was popular. His snakes were large, aggressive rattlers. Their tips hissed like tin cans of pebbles and their scales were cream colored with black diamond heads. Reina was the older of the two with noticeably longer fangs. She often appeared sheepish, hiding her eyes beneath an inner lid of white. Corporal was different. His movements were precise, lingering, a flash of slit eyes. When Diego wasn't in bed with a woman, he allowed his snakes to sleep curled above his feet, their cold ribbed bodies as heavy as several cats.

The stage brightened and a ruby curtain swept apart over the platform, revealing Diego beneath the lights. With deer-like legs, he trotted and paused center stage, holding his audience in a piercing gaze. At twenty-one, he was slender with a graceful throat, his musculature trim from his day job working as a lineman at the Gates Factory, where he churned out rubber belts against the belligerent melody of machinery and the curses of strained men. He stood onstage in a sparkling dress shirt and purple trousers, his abundant black hair blue with pomade.

Taking a step back, Diego whistled with his pinkies hooked in his mouth. He lifted the lid from his wicker basket. The audience gasped.

Diego called to them. His Reina. His Corporal. The snakes rose together in a braid, their brawny bodies held apart, creating a space where Diego's face could be seen in the gap, calm and un-flinching, his eyes highlighted in black kohl and his mouth painted red. He reached for his snakes, lifting them higher by their fangs. The crowd roared as Diego released them from his grip and the reptiles fell to the floor, playing dead at their owner's feet. He nudged them with his wing-tipped shoes and clapped three times. The snakes blasted upward, diverging from one another in a V.

Lights dimmed. People cheered. Coins like hail clinked over the wooden stage. The entire world, even the glistening river and creek, darkened as Diego moved into his next trick.

"A reading, please." It was a small voice, then an ashen hand clutching a dime.

Before Luz stood a young woman, a redhead who seemed to rise into the air, her figure hidden beneath the billows of an emerald coat. It was one thing to be a white woman at the chile harvest. It was another thing to be a white woman alone. And certain Anglos scared Luz, how they hung signs in their businesses and grocery stores: NO DOGS OR NEGROES OR MEXICANS ALLOWED.

"Your name?" Luz asked.

"Eleanor Anne," said the girl quietly, as if she'd been trained to speak low. "And you're Little Light?"

Luz focused. She poured the tea. "Only my brother calls me that."

"I know Diego real well," said Eleanor Anne.

"He knows lots of girls real well," said Luz.

If Eleanor Anne thought Luz was being rude, she didn't show

it. Instead, the girl was eerily oblivious to anything outside herself. She had a smell like sugary perfume and she kept her coat buttoned clear to her throat, though the night was peacefully mild, as if the weather had offered the city a gift. Beneath her large green eyes were bruise-colored bags, and her thin lips were chapped, a scab running her center seam. Hopefulness mixed with dread beamed from every inch of the girl's heart-shaped face. She seemed somewhat older than Luz. Maybe nineteen or twenty. She had come from Denver's Park Hill neighborhood, near the edge of City Park. Her father owned a shipping business, she explained, and offered no further details. Luz kept her distance behind the table, edged back in her chair. She didn't like how Eleanor Anne had the slouched posture of a dog raised in a too-small cage.

Luz asked, "You come here with someone?"

"My brothers," said Eleanor Anne. "But they're playing a game somewhere, one with water." She finished her tea in slow swallows. Her teeth were square, shockingly so, and she had an air about her that was static, strangely still, as if the girl wasn't entirely alone, like there was someone else beside her steadying her hands. Luz felt sick with worry, a feeling she'd experienced only a handful of times—like when her father left and her mother wept into the night, her tears freezing solid on their cabin floor. She wished the girl would leave.

"Done!" Eleanor Anne handed Luz the mug.

Luz thanked her. She considered the leaves, their soaking shapes.

"Who taught you," asked Eleanor Anne, "to read tea leaves?"

"My mother," said Luz. "She said my great-grandmother had the sight, too."

"What was her name?"

"I don't know. No one told me."

"Where do you come from?" asked Eleanor Anne.

Intrusive, thought Luz. "The Lost Territory." She looked up for a moment before returning her gaze to the tea leaves with a placid expression. "And you?"

"Me?"

"Yeah, I don't suppose you *come* from here."

"Missouri," she said, "my father brought us to Denver when I was young."

"Long way from home. Your cup," Luz said dryly, "is filled with a clam, an owl, a brick. It probably means two men will fight over you."

Eleanor Anne told her she had no idea who those men could be. She was hardly seeing anyone, let alone multiple men. "How do you know it works? Your sight?"

"It doesn't *work*," said Luz, "but most of the time it goes in the right direction."

Eleanor Anne turned away, peering over her shoulder. Diego was onstage draped in his snakes. "What do they fight about, these men?"

Luz peered over the brim and into the hull of the white mug, eyeing the peculiar pattern of clumped leaves. Nothing immediate. No image of a person, street corner, discernible house or garden. Then something strange, off-putting, the tea leaves seeming to drift like a blizzard over golden plains until Luz saw a place she hadn't seen before, twilight, a grassland marked by a dirt road, a lighted caravan of horse-drawn wagons hobbling along the path. Small red trailers halted, and from their doors came acrobats, fire dancers, jugglers, clowns, and a little girl with straight bangs and a handsome face, a large hearty belly. The tallgrass prairie smelled of fire. They were in the fields behind barns and dingy tractors. Crows squawked and the few cottonwood trees shivered. A pack of white men and women had gathered, and the girl asked if they'd like to see a trick. She spoke English like a grown-up. "Like with cards?" asked a child among the audience, and the girl shook her head. She pulled a fire poker from a satchel. It was a foot long with a hawk's talon at one end and a spiral handle at the other. The girl plunged it down her small throat, turned the handle, and brought it out again, clean. "That's no trick," yelled a man from the crowd. "Better trick would be to gut yourself, gypsy." The pale mob laughed then, edging toward the girl as one.

Eleanor Anne said, "What do you see?"

Luz looked up, dimness in her eyes. "I don't know. Some kind of circle."

"A ring," said Eleanor Anne optimistically. "Maybe I'll be married."

"Sure," said Luz, with a forced smile. "Say," she said, "what's Missouri like?"

Eleanor Anne turned her face to the side, the tip of her pinched nose lopped away into shadow. "Flat," she said. "That's about it. Nothing like here."

Later the booths and white tents were empty. Warm winds off the river and creek scattered handbills and soiled napkins. Maria Josie and Lizette had gone home. Lone performers and mechanics were left on the riverbank, loading and unloading goldfish and Navajo blankets, storing mirrors, and tearing down carnival rides and the long spokes of the Ferris wheel. It was a no-man's-land layered beneath a ghastly silence. Diego sat cross-legged on his painted crates with his snakes at his feet in their basket. He smoked a pipe, a heavy plume engulfing his prominent face. They were waiting for Alfonso with his pickup truck. They'd soon load the Spanish door, crates and snakes, and Luz's tackle box and tea leaves, carting everything back home to Hornet Moon.

"How'd you make out?" Luz asked.

Diego placed a foot on his basket. "Not bad. Yourself?"

"Read for a few people. There was a girl tonight. Someone who knows you."

Diego laughed, short and ugly. "Oh yeah? Lots of girls know me."

"An Anglo girl," said Luz. "She was alone. There was something about her, a bad feeling."

Diego haggardly looked upon his sister and his sporadic stubble rose like the coat of a fearful animal. He shuffled through his pockets, presenting Luz with a silver bracelet, the imprint of a bear claw near the clasp. "Found this cleaning up," he said. "Ours now, Little Light."

TWO

❧

La Divisoria

The next morning Luz stood at her altar, crossing herself from forehead to heart, shoulder to shoulder. The soapbox on her corner of the floor was sprinkled with marigolds and uncooked rice and a damaged photograph of her mother and father, Sara and Benny, standing beside a tilted adobe church in the desert, their young faces distorted, as if someone had taken flint rock and scraped onto the photo, hoping for fire.

They were a family, Luz, Diego, and Maria Josie. They shared a one-bedroom apartment on the fifth floor of a tenement on the edge of downtown Denver, an Italianate with pediments and arched windows and alabaster bricks baking in sunlight, a building named Hornet Moon. Diego slept in the main room on a steel bed that pulled down from the stucco wall. His window looked upon the alley at the back entrance to a butcher's named Milton's Meats, a tiny world of trucks and flies and men working among pig and turkey carcasses. Maria Josie and Luz occupied the bedroom, a high-ceilinged space divided with a worn cotton sheet draped over ropes, one side for Luz and the other for Maria Josie. Their window opened to the street, a view walled in textures of bricks, doorways and fire escapes comfortably cross, a patch of visible sky. *Watchful giants,* Luz often thought of the buildings, as she gazed at her corner of the city through the fog of her own reflection. The apartment's most notable feature was the white-walled kitchen with an elegant Lorraine gas stove that Maria Josie had won during a card game, but beyond that, they had a half-broken icebox, their gas and electric was unreliable, and in the late evenings and early mornings they walked with candlelight to the shared bathtub down the hall.

"Little Light," Diego hollered from the other room. "Come here."

He was on the oak floor doing push-ups in his trousers, shirtless, Reina curved down his back in a coiled L. The snake flicked her forked tongue in greeting at Luz. Diego was up early before his shift at Gates. The main room smelled of his amber cologne and pomade and an undercurrent of ripe sweat and the gritty flesh stench of the butcher shop. Overalls hung from the long window, shading Corporal in his glass cage.

"Where you off to this hour?" Diego asked, eyeing Luz's curled hair, her blue sack dress winking beneath her threadbare winter coat.

It was laundry day, and Luz told Diego that he should've known. "If you paid attention to anyone but yourself." Three days a week, Luz and Lizette washed and pressed rich people's clothes at a washery off Colfax and York.

Diego said, "How you stand Lizette for that long? I'd wring my own neck."

Luz pointed to Reina. "There's worse company."

"Do me a favor." Diego went down. "Take Reina and put her in the cage. Bring me Corporal." Diego went up.

"No," Luz whined.

"She ain't gonna do nothing to ya. Shit, she likes you." Diego edged left shoulder forward, nudging Reina in Luz's direction. The girl snake flashed her sheepish expression. She lifted her endless throat.

"What about Corporal?"

Diego told her the snake was too lazy for violence. "Plus, he just ate."

Luz looked at the snake's middle, the mouse-shaped lump. She sighed and squeezed through the narrow aisle between Diego and the cage. He continued his push-ups as Reina bobbed over his back. Luz inched forward, her arms stiffly out, and in one swoop, lifted the chilly snake. "I hate you, I hate you, I hate you," she said to Diego as she slipped Reina into the cage, which smelled of dead rodents and hay. The girl snake flopped onto Corporal. He grunted.

"He talks now?" Luz said.

Diego laughed. He rolled onto his feet. "Maybe I should grab him myself." He stepped to the glass cage, diving his arms downward to Corporal. He lifted and cradled the snake before flinging Corporal over his back, a slapping sound as scales met skin.

Diego returned to the floor. This time between push-ups, he clapped.

Lizette lived on the Westside in a tilted orange house off Fox Street with her mother and father and four grimy brothers who threw tantrums and played vaqueros and bandidos with stick guns in the yard. Inside, they'd wail and slide down the banister in dirty socks. Tía Teresita and Tío Eduardo were usually only a passing storm, chasing one boy or another with a wooden spoon. *Don't make me break this over your little butts,* they'd holler. Steel pots of menudo and pintos steamed on the stove, and their tortillas, the kind made of corn instead of flour, rested in a wicker basket on the kitchen table. The houses of Fox Street were humble, small roomed, tiny yarded, and beautifully adorned with stone grottoes housing blue porcelain statues of La Virgen de Guadalupe.

If the Westsiders were considered poor, they didn't believe it, for many owned their own homes from the money they had earned at the rail yards, the slaughterhouses, the onion and beet fields, the cleaners, and hotels. Their lives were lived between farmland rows and the servants' back stairs. They had come to Denver from the Lost Territory, and farther south from current-day Mexico, places like Chihuahua and Durango and Jalisco. Many, including Teresita and Eduardo, had arrived after the bloodiest days of the Mexican Revolution. Maria Josie's mother, Simodecea, had been distantly related to Teresita's father, a jimador in Guadalajara. But one morning when Teresita was eleven years old, she had walked the agave rows to find her papa blindfolded and shot, a tiny hole in his head like an extra eardrum leaking blood into the earth.

Luz lifted the latch on Lizette's metal gate, stepping over yellowed grass, flattened in frost. She waved to her cousin, who was seated on the four-step concrete stoop beside their red wagon. "Ready?"

Lizette wore her new-used coat and was resting her chin on both hands, elbows on her knees. Her eyebrows were thin black lines, clownish and wandering as she reached to the ground beside her ankles in frilly socks. She raised a steel thermos. "Try some, prima," she said.

Luz took the thermos from her cousin. "What is it?" she asked.

"Coffee," Lizette said.

Luz sipped, and the bitter taste of alcohol stung the length of her throat. She coughed before she spat. "And what else?"

Lizette frowned. She stood from the ground, dusting herself off with both hands. "You are wasteful, you know that, Luz. I had to buy that."

Luz tilted her face. She kept it there.

"Actually," Lizette said, reaching for the red wagon, "Al made it in the bathtub."

Luz laughed. "Let's go."

They took turns pulling the wagon, their fists cupping cool metal. Before Speer Boulevard, where the Westside eased into downtown, the cousins paused near an open alley, trash heaped beside hibernating honeysuckles and lilacs.

"Hand me that baloney," Lizette said, motioning with an empty hand.

Luz reached into a paper bag on the wagon's left side. She unraveled spoiled meat from a checkered napkin, and handed it to Lizette, who then whistled and waited. From an abandoned coal shed at the far end of the alley came a small yelp that grew into a trotting pant. There he was, skinny legs and patchy fur, blinded eyes nothing but whites. Jorge, Guardian of the Westside.

"Sit," said Lizette, her forefinger out like a ruler.

Jorge growled before easing his legs elegantly to one side. Lizette dropped the meat onto the sidewalk and Jorge snapped into action, scarfing his food. As he finished, the fishy stench of bad meat lingered and a wet mark remained on the ground. Lizette swallowed the last of her morning coffee. She grimaced and wiped her mouth with the same hand she had used to serve the meat.

"In the flawed capitalistic system," she said, mocking Leon Jacob, a famous local radio announcer with a weekday show, "even the dogs must work to eat."

They crossed the creek where the city's grid shifted. The roadways widened, streets built for carriages and trolleys and white-out blizzards. They collected laundry from grand homes with bedded gardens, shrubbery shaped like tigers and bears. Most of the girls' route came from Alfonso, who, along with several other Filipinos, worked at the Park Lane Hotel. *Rich folks always need something,* he'd say in his musical accent. *But you can't ask. You have to know.* And Alfonso knew everything. For years, he had served the newspapermen, the silver barons, doctors with diplomas from Harvard and Yale, places Luz couldn't fathom. But she was thankful for the job. Some families tipped well, and every Christmas an architect named Miles Sweet sent the girls home with two hams and a sack of worn clothes, this time to keep.

As they walked, sunlight pressed through a sheer canopy of unfallen leaves. Beneath the cottonwood branches, the girls were centered and small, determined among the stone mansions and foursquare Victorians, their red wagon in tow.

"What do you think it's like?" Luz asked.

"What *what's* like?" said Lizette.

Luz lowered her voice, afraid houses could hear. "To live in homes like these."

"Boring," said Lizette. "Their lives are plain. We have all the adventure." She shouted again in her radio announcer voice: "The Incredible Lives of Westside Laundresses!"

Luz smiled. She wished she could feel the same way, but instead she felt locked out, and wondered why she even wanted in. "But they sure are beautiful."

"Don't be too impressed," said Lizette. "It's how they trick themselves into thinking they're better than we are."

They came to a stone house, where clumped together in a gunnysack at the side door were soiled diapers and a woman's nighties. The cousins hoisted the sodden bag from the ground and wrestled it into the wagon. Luz's left pinkie nail caught and broke on a loose thread—the pain seeped. Laundry days stained her fingernails, cracked her palms, dried her skin like scales, and over time, if she didn't stop lifting the heavy loads, Diego had warned Luz that her back would bend outward into a small mound.

"Your turn to pull," Luz said.

Lizette scrunched her nose. The air jittered with dying leaves. "If I'm pulling, we take the shortcut."

"You're kidding," Luz whined.

Their last stop lay on the other side of Cheesman, the old cemetery converted into a park. Though the headstones were gone, most of the bodies were still underground, and occasionally when Luz crossed the hilly grass, her mind filled with images of the dead. She'd seen babies, younger than two, withering with hunger, their eyes inconsolable in ravenous sorrow. Once she saw a glamorous blonde under a woolen blanket, a gunshot wound reddening her yellow hair. There were soldiers who had survived the Great War only to return home, death by suicide. A man missing half his skull. An Arapahoe warrior in gray paint, three arrows piercing his chest. That man, she could tell, was from an older burial, before the cemetery, before the city even existed.

"I pulled for most of the hill." Lizette stood bossy with her hands on her hips, her face sparkling with sweat, an even exhaustion. She grabbed the wagon. "We're taking the shortcut."

"Fine," Luz said. "But you better walk fast."

The park was a vast lily pad of rippling green, a pathway leading to a marble pavilion. A busy midmorning. Couples in the shade, resting on iron benches. Squirrels dived through high grass, their backsides rounded like small bears. A group of Anglo men in varsity sweaters played football. They came together and pulled apart like a pack of wolves. A stout one with auburn hair cradled the ball as he ran. He was quarterback, and he shouted a string of numbers and commands, words like "Mississippi" and "Omaha," but as the men plunged into a new play, his eyes fell upon the cousins and he hollered something the girls couldn't make out, as if he spoke in the tone of a barking dog.

Luz smacked Lizette's left hand, signaling caution.

"It's okay," Lizette whispered. "Ignore them. We're almost out."

The man yelled again, but by now the girls had edged around a thicket of maple trees, the land concealing them with affection.

"So, for the ceremony," said Lizette after some time. "I refuse to wear a veil." She mentioned her wedding to Alfonso often, though Luz knew in all likelihood they'd have to wait months or even years before Lizette could afford a dress, let alone a veil.

Luz spoke against the wind. "You think the church will let you do that?"

Lizette nodded, pausing the wagon and slowly sliding her arm down the metal handle. "No," she said. "Because they're always trying to hide a good thing. Like this face."

Luz laughed, and told her cousin that yes, she agreed.

They had almost left the park, veering toward the eastern gate, a path lined in oak trees with thick roots bulging at the base. White paper was affixed to a tree, just one flyer at first, then another and another, as if a fungus had overrun the bark. Maybe it was a sign for a missing cat, something for sale? Since the crash, people were selling odd things. Their houseplants. Their bookends. Renting their bathrooms as bedrooms. But the girls came closer and read the sign clearly, professionally printed and typed.

NOTICE

This Park Belongs to WHITE PROTESTANTS

NO GOOKS

SPICS

NIGGERS

Allowed

Or

Kikes, Catholics, Communists

"I can't believe I learned to read," Lizette said, ripping the notice from the bark. "So I could read bullshit like this." She balled the paper, anger like flames in her hands.

"Let's go," said Luz, looking over her shoulder, searching for people in the trees. "Now."

They left behind the lavish houses, the manicured lawns, that hateful bark. At the edge of Colfax, the city was an open vein. The hobbled tents of vagrants were pitched under faded awnings, policemen rode on horseback, and there were sounds of hollow hooves. A woman screamed from an open window. Somewhere glass shattered. A baby cried. Soaring pigeons caught sunlight, their oil-slick wings illuminated in a great flash. The city had a pace, a feeling. It seemed Luz could dive into the roadways, drown in the immensity of people and machines. In the distance, the Rocky Mountains embraced the skyline, that rift where the rivers decided to run west into the Pacific or downward and out into that faraway gulf. La Divisoria, the separation of it all, a continent split in two.

After some time, when the park and its bodies were far behind, Lizette said, "Sorry we went that way."

THREE

The Greeks

"There's been another killing," said Papa Tikas.

Luz was with Maria Josie in the Tikas Market, a tightly packed brick row where the Mexican, Colored, and Greek neighborhoods met. Papa Tikas sold the freshest meat and vegetables in Denver, unloading vibrant melons and apples and cuts of lamb each morning directly from the butchers' and farmers' trucks. Luz was in the bulk aisle beside the register, scooping pinto beans from wooden barrels into paper sacks. It was Thursday afternoon, and she wore her hair pinned away from her face. The market was calm, the selection thinned from an early morning rush.

"That same cop as last time?" said an older man in a Greek accent. "Business as usual for them."

"It might be, but my son is a determined lawyer." The ornate register dinged, and Papa Tikas handed the man his change. They were both nicely dressed, rings on their fingers, thick gold watches on their wrists. "He'll make it all the way to district attorney someday."

"A socialist as the DA. Can you imagine?"

Papa Tikas laughed. "Another way is possible. It wasn't so long ago—"

At the nape of her neck, Luz felt a callused hand. "Don't eavesdrop," said Maria Josie, making her way toward the dairy aisle.

Luz told her auntie that she wasn't, and rolled her eyes. She slipped past a group of viejos playing dominoes over a folding table in the foyer. The clip clap of their ivory pieces merged with the crackling sounds of the radio. *"In the early spring,"* President Roosevelt's assured voice rang out, *"there were actually and proportionally more people out of work in this country than in any other nation in the world. . . . Our troubles will not be over tomorrow, but we are on our way."* Whenever Luz heard the president's announcements on the radio she imagined him tall, gray-eyed, grandfatherly with his cane and leg braces. Since he had taken office, people seemed more hopeful about finding work. But even with jobs, no matter how much Luz or Maria Josie or even Diego worked, they were still poor, as if their position in life had been permanently decided generations before.

"What about pork chops?" Luz called across the store.

Maria Josie stood on the checkered floor, studying her grocery list. After some time, she slid the paper back into her trouser pocket. Her cropped hair stayed against her head as she shook her head *no.* "Not this week, jita."

Luz nodded in annoyed acceptance. She was hungry and felt that way often. A breeze rushed the market aisles, stirring smells of garlic and lemon and clove. Along the walls were religious icons, gold-leafed and glinting, a dragon slayed by Saint George, a saint Luz always mistook for San Miguel. They must be the same, or at the very least, cousins.

"How we doing on rice?" Maria Josie asked loudly.

Luz said they were fine, and didn't mention that Lizette had been giving her free rice from Alfonso, who had been stealing it from work.

Maria Josie was scanning shelves, clearly running calculations in her mind, cutting a penny here, a nickel there. In her midthirties, she had a young face and black hair stringed gray along the temples. She often wore men's clothing and was sometimes mistaken for one by strangers, strangers who yelled names at Maria Josie, names Luz was never to repeat. Maria Josie preferred the company of women, though she didn't state this out loud. Sometimes she stayed the night someplace else, and every once in a while, she'd bring a woman friend back to Hornet Moon, where they'd smoke cigarettes and drink tequila in the kitchen until dawn. More than once, Luz remembered walking the shared hallway with a lit candle, glimpsing her auntie embracing a woman near the tenement stairs, her elegant hand rushing long hair.

"My light." It was Papa Tikas from behind the counter. "Why do you have the strained face of a scholar?"

"Hi, Papa Tikas," Luz said with a smile.

"You're a beauty," he said, waving his arms to the tin ceiling. "But you know what else you are, Luz? You're smart. What're you thinking of?" Papa Tikas worked his hands through his canvas apron, his white eyebrows lifting.

No one besides Papa Tikas ever asked Luz about her thoughts, and the question made her feel warmth, a worthiness. "My auntie," she said, motioning at Maria Josie, who walked toward the register with a meager basket.

"Ah," he said, "who could ever forget the prodigious Maria Josefina."

Maria Josie waved her left hand in the air, as if to say, *Nonsense.* She took some bananas from Luz's basket, directing her to put the rest of her groceries back.

Papa Tikas weighed the fruit and flour, speaking to Maria Josie about the weather, the stray cat he had found sleeping in the milk crates behind the shop, his bad case of *ar-ther-rite-us.*

"You gotta put clove oil on your joints," Maria Josie told him.

Papa Tikas nodded with his whole body. It was so much easier, he claimed, to complain about problems than do something about it. "The gift of gab," he said, looking at Maria Josie with precision. He took her change and handed over three paper sacks. "Looking forward to the party?"

Maria Josie chuckled, her breasts lifting as one long shelf. "Oh, a dance is for young people. But how proud you must be that David has his own office now."

Papa Tikas's only son, David, had just opened his own law practice after working for a large firm for several years. He had gone east and graduated from Columbia Law School, bringing back mysterious seashells, potent Chinese herbs, and several lanky, unadorned Anglo girlfriends. Luz was only a child when he first left, but whenever he was home for break, she caught herself gazing at him in the store—his body was as sculpted as an athlete's, and his eyelashes were full, like clumps of dust. Once, around Christmastime, Luz watched David shake out his curly brown hair after walking in from the snow. Flecks of water ran down his face and jacket, beading the skin around his neck. Luz was fifteen then and wanted nothing more than to run her tongue along his Adam's apple. She had never wanted something like that, and it startled her that she could.

"Proud, yes," said Papa Tikas, "but also anxious." He told Maria Josie that David had become quite the radical, fighting for one cause or another. Fair wages. Affordable rent. It was a noble heritage, he explained. In his own youth, Papa Tikas had been an organizer, assisting his fellow coal miners in the Lost Territory, but it was dangerous—many of his compadres were murdered by company guards, those hired by Rockefeller to corral striking miners into obedience. "He means well, but David only knows the life of a successful shopkeeper's son." Papa Tikas winked before turning to Luz. "You and Diego will be there, no?"

Luz nodded. "And Lizette with Alfonso."

"Of course," he said, chuckling. "Your loudest accessory."

On the way home, riding along Sixteenth Street, the streetcar turned a sharp corner, sending Luz and Maria Josie swaying to the right in the back section. Their grocery sacks toppled from their laps, carrots and onions rolling over booted ankles. Luz gathered the items from the dirty floor, scrambling on her knees, arms fumbling as if panning for gold. When her hands fell upon several pounds of pork, a good cut with lots of fat, wrapped in wax paper, she knew immediately the meat had come from Papa Tikas. Either a gift or a handout, and sometimes those were the same thing. Luz shamefully handed the bundled meat back to Maria Josie.

"Damn that man," she said, turning away from Luz.

Luz said quietly in Spanish, "I won't tell Diego it was free."

FOUR

The Trouble with Men

They parked on Curtis Street and scrambled out of Alfonso's busted-up Chevy in a line of dress clothes, a click-clack of Luz's and Lizette's pumps. David's party was at the end of a strip of dance halls with names like Royal, Empress, Colonial, and Strand. Dime girls danced in rosy windows while corner Romas sold hash and breathed fire from sticks. The night smelled of the far-off meatpacking plant's manure and metal, and soon mixed with the scent of marijuana and perfumed skin. Diego and Alfonso ducked into an alleyway, their black hair glinting, their secondhand wing-tipped shoes polished bright. They sparked a joint and told Lizette and Luz to keep watch.

"You better not get too owled," said Lizette. "David won't like that."

"Let that pendejo get mad," said Alfonso, inhaling so deeply that his face resembled a skull. He offered a hit to Diego, who refused and flicked the joint quick and red like a small comet launched into the sky. The alleyway was dotted with stagnant pools of water among dead weeds and fuming sewers. Feral cats shifted in shadows. Beyond brick walls, spotlights rose into the night, white masts shooting into the sky like swords. The air held the strange stillness of oncoming snow. No breeze, only lingering smoke.

"Come on, you guys," Luz said. "We'll miss the food."

Rainbow Hall's enormous brass doors opened to a lobby that ended in a crushed velvet curtain beneath a stucco arch. In the main room, black bears and trout were carved into stone walls. The ceiling was an elaborate mosaic of covered wagons sailing the plains, their wheels trailed by hordes of buffalo.

Nearly a hundred people had gathered to celebrate David. The space was swampy with their heat. Bushels of roses and white orchids covered dozens of round tables. Cedar wreaths extended from the walls. On an elevated stage, old men played mandolin and guitar, a bobbing accordion, the room exhaling with music and laughter.

"Coats, please." Papa Tikas had approached them, placing his palms over Luz's shoulders. He smelled of licorice and paper, something vaguely leather. In a forest-colored suit, he bowed to kiss Luz's and Lizette's hands. Lips warm and wet. He greeted Diego and Alfonso with steady embraces. Lizette slid out of her disintegrating fur jacket, passing it over on a hooked hand. Papa Tikas hugged the pelt with one arm, reaching for Luz's wool jacket with the other. He studied the girls' red satin dresses. Lizette had made them herself, no pattern or sewing machine needed. "Tonight, we get twins," he said.

They followed as he weaved through aisles, embracing family and friends, kissing the cheeks of gorgeous women and their ancient grandmothers, parting the thicket of elbows and shoulders, until, finally, they arrived at a lengthy table stretched regal with caviar, eggplant, grape leaves, racks of lamb, fried potatoes, veal sausages, pastries. The scent was overwhelming, fats and yeasts, the citrus of flowers. Luz nudged Lizette, as if to say *Impossible*.

"Papa Tikas," said Lizette, in a babyish voice. "Are you really Papa Noël?"

"Kouklitsa," he said, before stepping away.

During dinner, the glowing chandeliers dimmed and one of David's cousins announced it was time for the Kalamatiano. The dance floor bloomed, Orthodox girls, newly married couples, children running, scampering over wooden floors. They linked arms in a wide, meandering circle, footwork beating back and forth. The floor thumped with movement.

Luz stayed in her seat, picked at her plate and worried over who'd eventually ask her to dance. She was seventeen years old, eighteen in a few months, and Luz worried something was broken about her. She had never had a true suitor, and waiting for love felt like searching the horizon for a figure in the distance, walking toward her from darkened clouds.

Across the table, Diego twirled a small meaty bone between his fingers. Lizette pretended to poke Alfonso with an asparagus spear, and he bent down, disappearing under the table for a moment before revealing a metal flask. The party was abundant with red wine, but Papa Tikas didn't want any fighting at his parties, so he rarely allowed hard liquor. Alfonso handed the flask to Lizette, who drank before passing it to Luz. The liquor tasted cheap and stale and went warmly down her throat.

"Why you always have that hillbilly shit?" Diego asked.

"Made it myself, hombre. I'll bring the good stuff next time." Alfonso laughed. He yeehawed and slapped his knee. He was good for Lizette, Luz thought. A balance. They'd met at Saint Cajetan's Memorial Day barbecue. In the green plaza, Alfonso stepped to their table in the springtime weather, the air full with apple blossoms and drifting cottonwood saplings. "Señorita," he said, tipping his ten-gallon hat, "the name's Al." He thought he was a real cowboy, always dressing in boots and hats and sterling buckles. He'd come to Colorado from the Philippines, a place Luz had never heard of before she'd met him. There were several men on the boat. It smelled faintly of vomit and was filled with young and old alike—there was a gambler named Miguel who'd lost an eye and spent the entire voyage squinting without depth at the horizon. They arrived in San Francisco, but Alfonso wanted the mountains, the desert, a place with no oceans anywhere in sight. "On all the maps, Colorado looked wild," he once said, "though no one mentioned it'd be so hard to breathe."

They were halfway drunk now—everyone, that is, except for Diego. Lizette had rushed with Alfonso to the dance floor, her shapely hips knocking couples out of her way like a strong tide. Diego remained at the table with Luz. He slumped in his chair, rolled his shirtsleeves to reveal the small snake tattoo on his left arm, just above his elbow. As the booze worked through Luz's veins, she felt cradled by the room. She asked Diego if he was all right, but either he didn't hear her, or he didn't care. Sometimes men were like that, treating a girl's voice as if it had slipped from her mouth and fallen directly into a pit.

Lizette sashayed back to the table then and bumped Diego with the back of her hand. "You're being a real party pooper," she said. "Al's going in search of more hooch. Want any?"

Diego sipped his water. He told her no, thank you.

"You know," said Lizette, "I was reading a book on—"

"*You*," Diego said, "were reading a book?"

Lizette sat down. "I'm just all beauty and no brains. That's what my family thinks of me, right?"

"No, not in the slightest," Luz shook her head. "It's all hips and no brains."

Lizette shot her cousin a dirty look. She smoothed the lap of her dress, keeping her eyes on her palms as if she were reading a fortune. "This book said there will be no drinking water by the year 1955. Too many Anglos coming to the Southwest region. It'll be like a war over water."

Diego frowned, as though he were considering something very serious. He said, "Don't worry about it, prima. You can keep drinking what Al mixes in the bathtub."

"My goodness," said a high hoarse voice. "My little feetsies are killing me."

Luz was startled as David and his blond date rushed the table, plopping themselves into open seats. They were laughing and catching their breath, and they smelled strongly of whiskey. David's curls had gone limp with sweat and the blonde's makeup was smudged beneath her eyes, a white woman with lengthy teeth and collarbones like metal hangers, her cleavage wagging.

"How the hell is everyone?" said David. "Glad you could make it."

Lizette made her hands into a cone and shouted, "Congratulations, David. Real great news."

"Thanks." He beamed. "Hey, where's Maria Josie? Off stealing someone's wife?"

"Come to think of it," Diego said. "I haven't seen your ma all night."

David ignored Diego and straightened his bowtie. He was the only person in Rainbow Hall wearing a tuxedo. And why not? It was his night. "Meet Elizabeth," he said. "Elizabeth, the Lopez family."

"Elizabeth Horn," the blonde said, fanning herself with a napkin. On an empty chair, she stretched her legs and slid off her shoes. There was a smell like spoiled milk. "Now, will one of you dolls take this maniac out for a spin? I need a rest!"

Lizette said no, that she was exhausted. "Plus, I'm waiting for Al."

David said, "Always wanted to dance with a fortune-teller, anyway."

"I'm not much of a dancer," said Luz.

"Or a fortune-teller," said Diego.

David placed his hands over Luz's shoulders, his grip like his father's, warm and dense. "We'll go slow." He dropped his hands to her wrists and guided her up from the table. A puppet without a string, Luz thought.

"Oh, you're doing me the greatest favor," said Elizabeth Horn, lighting a thin cigarette.

The song wasn't slow, and David pulled Luz closer than he should. The frame made by their arms was more like a root than a box. Her breasts flattened into his chest as they danced deeper into the crowd. He wasn't the best dancer at Rainbow Hall, but he was effortless, his movements as natural as taking a breath or falling asleep. His eyes were halfway closed like those of the shiftless who camped in the alleys. Luz noticed he hadn't aged, but he'd grown broader in his shoulders and waist, more substantial in form.

"Why lie?" David whispered. "You know how to dance."

"It depends on who you're asking. Diego says I'm lousy."

"You've got quite the step. I'm sure most men who aren't your brother would agree." David placed his palm on Luz's left hip, squeezed. "You know, I remember when you were this tall."

"Can't stay little forever, right?"

David moved his face along Luz's neck. The fullness of his lips grazed her throat. "No, you sure can't."

Luz breathed. She felt a dim pulse between her legs, and her face burned red. She placed her cheek against his shoulder and watched the ballroom spin sideways. The room stretched with the twirling faces of the crowd. "Congratulations, by the way. Everyone's so proud."

David plunged Luz into a dip. Her hair spread and caught around her nose and mouth until everything was upside down. She used to play like that as a little girl. She'd hang from a dead juniper branch, imagine she walked barefoot among the clouds, breathed sand for air, lay upon the sky as her bed. The air was always so sweet and full, so alive with sage and thistle. Though Rainbow Hall's tin ceiling glimmered with gold, it was nothing compared to the vastness of her past. Luz felt sad then, as if she missed her mother and father, their decrepit cabin. David then raveled Luz upward. She forced a smile, shaken and disoriented. Near the front doors, an Anglo girl stood in an emerald coat. Her red hair was fire against her ghastly skin. Her eyes were punched black and her mouth was a tenuous line. Eleanor Anne? Could it be?

"Do you know her?" Luz pointed toward the doors, kept time. "The girl in the green coat." She gestured again, but stopped. No one stood beside the entrance. The hallway was lonely in red carpet. Empty. "She was just there. I know—"

"Who?" David asked, looking around.

Luz reached for her mouth. Pain seeped from her molars into her jaw, spilling from one section of her face to another. She turned away from David and spat into her hands, expecting blood but finding only saliva. "I'm so sorry," she muttered. "I need air. I'm sorry."

Outside Luz shielded her face with the bottom of her dress, her legs exposed as she hobbled down the alley. She stared at the front end of a pickup truck, headlights blasting warmth into her eyes. Silhouettes shifted in black lines, and the sounds of the truck's engine sputtered among footsteps. Luz staggered forward, her pumps crunching gravel, her breath a silvery cloud. She heard muffled sounds, broken coughs. She then saw Diego pinned to the truck's metal hood. Two men held his arms outward like wings, while a third man, dressed nicely in white suspenders, heaved with something heavy in his hands. A brick. The man slammed it into Diego's jaw. The slab gleamed wetter as he brought it down again and again, a sound like a mallet upon meat. The men had the movements of work, repetition, comradery. When they dropped Diego where he stood, his body made a sound like nothing else. A limp sack, the cold ground. The men looked up and one pointed his bloodied hands directly at Luz. "Was this in your tea?" he said, and then loaded himself into the truck along with the others as they barreled away. Luz screamed at the ribbon of Diego's blood, luminous and long like a tongue stretched from his mouth to his belly.

FIVE

Night Owl

Teresita suffered from insomnia and was awake fixing posole when the men rushed into her kitchen, tossed cups and plates from her table, and dropped Diego onto the oilcloth. Luz and Lizette followed like flower girls, their eyes matted and red from weeping the entire ride to Fox Street. The kitchen swelled with voices, the slap of a spoon on the oven's edge, a knife slicing pork. A single lightbulb swung over the table, casting bold shadows over Alfonso, David, Papa Tikas, Tío Eduardo, a handful of others, and a halfway-conscious Diego. His breathing was very slow and he could not speak. Luz avoided looking at him. She preferred the men's scuffed shoes, the pristine linoleum, her ankles smeared with dust and blood. It was a little after midnight, but the night had expanded into something else, something immeasurable and void.

Teresita yanked her daughter's arm, directing Lizette to give the men glasses of milk and bowls of yesterday's menudo. "Sober those drunks up," she said. "This is unacceptable. All of you," Teresita shouted, her wooden spoon high as a shield, "get the hell out of my kitchen."

The men were a small mob in their crunched shirtsleeves and wetted hair. Maria Josie was with them, too—David had driven to Hornet Moon, thrown rocks at the windows until she woke up, a woman beside her (they had said in snide remarks) she left behind as she rushed out. Their armpits were damp and their alcoholic stench was thick. Voices caught like fire. Anguish grew or diminished within seconds. The room was sick with fear. Papa Tikas raised both arms, as if to argue with Teresita. His velvet jacket lay lazily over one shoulder and his watch face was speckled in blood. He muttered into a clenched fist before retreating from the kitchen, the other men following as Lizette trailed them with food, the glasses of milk bone-white against the pewter tray. The men debated their way into the next room, cursing in all their languages. Teresita told Luz to stand at the counter, finish chopping pork for tomorrow's meal. "Wash your hands," she said, and Luz felt sobs returning to her face, but out of fear of Teresita's anger she sealed that part of herself away. She focused on the meat, the faint and spiraled veins, and as she cut, Luz noticed that her red satin dress was darker in all the places where she'd cradled her brother's head to her body, crying out for help in the empty alley.

Teresita set her spoon on the stove. She wiped her hands over her beige apron, working the flesh between her fingers. She was a beauty like Lizette, though motherhood had increased her body, left her breasts full and low, her forehead in a constant pinch. Her black hair was braided down her left shoulder, and she wore strings of turquoise clipped into each ear. She had bronze skin, a wide and regal nose, and intimidating black eyes that were wet like a cow's. Bending over Diego, Teresita's form was commanding. The smell of his body mixed with the scent of hominy, like pennies, turned soil, very alive. She lifted his chin with two fingers, turned his neck side to side. Sniffed.

Luz turned away and returned to her pork.

Teresita said, "Better get used to it, mija. Soon you'll be a wife and a mother. They blow themselves up in mines, shatter bones with gears, crush their faces with rocks. Who do you think fixes all that?"

There was commotion from the other room then, a pounding on the front door. Luz heard Maria Josie's voice rise above the men. A woman screeched from the stoop, pleading to be allowed inside the home. The woman said that she loved Diego, her voice rhythmic with tears. *Eleanor Anne,* Luz thought, and then Maria Josie shouted, firm and final, "Can't you see you've done enough? You'll get us all killed if they followed you here." Then the door was slammed.

Lizette reentered the kitchen with an empty tray. She gave the table and Diego a sidelong glance. She looked like herself but as a little girl. Her eyes met Luz's and together they understood each other, now fluent in fear.

"He needs a sew," Teresita said. "Get the white thread. Break some ice."

Lizette reached first for the metal pick in the sink. Beside Luz at the counter, she hacked at a block of ice before plunging her hands into a junk drawer filled with rubber bands, matchboxes, needles, and twine. Their movements were synced, two girls working away in a kitchen, as if food were spread across the table instead of their semiconscious kin. Teresita flicked on the radio. She moved the dial from a mystery serial and past Leon Jacob until she landed on a lonesome ranchera, the emotional notes held within her throat, a humming above the table.

Lizette brought her mother the thread, and Teresita pulled an arm's length against the lighted room and snapped it with her teeth. Diego groaned across the table. Beneath her apron, Teresita wore a gossamer nightdress, the cotton style of peasant girls. She almost seemed younger than Lizette or no age at all. She pulled a chair near Diego's face and told the girls they could watch, if they wanted. "I won't make you fix him this time, but it'll serve you both to learn." She got to work, her nimble fingers diving into Diego's skin as though he were a quilt. Luz was ashamed of herself as she moved to the open doorway between the kitchen and the other room. She couldn't look at the garbled openings in her brother's face.

"There, that should do it," said Teresita, tying the thread in a bow, Diego's moans escaping his mouth. "Easy does it, Nephew. Easy does it."

SIX

To the Edges

For seven days, Maria Josie sat at Diego's bedside, reading aloud from an old copy of *Don Quixote*, breaking only for meals, sleep, and her long shifts at the mirror factory. Between the book's pages, Maria Josie would glance up with a watchful gaze, casually, as if checking the clock. It had snowed, padding the exterior brick and rickety roof in a pleasing weight. Several times a day, Luz brought Maria Josie water with iodine and an herb called plumajillo. She'd walk swiftly to the nightstand and place the white dish beside wilted lilies and dried marigolds and heaps of bloody gauze and wooden rosaries. There were santo candles burned into liquid wax. San Miguel, glowing from his eyes. The bedroom smelled like sickness, a plumy stench that clung to Luz's clothes and hair. She'd open the windows only to mingle the smells of illness with carcasses and smog. Reina and Corporal looked on from their glass cage, and because Maria Josie was afraid of them Luz took over their feedings. Sunlight would warm their faces as she dropped mice into the cage.

"Any better?" Luz asked one afternoon, sprinkling hay into the terrarium.

Maria Josie sat beside Diego, cleaning her glasses. "See for yourself."

From across the room, Luz considered Diego's face. It was the size that frightened her most, the inhumanness of his proportion. "I just don't understand why'd they do it. Why Diego?" she asked with sadness, thinking of the brick slammed into her brother, over and over.

Maria Josie grimaced, curving her arm in a flannel jacket over the chair's back. "They're men, white men." She pushed forward and gripped Diego's foot, small and paw-like beneath his quilt. "That's what they do."

On Thursday afternoon, Luz returned home from washday. She was surprised to see Diego wasn't in bed. He was seated in a white chair with his face to the window, the orange curtains tied in great bows, his back lumped forward in gray pajamas. Maria Josie wasn't home, and the apartment felt emptier without her. From the roof, there were sounds of melting snow. In the hallway, Luz slipped off her winter coat and hung it on the rack. She hurried toward her bedroom, afraid of seeing her brother mangled, the image of his new face, a sharp pain in her heart.

"Can't say hello?" Diego said, his voice hissing, ugly.

Luz paused. She mouthed *goddammit* to herself before reluctantly stepping into the main room. The floorboards shifted.

"I heard you found me." Diego kept his face to the window.

The room was bright. The bed had been stripped of its sheets, and a sagging pinstriped mattress was exposed. The nightstand's bloody gauze was gone and the room smelled of sunshine and wet pavement. "I picked up your teeth," she said. "The ones I could find." Luz looked to a clay bowl on the bureau.

Diego laughed, rattling the floor. "How many?"

"Five."

"Well, shit," he said. "Tooth fairy owes me."

Jazz came over the radio, a lone horn whining. Luz went to the bureau, clinked bottles of cologne as she eyed Reina along the windowsill with her vertebrae in four peaks, sacred mountains across her back. "Have they ate?" she asked.

"First thing this morning."

Diego swiveled around then, facing Luz in polished light. His swelling had eased, though his jawline was lopsided and curdled, as if the upper skin had fused to his throat. Razor-thin lines traced the shaved sides of his head, ending at his mashed mouth, where Teresita's stitching resembled train tracks. Diego's face went from purple to green, yellow to black. Luz could see through a hole in his left cheek, clear into his mouth, to the bed of his tongue. In his lap, Corporal was funneled in a dark pile, and Luz must have made a face because Diego winced. He seemed in pain some-where inside his throat. Bending forward, he gave Corporal a nudge, the snake sliding like a puddle off Diego's blanketed lap. Luz was angry with herself, angry that part of her blamed her brother, for everything.

"Why were you outside the party?" she asked.

"I had a bad feeling, thought I should get going, but they caught me in the doorway."

"Who did?"

"Eleanor's people. Her brothers, her father."

"Why hasn't anyone called the police?"

"Come on, Little Light. You know why."

Luz knew as well as anyone that those men probably were the police, or at the very least, associated with them. The orange curtain wavered then and Reina darted her face around the edges of the bow.

Diego said after a long while, "They've let me go at Gates."

"What will you do? No one has shifts."

"All snakes, all the time." Diego struggled through a laugh, his cheek drafty through the stitched hole. "I'll go north. There's work in the fields."

Luz pictured her brother wading through a sea of knee-high crops, laboring over mud-caked beets, buried in long green rows, the sky ablaze with dust and clouds and locusts. "You're leaving?" she asked, her voice clipped with sorrow.

"Maria Josie's asked me to get going."

"But we came here together."

"And I'm no longer welcome."

"Why'd they do it, Diego?" Luz asked. "Tell me what happened."

Her brother wouldn't answer. He tilted his face, straightened his shoulders. Diego pointed to the window. "Look," he said. "Reina won't sit with me."

"Of course she will," said Luz.

Diego reached toward Reina, but the snake slinked behind the curtains, fluttering as if by a breeze. "No," he said, "she's afraid."

Within a week, most of Diego's things were cleared out of the main room. No velvet capes, no satin dress shirts, no hawk feathers or colognes. He had packed a yellowed satchel given to him by Maria Josie. The bag's leather was worn smooth and resembled a dried kidney. Deceptively large, it swallowed bars of soap, a boar-bristle brush, trousers, and dress shirts. Most everything else Diego sold or gave away. As for the snakes, on his last night in Denver, Luz followed Diego as he carried them in their wicker basket down the tenement's stairs and into the street. It was twilight. The streetlamps were lit. The air was crisp.

"You can come with us to the creek," he said. "Or stay. It's up to you."

"I can't watch," said Luz.

Diego tipped his hat. "A quick spade to the head. That's all."

"Why can't they stay with us?"

He raised the basket some, lightly twirling it by the roped handle. "They aren't meant to be without me. Besides, Maria Josie would kill them anyway."

Luz greeted the snakes one last time, giving their basket a tap before sliding off the lid. At the bottom, Reina was on top of Corporal, sleeping over his back as if he were a cot. Luz had known the snakes almost half her life. She'd miss them, awake in the middle of the night, cold and sifting like soil, a bedroom away. They seemed like protection. Against what, Luz wasn't sure.

"They're mine, Little Light," Diego said, as if he could feel Luz's questioning.

"Fine," she said. "Goodbye, snakes."

It was a little after eleven when Diego returned. Luz heard his key, the creak of hinges. She was alone at the kitchen table, the radio on a news program. Bonnie Parker and Clyde Barrow were wanted again, this time for murder. They had been hiding out in Dallas, but risked everything to see their families. Luz understood why outlaws would do that. It must be lonely going from town to town.

A Dallas grand jury had just delivered a murder indictment, and Luz wondered what that meant.

Diego shot Luz a look of dread, and the room charged with a new feeling. Grief. He had on coveralls and his hair was cut short. His face was clean-shaven and he walked, slump-shouldered, in a pair of new work boots, taking a seat across from Luz. He tossed an envelope onto the table.

"Go on," he said. "Open it."

Luz tore the seal with a fork's prong, revealing fifty dollars and the silver bear claw pendant. "Thank you, Brother."

"I pawned the chain, but the charm is nice. Should cover some of the rent next month."

"Was it quick? Reina and Corporal?"

Diego rubbed his face with both hands, as if he could wipe off his skin, remold his expression into something less revealing. "How about you read for me?"

"Your leaves?"

"Nah, the ending of *Don Quixote*. Yes, my leaves."

"I don't want to, Diego. I don't want to see nothing else."

On the radio, a woman howled and the detective shouted, *In all the alleyways, you crept into this one, you son of a bitch.* Diego leaned from his chair and shut off the radio. "Send me away with some hopefulness."

Luz finally agreed, boiling water on the stove, the kettle screaming. She poured the steaming water into a porcelain cup with blue flowers along the brim. The tea was rooibos, and Luz watched carefully as Diego sipped. She studied his face, told herself to remember. Who knew when she'd see him again? Across his neck was a crease, a faint wrinkle cutting his throat. His lips were scabbed purple along the bottom. He had healed somewhat, and Alfonso had found a friend who fitted Diego's mouth with porcelain teeth, paid for with a debt. His jawline was nearly back to normal, though it appeared more square than before. It was strange, Luz thought, how one night altered so much.

Diego finished. He handed his sister the cup. "Before you go in, how's it work? The things you see."

Luz was surprised. It wasn't like Diego to ask questions about other people. The cup was cold, as if it had never been filled with tea. "You know how it works."

"You see the future?"

"No, it's like a road. Sometimes, even with my memories, I get confused. I don't know if something happened, or if it could have happened. People are unpredictable, but there're only so many roads."

"That's no fortune at all," he said with a smirk. "Go on with it then."

Luz considered the cup. The black leaves were pushed to one side, leaking brown like spewed tobacco. The dark flakes blurred and soon Luz heard the sharp sounds of a pearl-handled razor against skin. It seemed like early morning and in her mind she saw their father standing in a singular column of sunlight before an open window. He wore no shirt and gazed into a wire-hanging mirror to his left, his suspenders resting against his thighs, circles of light beaded over his pale body. As the hairs fell from his face, Luz could see his cheeks, their delicate bones and deep dimples a wonderful surprise. She was a little girl again, before her father had left them, before he broke her heart at eight years old, and she cried herself to sleep every night until Diego would hold her, telling his sister it would be okay. Luz shook her head. No matter how many years had passed since their father had left, the image of him made her want to cry.

"Papa," she said at last. "I just see Papa. No one else."

Diego laughed luridly. "How is that deadbeat?"

"You have his markings on you," said Luz. "Like a scar."

"Well, shit," said Diego. "Who believes any of that bull, anyway?"

"I do," said Luz.

Before he left for good that night, Diego stood on the sidewalk with his satchel and hat. The neighborhood was cast in black and white, the moon full with abundant light. Street cats patrolled their territory, and brackish heaps of dirty snow rested in the gutters, melting slowly into the dark. He'd walk to the train station, and from there, Luz had no idea where her brother would go. She could sense his feelings of powerlessness. The night wind blew ugly through skeletal trees.

Diego said, "Our people never been this far north before, where I'm headed."

"Maybe you'll like it better."

"Shit, I still miss the Lost Territory. That's our home. Everything else is edges."

"I'll write you whenever I can," said Luz. "I'll tell you all about the neighborhood, all about Lizette, the dances. Everything."

He smoothed his sister's hair, kissed her forehead with his damaged mouth. "I love you, Little Light, and I promise I'll be back for you."

Hours later, Maria Josie brought the coolness of the night into the apartment on the shell of her jacket. With matter-of-factness, she said hello to Luz and hung her coat in the hallway. There were small cuts along her knuckles and wrists, tiny slashes from mirror shards that she'd later cover in a piñon salve. Maria Josie pushed a toothpick from one side of her mouth to the other. Luz studied her face as they stood beneath a dangling light in the hallway. There were shadows under her eyelashes, fanning, thick flaps. They were inches apart, and the claylike base of Maria Josie's skin gleamed.

"Why are you doing this to Diego?" Luz asked.

"I have my reasons, Luz." Maria Josie cleared her throat, removed the toothpick with a flicked wrist. "You feel a way now, but over time, it'll change."

"No, it won't. I have no brother now. I'm alone."

"You remember when you came here? When your papa left you," said Maria Josie. "I promise you that was the lowest you'll ever feel. No man will make you feel worse than that. Not even Diego."

The hallway resembled a cave with humid air and bowed walls where Luz looked to their shadows like puppets. She was angry with Maria Josie, could feel it leaking out into the apartment, this rage. Was there nothing she could control? No constant besides work and those she loved leaving? At seventeen years old, Luz's back often ached from hauling laundry across town, she had split toenails from too-small shoes, and a single worry line developing down her forehead like a crack in her skull.

"You just hate all men," said Luz and waited to be slapped, but it didn't come.

Maria Josie put her hands into her trouser pockets. Her forearms were corded and she smelled of sand. "When you first came here, to this apartment, you sat down on my floor with a little pillow sack filled with good shoes and clean underpants. Nothing else. You had no mama or papa. Only me and Diego, and what did I tell you? I said you could stay with me if you were good people, pulled your weight, weren't hurtful or cruel because of the fate befallen you. Ever since you were little, I've protected and watched you both. If I say it's time for Diego to move on, he needs to leave. You must trust me, Luz." With that, Maria Josie went toward their bedroom, turning back for only a moment. "You have a great light inside you, and I'm sorry you've known such loss at this young age."

Gently, she closed her door.

SEVEN

A Getaway Car

The Lost Territory, 1922–24

Maria Josie had once appeared at the cabin where Luz lived with her mother and father and Diego, high in the desert mountains, in that place called Huerfano. As if swirled into being through wind and sparkling snowmelt, she arrived in summer with no carriage or automobile or even a horse. It was nighttime and the sky was marbled in stars. She wore her hair in a tightly knit bun, long beaded earrings pouring like water onto her collarbones. Maria Josie was frantic, crying. She was strong and beautiful in a floral print dress. And pregnant. Luz saw it right away, the swell of life at her center.

"Please come with me, hermana," Maria Josie pleaded. "I am begging you. You can't live at the mercy of a man who beats you, who won't even marry you."

There was shouting, Mama standing before the door, pressing hard with her open palm, turning her own sister away. "What do you want me to do? Abandon my family?"

"Bring them," Maria Josie cried. She turned to Luz, peering through the cabin door. "Baby Luz, come with me. I'm your auntie. I've come to get you all."

Mama was closing the door now, the room moving from starlight into a walled darkness. "He'll be back from the saloon. You trying to get us all killed?"

Luz stayed motionless in the semi-dark, allowing her terror to widen, to sweep across the dirt floor, over the stove and washbasin and rocking chair. Her mother and auntie began speaking a language Luz didn't know. It wasn't the Spanish they spoke, the English, or even the French of her father. It was Tiwa, Diego told her later, and Luz found it lovely even as Maria Josie cried out in its sounds before embracing her sister, rushing through the cabin dimness to hug Luz and Diego, her belly pressing into them with force. She then disappeared into the night in the same way she came.

"Whatcha see?" Luz asked Diego a couple of years later as they stood on a granite boulder. It was 1924 and she was eight years old. The land was stretched with the movements and temperament of sleeping volcanoes, high desert dust, and that lengthy coal vein beneath their feet. "A trap?"

Diego was bent over a long crevice in the earth, his back to his little sister. He was hatless with dark hair spiked above his neck. They were among purple wildflowers, tall grass, and red willows, the laughter of a stream. *Those mountains over there*, their mother would say, pointing southbound. *Your grandfather was born of those mountains, and these mountains here*, she'd add, *they cradle the Rio Grande*. She taught the children to hold their hands against the sunlight and wind, to feel the sensation of home against their palms. Santuario, she'd tell them, as they hung laundry on the line, picked chokecherries from the riverbanks, collected sage and oshá from the roadsides.

That morning, there had been a note across their schoolhouse door. Mrs. Oberdorf was sick, Diego read, and the children were not under any circumstances to enter the one-room schoolhouse, which seemed more like a barn to Luz than a place for learning. She hated the way Mrs. Oberdorf made her feel. She spoke to the children in the mining camp very slowly, as if they couldn't understand English, and only Anglo students were allowed to sit near the front. Spanish and Indian and all the other languages weren't allowed, and Diego, who often blurred several languages at once, frequently received a ruler to the hand or even a whack across the face. But on this mild morning in early October, school was canceled and Mrs. Oberdorf was at home *coughing up blood into a washbasin,* Diego claimed. *Hopefully a consumptive.*

Diego soon let out a wild yelp at the edge of the human-sized fissure in the rock. The air was cooler above the crack, resting there like oil in water. He had taken his coiled walking stick and banged around the insides of the earth. "Holy smokes!" he yelled and knifed into the gap, retrieving from the depths a baby rattlesnake wrapped around the warped end of his stick. "Look," he said to Luz, raising his staff, the snake motionless and draped.

"Nasty," Luz said. "Move it away from me."

"This is no 'it,'" Diego said. "She's a girl, can't ya see?"

"Nuh-uh." Luz shook her head. "Why was she down there?"

"Because someone wanted her gone," Diego said. "But I'll save her." The baby girl snake unraveled herself, stretching the entire length of her scaled body down the stick until her forked tongue poked from her mouth and grazed the edge of Diego's right hand. "Reina," he said. "That's what I'll call you."

Diego raised the stick vigorously as if against a great sea, unintentionally smacking an overhanging branch. An angry hum exploded from the mummy-wrapped nest now lying cracked at his feet.

Wasps poured into the sky.

"Di-ego," Luz stammered.

"Run," Diego hollered. "Fast, and into the water." He unhooked Reina from the stick and brushed wasps from the snake's face before sliding her into his book bag.

Luz tore down the mountainside, her booties kicking up stones and loose dirt as she padded the ground in her little footsteps. The morning sun was shifting into afternoon, a large hot globe with wasps all around, as if Luz's eyesight had cracked into yellow and black. Her heart pounded drum-like in her chest, and she called out to Diego across the land. "Are they getting you, Brother? Are they?"

Then, jump. Splash. A red hot pain turned cold.

Stung and swollen, somewhat dry but still mostly wet, the children came over the hillside toward their block of company cabins. Their mother was away in the big town, Saguarita, as she was every Wednesday, selling jars of chokecherry jelly in specially woven baskets. Their father was deep underground in the coal mines. He worked the winds, the sunless shafts where men were often blown to bits, suffocated, trapped. The miners kept yellow canaries in square cages, their lungs and the lungs of their wives and children all webbed in nighttime-colored muck.

"I'd rather die by a bear," Luz said matter-of-factly. She felt pain around her left wrist and her own neck, but couldn't find any marks, and as they rushed home, she pleaded with the mountains not to let a creature so obnoxious as a wasp kill them dead. "At least that's extraordinary."

Diego spoke with a strange mindfulness in his voice. "Don't say that, Little Light. Gives me a bad feeling." They were going to be fine—just needed some salve, he explained, and Diego knew where his mother kept it in the kitchen with all her tinctures and dried flowers, roots and herbs. He had been bitten by snakes and spiders in the past, and he recognized that certain insects and some plants were filled with poisons. "Ways to protect themselves, really," he told his little sister. "They don't do it to hurt us. They just don't want to die themselves."

"Nobody wants to die," Luz said. "But you don't see me going around stinging and hurting people."

As they walked alongside the outer edge of the cabins, Diego gently pulled his little sister's braid. "Someday you might."

They came over the rocky hillside, looking down at their one-room cabin, the third on the left, away from the coal furnaces. The air was choked with black smoke, and all around freshly cleaned clothes blew across wiry lines, dirtied once again, absorbing dust.

Then there was a sight Luz hadn't seen before.

"What is *that*?" she said as they stepped over the trail, pointing with surprise at a black automobile rounded like a cockroach parked alongside their cabin.

"A Model T." Diego stopped walking. "The mine's superintendent has one," he said. "Some of the older Italian and Black boys got to ride in it once." Diego slung his book bag from his right side, paused at an old fruit crate. Delicately, he pried the baby snake from his bag as if he were removing a single eyelash from a cheek. "Shhhh," he told the snake, before placing her in the crate and motioning for Luz to follow him into the cabin.

"Wow," said Luz. "Do you think we'll get to ride in a car?"

"I don't think so," he whispered, and they stepped inside.

In the cabin, divided with once-white sheets, their father stood tall among the fabric, many papers in his hands. The room smelled of oil and leather, etchings of chile powder. His shoulders were visible in thin suspenders, the outline of his jaw. Their father looked at his children with insulted surprise, shoving paperwork into an open travel chest. He was in a hurry, mildly out of breath.

"Why aren't you two at school?" he asked with clipped irritation.

"Papa," Luz said, waving her arms into the air. "We were stung! By wasps."

"School's canceled," said Diego, stepping toward his mother's collection of medicines along the windowsill. He pulled a glass vial from a low wooden shelf. He began applying dabs of the liquid first to Luz's arms and then along his own neck. "Mrs. Oberdorf is sick," he said, and then, with further consideration, added, "She's coughing up blood."

"Blood?" said Benny, his Belgian-French accent thick. "Best you children stay away."

"What're you doing home, Papa?" said Luz, sweetly. She ran to her father's side, hugging him hard around his sinewy legs.

Benny kneeled. He ran his hands along Luz's black braid and kissed her on the forehead. "I have to go away on a trip, my baby girl."

"In the automobile?"

"Yes, baby girl."

Near their father's feet, the travel chest was filled with his wool coats and work boots, a smattering of script and some government money, too. Luz expected a fierce punishment to rain down on her and Diego for getting stung, but their father only shoved more papers into the trunk and slammed closed the door with its brass lock. Benny then stood, his shoulders grazing the hanging sheets, the cloth fluttering like a visible wind.

"You two help me load up. This trunk here and another out back."

Diego cautiously walked around his father, eyeing the chest. "Why do you have Mama's money in there?" he asked. "Her silver, her turquoise?"

Benny hardened his posture. "Your mother's money?"

"Yes," Diego hissed. "We need that money, so we can leave this damn coal camp someday."

Their father paused for a moment before lifting his right arm and slapping Diego, as hard as he could, palm-side in the face. The sound was like splitting wood. "Everything here is mine," he said.

Diego let out one groan, but he clenched his mouth, keeping anything else inside.

Luz stepped back out of reaction. She was used to her father's temper. One moment he could be euphoric, singing Belgian songs, strumming his mandolin, kissing their mother and lifting Luz high into the air, swinging her with joy around the cabin. But like a thunderstorm flooding the plains, their father often changed, a violence bursting from his mouth and hands, usually directed at their mother. When that happened, Diego would walk Luz around the camp, telling her stories about the mountains, the names of the trees, the pictures in the stars.

"Don't you question me, Son," he said. "Get the trunks now."

Diego helped their father load up the automobile with a pained expression. Luz sat outside on a tree stump, surrounded by the haze of dirt from their hauling feet. When they had finished and the cockroach car was filled with every artifact of their father's existence, Benny walked through the sunlight cascade, taking a seat behind the steering wheel. He started the engine and drove off in a rumble, the automobile gaining speed, a foggy pillar dispersing into the air. It went on like that for some time, rocking back and forth, until, suddenly, the car stopped and Benny jerked open his door. He stepped down and ran toward the cabin.

Luz yelled, "Did you forget something, Papa?"

"Yes," he said, trotting to her feet. He hunched over, sucking in a huge breath. With Luz in his arms, he lifted her into the sky, swirling her in a circle, the entire world a colorful blur. She focused on her father's face—his freshly shaven cheeks, his green eyes, the slight upcurve of his lip. When Benny set Luz back down, he kissed her face and touched her hair one last time. Luz gazed at her father as tears flooded his reddened eyes. He was turning away from her now, hiding his crying against the landscape.

It was the first time it happened, that Luz suddenly understood something unsaid. She knew, sensed it in her hands and heart, a feeling spreading like ice water to her mind. Her father was a liar, and he was leaving and not coming back.

She began to cry as she had as a baby, thick, rolling, guttural. Luz held on to Benny's shirtsleeves, pulled his hands to her face.

"Papa," she said, in agony.

He pushed his daughter away from his light skin, and in the haste of parting said, "Be a good girl, my baby, my little light."

Luz would look back on that day with a certain amount of shame. Even then, at eight years old, she felt foolish not to sense what came next—the long winter without adequate food, the blizzard nights when the hearth inside the company cabin grew ice, and those terrible and more terrible things her mother was forced to

endure in that mining camp of men. But how could she have fore-
seen that her father, Benny Alphonse Dumont, would abandon
his family so calmly it was as if he were tossing out a pair of heavily worn boots? And, more important, how was Luz to know, at
such a young age, that everything, good or bad, is eventually taken
away?

PART 2

EIGHT

The Inner Self

The Lost Territory, 1892

Pidre settled in a town named Animas, the inner self, the soul. It was seated against the railroad and a wide river that flowed down from the San Juan Mountains near the emergence point, where his people had crawled out of the earth at the beginning of time. He took jobs in saloons, swept out horse stables, kept his money under a horsehair mattress in his boarding room. It was demanding work, but for every cent made, Pidre knew he could turn it into ten more.

The town was different from the village. The train's steam rolled through the sky like a hovering ghost, coating everything in its wake in dark soot. French, Spanish, Diné, Apache, any kind of man you could dream of frequented the town. Pidre walked the muddy and bustling streets with a sense of reverence and determination. He tipped his beaver cap to other Indios in European garments, the freedmen in elegant suits. He savored baked goods made by women from lands as far away as Greece and Italy. At lunch counters, his tin pail in hand, he smiled and waved and compared the shape of his eyes to those from the East, the Chinese rail workers, the Japanese farmers. As it was in Pardona, citizens of Animas enjoyed his optimism, his undying work ethic, his childlike wonder at the simplest acts of beauty, a bursting sunset, peeling a grapefruit from the coasts of Califas. But Animas could be an ugly place, too, where those deemed criminal were strung up in the town plaza, death by hanging, a distinct American bloodlust.

After three years in the town, Pidre had saved enough for an investment. He considered his options delicately. Many of his compadres had wasted their earnings on silver claims that ran dry in a matter of months. He could put down a payment on a hotel, a small cattle ranch, a brothel perhaps, or maybe a saloon. One morning as Pidre paced the slim walkways of his boardinghouse, considering his many options, his hands wringing at his center, an Irish miner and fellow boarder named Michael "Mickey" Garrett stopped him before the staircase. Mickey was wearing new boots that he claimed were made of ostrich. They were purple with black dots and raised spikes. He stood before Pidre on the middle step, lifted his right foot, and said, "Take a look. Bet they taste like chicken."

Pidre contemplated the boots for several seconds. He said, "Very pretty, Mickey."

Mickey lumbered to the top of the stairs and stood before the narrow windows overlooking Main Street. He gripped Pidre's forearm, guiding him to the eastern view. Men exited brothels and saloons with sore eyes. They held their hands to their foreheads and stumbled toward their horses and boardinghouses. The sun glistened over the mud streets and brick buildings, making the town appear, if only for a few short minutes, pristine. "Do you want to know where I got 'em?"

"No, not particularly," said Pidre.

Mickey laughed. He had a ruddy nose and a dirty beard.

Pidre reached out and smoothed his friend's neck. "Put some salve in it. The ladies will appreciate that."

"Haven't seen a proper woman since I left Dublin." Mickey's bluish eyes widened and he pointed toward Fourth Avenue. "That man there," he said, "the one with the cane. He sold me the boots."

A slim man in a French top hat walked the street in languorous strides. He held a decorative silver-capped cane in his left hand, though he barely tapped the ground as he moved. He didn't stop every few steps to nod and offer morning remarks to shopkeepers or passersby. He simply went forward as if he knew no one and didn't want to. The man seemed interesting, notable even. "Why should I care?" Pidre said.

"Because," said Mickey, "he's got something you'd like to see."

At week's end Mickey and Pidre rode on horseback to the farthest corner of town to a section that wasn't incorporated into Animas. It was a no-man's-land, dropped into the Lost Territory, marked by no imaginary or geographic borders. It was nearing nightfall. They approached a wooden cabin beside a bend in the river that was so wide and deep it appeared as a dim blue lake. It was early autumn. The aspens were ablaze. The men walked in their boots, sounds of cacti crunching beneath their feet until the noises deadened at the red sandstone walls of the canyon. They entered the cabin with their hats in their hands and their pistols in their sleeves.

His name was Otto Fitzpatrick and he sat before the fireplace in a rocking chair, a spittoon at his feet, his silver hair in strings around his cavernous face. Had they not known who he was, they would have assumed he was a wild man who lived off the land and ate mostly crows and squirrels. But Otto Fitzpatrick, a trader, had recently come by rail from New York City and brought with him trunks of the latest Parisian men's fashions, electric lamps, anthropology books on the Native peoples of the American West, good liquor, and trading cards. The cabin was an emporium open only by invite. Pidre hadn't encountered a trader like him before. Mickey had told him that Otto Fitzpatrick came from a family of Wall Street investors and vast landowners of the American South. "It's a game to him," Mickey had said on the wagon ride over. "He's a competitive son of a gun."

"Mr. Fitzpatrick, I've got a buddy of mine here for you." Mickey spoke loudly and kneeled on his left leg.

Otto stared into the fire. He spat tobacco at his feet. The sound was like a bullet in rain. "Repeat yourself. I didn't catch a thing."

Mickey went to speak again, but Pidre interrupted him. He said in Tiwa, "I hear you have something to show me."

Otto's face was unshaven, and as he heard the sounds of Pidre's mother tongue, he rolled his stubbled cheeks into a type of smile that was portentous yet welcoming. He answered in Tiwa with nearly impeccable pronunciation. "Northern pueblos? A resilient people if I ever encountered some. Who exactly is your clan, son?"

"Pardona," said Pidre. "I come from the Sleepy Prophet. She raised me up, but before that, they don't know. I am Winter People."

Mickey walked toward the fireplace. He swiped his hands across the mantel and knocked over a coyote skull that made a shattering sound against the floor. "You don't hear me talking Gaelic just cos I can."

Otto worked his jaw with slow fingers and got to his feet. A smell like leather and cedar filled the room. "Ah, the mick has linguistic talents, too. Well, come with me. I'll take you out back."

It was hard to believe such a thing existed. Some twenty yards behind Otto's cabin was a low trail that disappeared into juniper bushes and came out at a meadow surrounded by red cliffs. In the center of the cliffs, some fifty feet high, a massive alcove gaped in the stone wall like an open, toothless mouth. A cedar tree grew in the center, dressed in sunlight, a blazing luminous cloak. In the span of several minutes the colors of the alcove shifted from scarlet to violet with a burned section of cedar the only indication of neutral color.

"Follow me up," Otto said, heading toward a wooden ladder at the alcove's left side. It looked as though it'd snap in a wind gust.

Mickey and Pidre shivered inside the alcove, some twenty degrees cooler. Otto pulled a kerosene lantern from his satchel, illuminating the stone surface with warm light. The sun set as the men walked in deafening echoes throughout the cold space. Moss flourished along the rear wall where water dripped from the mesa above. The cedar tree, the only vegetation apart from the moss, twisted its trunk toward the ceiling light. Pidre smiled at the sight of Venus. The violent planet blinked through a crack in the stone ceiling. The walls were blackened by three-hundred-year-old smoke.

"The ancient ones," said Pidre, "they lived here and abandoned it."

"Sometimes it's best to move on," said Otto, running his hands along the cool rocks. "Maybe something better was waiting for them elsewhere."

"Perhaps. Perhaps," said Pidre.

He watched as more stars appeared, a dazzling quilt of sky. He kicked the base of the cedar. Tiptoed between worn footpaths. Ran his hands over the smoke-stained walls. The air smelled sharp of greenery and dirt, a rich earthen soil, a windy calm. Across the stone ceiling Pidre made out the sight of an ancient one's handprint, permanent in black smoke. "What do you reckon this space is good for in today's world, Otto?"

Otto pushed his silver hair away from his face. He raised a bedraggled left hand. He told the men to listen. He gathered air in his lungs and sang out a long and soulful note. *Home, home on the range.* The notes slipped between rock and cedar and wind for a dozen or more echoes, repeating and playing against the four directions, across the earth, the stars, traveling inside the men's hearts. "It's a theater," said Otto. "And a fine one at that."

Pidre gripped Mickey's shoulders, as if to say, *Good work, brother.* "How much you want?"

Otto kneeled. He picked up a few pebbles, spattering them out of his hand and over the alcove's edge. "I'd like a good business in here. A place to put Animas on the map. A man who knows how to bring people. My cabin included."

"Now how much is that in U.S. currency?" Pidre mirrored Otto's hand movements, plucking pebbles from the earth, tossing them over the ledge.

"One thousand dollars. And I want ten percent of the monthly revenue for the first three years. If those terms are suitable for you," said Otto, "then I'll have papers drafted, make it official."

Pidre didn't admit to Otto that he couldn't read any papers, but he was glad to have found a friend, someone who could decipher the written language of white men.

Mickey nodded and spoke up. "And I can help with any *fine* details."

Pidre looked to the night sky, where the ancient and cracked face of the Sleepy Prophet appeared in a starry cloud. Her eyes were closed and her mouth was held in a tight sneer. Reaching into his trouser pockets, Pidre found his pipe and tin filled with moist tobacco. He offered a pinch each to Mickey and Otto. All three men stood in the giant and empty alcove smoking under starlight, the sounds of their lighters flickering against the rocks, the echoes of their breath heavy in the sand.

That night, in cold sweats, Pidre saw his theater blooming before him, and he felt the presence of a woman traveling by wagon, somehow, faster than the iron horse.

MEXICAN SHARPSHOOTER'S HUSBAND MET HORRIBLE DEATH

Santa Fe, N.M., September 12, 1887. Mexican Sharpshooter Simodecea Salazar-Smith fatally shot husband Wiley Smith in face during Wild West circus, killing him instantly. A caged black bear had gotten loose and charged Mrs. Salazar-Smith during her performance in which she shoots a deck of cards from atop her husband's head. Mrs. Salazar-Smith is recovering with broken bones in both legs where the black bear mauled her. The animal weighed 250 pounds.

Jack Wesley's Wild West Show came to Animas in late summer. The show bills lined the street poles and horse stables, white banners with red and blue lettering, advertising bear wrestlers, vaqueros, trick riders, sharpshooters, and more. The townspeople didn't know what to expect from the infamous Jack Wesley show. There were murmurs in the saloons and storefronts—talk of an opening day parade, mentions of historical battle reenactments, the great and embellished drama of how the West was won, or, as Pidre looked at it, lost. He had spent several months anticipating the show's arrival. The performers had finished a European tour, several stops on the East Coast, rolling inward to those industrial towns like Indianapolis, Detroit, and Kansas City. Mickey first told Pidre about the Wild West shows. There, he explained, Pidre could find performers to fill his amphitheater with their nearly divine talents.

"I hear the bear guy, his contract is up after these last couple spots," Mickey said to Pidre over a bottle of mezcal. They were enclosed in the dark wood of Ma Chelington's gin mill. Amber chutes of sunlight licked the uneven floorboards whenever a new patron passed through the batwing doors. The saloon smelled strongly of men—sweat, gunpowder, and rye.

Pidre took a swill of his drink. He dabbed around his mouth with a black kerchief. "I don't want no wild animals. I can settle for trick riders, but a bear? That don't seem right."

"And imagine the shit! Well, 'pose it's no worse than horse shit." Mickey laughed in a gruff way and smacked his thigh, his dusty trousers releasing a brownish haze between them.

Pidre smiled and shook his head. "I'd rather stay away from bears."

"Suit yourself," said Mickey. "But these sons of bitches always want to be within an inch of death."

Pidre glanced through the darkened saloon windows. Outside, in the afternoon sun, horses and passersby moved as if in shadows, some shallow and hazy representation of themselves. It reminded Pidre of the hours before waking, long after the mind has gone to sleep, when our world meets the world beyond, and spirits shuffle soundlessly in the night.

On a Wednesday morning, Jack Wesley's Wild West Show arrived in Animas by train, dozens of black and red cars charging in from the east, smog raining reverse into the sky. That morning was unseasonably warm, and as performers opened their car doors and stepped out onto the narrow decks, they appeared brilliant in white sunlight. The women wore high leather skirts, draped in fringe, sashaying their capable arms through the dry mountain breeze. Vaqueros and cowboys leaned over the rails, clasping on to the train's ladders in their buckskin gauntlet gloves. The people of Animas gasped and cheered, showered the performers with handfuls of candy and cigarettes. Graceful white horses rested their muzzles through gaps in their stock cars. The air was rich with the stench of gunpowder and manure.

From a hillside, Pidre studied the commotion, squatting above his spurs, rolling a piece of white sage in his palm. There was something ominous about the advent of Jack Wesley's Wild West Show. And though he couldn't fully grasp the eventual consequences of that day, as he was peering at those jubilant train cars screeching to a halt, Pidre felt some unknowable stone dropped into the pool of his destiny.

That evening, Mickey and Pidre dressed in their finest—topcoats and beaver pelts, the ostrich boots and silver buckles. They set out for the makeshift fairgrounds, the white beams of gas spotlights eclipsing the heavens, appearing to trample and flatten the stars. The sounds of the Wild West show boomed throughout canyon walls—a pistol crack, a long rifle's pinging bullet, the exasperated neigh of a horse, the shriek of a female trick rider, the roar of a hungry crowd. The temperature had dropped and the men breathed fog as they walked through the carnival's wooden and lighted arch. The main stage was housed in a red tent, the big top, as Pidre had learned from the other traveling circuses that came through the Lost Territory. But Jack Wesley's show was different.

As they walked the crowded fairgrounds, Pidre made note of the different acts. A side tent featuring a real-live authentic train robbery and another with a brightly lit sign: INDIAN WAR BATTLE REENACTMENT. The circus goers were mostly Anglos from Animas and the nearby ranches and villages. They hungrily entered the tents, their eyes wide with amazement, their mouths open and full of half-chewed kettle corn. It was in that moment that Pidre realized he had entered the strange world of Anglo myth, characters resurrected from the language of story, populating the realm of the living, side by side, if only for one night and one night only. Pidre came from storytelling people, but as he passed a big top devoted to the reenactment of *Custer's Last Stand*, he couldn't help but think that Anglos were perhaps the most dangerous storytellers of all—for they believed only their own words, and they allowed their stories to trample the truths of nearly every other man on Earth.

At a little past eight, Mickey and Pidre took their seats in the top row of the main tent, the wooden bleachers sticky with beer, the tent's crimson walls coloring the arena like a wound. The sawdust floor was scabbed and uneven, clumped in areas where drunks had vomited or were too lazy to relieve themselves in the outside stalls. The bleachers were filled with single men, working women, small children with coal-smeared faces. While Pidre recognized several of the town's people, the crowd was far larger than expected. They had come for the main attraction, a bear wrestler named Wilston Montez from Wyoming. He was rumored to be of Spanish and German lineage, a solid man with an enormous egg-shaped head, his face tattooed in inky pathways around his mouth and nose. He was shirtless and wore leather trousers, oddly flesh-colored. In some ways, Pidre noticed that Wilston Montez resembled a skinned and defeated bear himself.

Mickey handed Pidre a whiskey-filled flask from his coat and pointed to the arena's center where a vast silk curtain draped from the ceiling with ropes. A bedraggled clown sat on a barrel—face down, legs crossed—silent under the faintest spotlight. The clown appeared neither male nor female, but rather some in-between state, their face painted orange and red, their hair a marvelous blue. The clown drew silent stares as they tapped their long-shoed right foot against the barrel, a loud, rhythmic thwack. Then a drum line appeared, and the red tent erupted in marching music. The silk curtain fluttered and rose as if by a great wind and Wilston Montez materialized at the heart of the arena. The clown stood from their barrel and tumbled away. Wilston stepped down from the crate, revealing the great expanse of his musculature in rippled form.

"He's a wild man," Mickey said with a sparkle in his voice. "Hunted lions, sailed with pirates, trafficked in guns."

"And now he kills bears," said Pidre with an air of annoyance. "I suppose we're all animals to him, then."

If Mickey heard Pidre, he didn't let him know and instead drank heavily from his flask. The arena went black, and lights reflected inside the audience's eyes. They were silent and eager. They were greedy for death.

And then, the bear.

The animal emerged in iron shackles from the tent's open door. Half a dozen men led the black beast, bound and already bloody, its claws bent inward and deformed. The pink and meaty side of the animal's paws were cadaverous, as if by stigmata. Beneath the rising jeers of the crowd, Pidre could hear the bear's agonizing shrieks, an extended lonesome plea.

"My god, Mickey," Pidre said, dropping his face between his hands. "For shit's sake, it's damn near dead."

The bear had been unshackled by its handlers and was now face-to-face with Wilston, who promptly grabbed the animal's scarred snout and pushed the bear's contorted face into rancid sawdust. He began beating the bear's humped back with his fist. The bear grunted and Wilston reached for the animal's discarded chains. He roped the iron shackles around the bear's neck and pulled, impressive in his ability to drag the creature in a half-moon. But the bear was sickly, underfed, and Pidre knew that it was as close to death as possible while still being kept alive. That was a dangerous state—the line between the living and dead collapsed—and only evil could come of it. Wilston paused and held up his right hand to his ear, motioning for the crowd to raise their voices. He laughed maniacally. He grinned with mossy teeth. He pulled a blade from his flesh-colored trousers, taunting the animal with his flickering knife. The bear cried. There is no other way to say this. Pidre's eyes welled with tears as the animal moaned in agony with its mouth opened to the crowd. For the first time, Pidre saw that every tooth in the bear's mouth had been hastily removed, leaving behind a serrated bed of blackened gums.

"Let's get going," Pidre said to Mickey. "I don't want to see no more."

Mickey had gotten good and drunk. He was an agreeable man

and shrugged off Pidre's request with little protest. "You're the boss," he said.

They stood to exit the tent, navigating the bleachers, Pidre avoiding the sight of the tragic bear being beaten with leather straps by Wilston Montez. The crowd was louder than before and the ripe smells of their perspiration and abundant liquor mingled with the scent of the bear's glandular fear.

They were nearly out of the fairgrounds when Mickey pointed to a side tent, an oblong bluish womb: SIMODECEA SALAZAR-SMITH, MEXICAN BLACK WIDOW, A SHOT BETTER THAN ANY MAN! WATCH HER SHOOT CARDS, GLASS MARBLES, BOTTLES, CLAY PIGEONS, HOLES THROUGH DIMES, THE FLAMES OFF CAN-DLES, AND MUCH MUCH MORE!

"Now that's a sad story," Mickey said, stepping toward the bulletin board, running his hand over the dusty boards. "She's the one who killed her true love. Shot him clean through the head, took off half his face. They couldn't have an open casket, they say."

Pidre glanced at the sign and snorted. "Still performing after all that?"

"They say she started at eleven years old. It's the only life she knows."

Pidre stroked his smooth jawline and looked beyond the bulletin board through an opening in the tent flap. The rounded showground was half the size of the big top and hazy with smoke. There were sounds like songbirds confused by night. Forlorn whistles. A sterling gasp. As if pulled inward by an unseen embrace, Pidre guided himself and Mickey into the smallish tent. The crowd was sparse and the sawdust was clean, smelling of pine.

At first, it was difficult to see what drew the steady gazes of the serene crowd. Their eyes were wells of concentration, and their faces gleamed with gratitude, as if visited by a saint. Pidre heard the sonorous crack of gunfire. High on a wooden platform, she was a stately woman in a beaded gown, glistening in white fringe, her black hair braided down her back. Simodecea Salazar-Smith looked into a shard of broken glass like lightning in her left hand. And then with her long rifle aimed over her right shoulder, she shot.

"What's she shooting at, Mickey?" Pidre asked, dumfounded.

Mickey chuckled. He lightly elbowed Pidre. "Watch. She's reloading."

Simodecea leaned over her perch and waved to the crowd. They cooed, as if in love. One of Jack Wesley's workers had stepped into the ring. The man wore black and carried a metal bucket. Simodecea locked eyes with him and seemingly mouthed a countdown. Then, as if terrified by her aim, he tossed the bucket into the air and ran for his life, water splashing around him in a dome. Simodecea repositioned her rifle and pulled the trigger. The man in black reappeared and sifted his hands through the sawdust until he held up a gold coin with a bullet hole at its center. The crowd gasped with delight. Simodecea laughed and flipped her braid.

"He planted that coin," shouted an audience member. "What a joke. I want my money back, you crooks. A bunch of charlatans." He wavered, piss drunk near the left-side bleachers. In his right hand, he clasped a tin cup overflowing with Jack Wesley's watery beer.

Mickey chuckled. "Oh, Christ. Have some faith." He patted Pidre on the back. "I wouldn't test this one."

Pidre watched Simodecea's reaction with great interest. She winced as the man continued shouting from below. Some of the crowd yelled for him to quiet down. They threw their kettle corn. They hushed him and moved seats. But the drunken man didn't stop and Simodecea seemed taken out of her next trick. Her face flickered with annoyance and as her already sparse audience stood to leave, Simodecea twisted over the ledge, locked her skirted legs along the side, unraveled herself upside-down, and dangled like an elegant insect. She aimed her rifle and shot.

The drunken man's beer erupted across his face and chest. He screamed, shrill and child-like, as he fumbled with his hands over his body. "The bitch shot at me!"

"Leave," said Simodecea, raveling herself upright. "Now."

The man scrambled through the tent flaps, shaken and disoriented. Pidre laughed and felt his heart racing. "She's the one," he said.

Mickey removed his hat and shrugged. "And how do you expect to lure her away from this sparkling gig?"

Later, outside her dressing room, Pidre held his hat in his hands, wishing he had a bouquet of roses rather than palms wet with fear. Mickey kept watch for any handlers who'd push them away before Pidre could approach Simodecea with his offer, but they didn't have to wait very long, for she came rushing through in a flurry of fringe. She removed her beaded headpiece with quick hands and wore her gun across her back with a thin leather strap. As she approached her dressing room door, she spotted Pidre and rolled her deliriously black eyes. Pidre laughed and offered a handshake.

Simodecea looked at his hand as if he had offered her a half-eaten sandwich and kept walking into her dressing room, leaving the door open as she sat at her red vanity, staring hard at herself in the oval mirror. "What do you want?" she said.

"Señorita," Pidre said, "I just saw you and felt compelled to know you. The strongest feeling came over me."

"It's Señora, Señora Salazar-Smith."

Pidre apologized. He told her of course. "May I ask, are you happy in your current contract?"

Simodecea flung her head back. She was in the process of undoing her braid, and her laugh sparked into the air around them. "You're a poacher? Oh, darling. No one wants to poach me now. You're five years too late."

"And why's that?"

"Because I don't shoot at live targets anymore. Well, unless they're a real asshole."

Pidre told her he understood. He stepped slightly forward into her dressing room, hesitating to go farther until Simodecea locked eyes with him and nodded. "If you please forgive me," he said, "I think your talent and artistry speaks for itself. You dazzle without death."

"I am Death, haven't you heard?"

"No, Death protects you. She's all around you, even now."

"What traveling circus are you with, Mr.—?"

"Lopez, Pidre Lopez, and I'm not a circus man. I have a theater made of red stone. I need my star attraction, and I want you."

Simodecea laughed and turned sideways at her vanity, removing her stockings, her left leg kicked high into the air. "Well, that's very sweet of you, Pidre Lopez."

"You can name your price," Pidre said.

Simodecea thought on it for some time. "No live targets? No moving around?"

"No. None of that."

"One more thing," Simodecea said. "No goddamn bears?"

NINE

Women Without Men

Denver, 1934

Luz plunged a white sheet with bloodstains into a bucket of soapy water, pressing against a glass ribbed washboard. Still, blood remained and Luz quietly cursed. It was January and the washery was airy with linoleum floors, large steel tubs, mothers and daughters shouting at one another through the sharpness of lye.

"Why don't they just throw these out?" she said to Lizette, who was beside her, folding men's shirts over a metal table. "They have enough money."

Lizette gave the sheet a sidelong glance. "Because they're cheap. Use the cold water," she said. "Mama showed me. I had a lady's blouse once, all covered in blood, the lacey bib mostly. She said she'd pay me extra if I got it out. Lemon and ice water."

"What happened to her blouse?" asked Luz with concern.

Lizette shrugged. "Nosebleeds?"

"Sure," said Luz with a bad feeling, knowing that probably

wasn't the truth. She had seen her own mother covered in blood from her father's blows more times than she'd like to remember.

A small boy in overalls wheeled a cart beside Luz and Lizette, looking on with a curious face, brown eyes like oiled skillets. The boy stood on the base of the cart and let out yippee sounds, his voice climbing the washery walls.

Lizette huffed, smacking the crisp sleeve of a white shirt across the table. "You gotta go, kid," she said.

The boy looked at her, defiant. "Where?"

"Not here," she said.

"But I'm bored," he said, glancing at his mother a few tables over, covered in children, a baby hanging from her body in a sling, another in a carriage at her side, an older girl helping with the wash. The woman looked like a singing mother doll, the kind Luz had seen in Maria Josie's old things hidden in the cedar box beneath her bed.

"He's fine," said Luz. "He's just playing."

"Well please play over by the john," said Lizette. "That area is empty."

The boy nodded. "Fine," he said. "But only because *you're* being nice." He pushed the screeching cart toward the sounds of a flushing toilet.

Luz looked at Lizette, the way her strong arms pressed fabric, smoothing and clearing, laying collars flat. "Are you afraid of it?"

"Of what, Luz?"

"Of *it*," she whispered. "Having a baby. You know, a kid."

Lizette told Luz that she had no idea what she was talking about. "Why would I be afraid of that?" It was clear that her cousin was hiding a truth, a lot like lying.

"Because," she whispered. "You and Alfonso." Luz pursed her lips. "I'd be afraid."

Another baby cried, this one on the floor in dirty socks. She softly pulled at the hem of her mother's skirt. Luz saw herself in that tug, recalled the way she had once reached for her mother's waist. *Pick me up, lift me.* After her father left, Mama drank so much she couldn't tell night from day. Her eyes didn't focus—they glimmered black and wet, as if she lived in a realm without sunrise, stuck inside the ether of her own design. She refused to leave that place, convinced Benny would come back for her someday.

When Luz thought of her mother, she often cried and over time, it was as if a large moon had eclipsed the memories of her. Still, sometimes images of her past came swiftly. There was a man once who stumbled into the other side of the cabin, through the hanging sheets and onto little Luz's bed. Diego woke up, brandishing a knife which he held to the man's throat until he scrambled his way out of their cabin in untied boots and unbuttoned blue jeans.

"I bet it's hard to have a kid, to be a mother," Luz said after some time.

Lizette cleared her throat. She reached for another shirt. "There are ways around it. You don't have to make a baby every time. Jeez, prima. Don't ya know that?"

Luz didn't know that, but she acted as if she did. "Maria Josie makes it seem like you'll ruin your life just kissing."

Lizette laughed. "Look, sometimes you just want to feel good. Otherwise, someone like Diego, he should have a million babies by now."

"Shit," said Luz. "Maybe he does?" They both laughed a long time until a chunk of sorrow pitted Luz's guts.

That night, Luz weaved between sleeplessness and dreams. She missed Diego more than she thought possible. Her pillow was soggy with silent tears, and her chest ached with the feeling of being emptied of her parts. In the room's shadows, Luz remembered when they first came to Denver in a train's cattle car of people traveling from the Lost Territory, lice and stench jumping from their bodies. Viejos spoke their dialect Spanish. Some prayed in Tewa or Tiwa, others Diné. It was night and very cold. The mountains were jagged peaks. Luz had watched the stars blink through the open roof.

"Are we almost there?" she had asked, snagging Diego's sleeve.

"Soon, Little Light," he said.

They were seated beside an old man who wore his sweat-salted braids tucked beneath a black bandanna. He sat on a worn trunk that smelled of copal, his trousered kneecaps bulging like roots. His eyes were whitish pools, and his mouth was folded like a brittle and fallen leaf. Apache, Luz noted by the buckskin medicine pouch with a man riding a horse stitched in blue and black beads dangling around his neck. He spoke his language into the air, keeping his face straight ahead, his eyes locked on some unknown point in space. When neither Luz nor Diego answered, the old man spoke again, this time in Spanish, and asked who were their people.

"The Lopezes from Animas," said Diego.

The old man turned and lifted his waxy and fat palm, placing it on Luz's forehead. A coolness moved into her. "Your elders are in the little one." The old man chuckled and nudged Diego with his thin arm. "Take care of her."

Diego had been gone now over two months. Maria Josie worked longer and harder than anyone, but she was still a woman and was paid like one, too, and so there was a search for a boarder, someone to split Diego's portion of the rent, to pitch in for flour and beans, to let others know that a man resided there. It wasn't that Maria Josie believed a man could protect them any more than she could, but the image of a man served a purpose, just as those wooden painted owls perched along the fire escape. A scarecrow, that was all. Because of this, Maria Josie had to be very careful with her selection. "You cannot trust a man," she explained to Luz. "Nearly all have some kind of deficiency, some malformation. They've been hurt a lot, menfolk, but they do most of the hurting, too."

There were referrals from aunties at Saint Cajetan's, their nephews or godsons, railroad workers in their early twenties, lonely men roaming mountains and plains, many having grown up watching their fathers beat their mothers like dogs. The first three men Maria Josie interviewed all left her with a cold feeling, as if a part of them hated her simply for being a woman, and Luz said one of them, a shortish man with a smell like socks, brushed her backside as he moved to exit the front hall. After that, Maria Josie said the hell with men, and she took in a young woman boarder named Milli Alonzo, the cousin of their postman, fleeing the tyranny of her father's rancho in the Lost Territory. Things went well at first. Milli kept to herself in the main room, only stepping out in a cloud of Shalimar perfume in the evenings for her shift at a supper club called Michael J's, but after some weeks it was clear that Milli didn't actually work at the club. She went to the train station instead. That's where they all worked, those girls. Maria Josie had told Luz she didn't give two shits that Milli was waiting for soldiers to unload from the trains, taking them upstairs into those rooms by the hour. But what Maria Josie couldn't tolerate was a thief. Milli stole from Maria Josie, a quartz rosary, gifted to her by her mother. *Simo* had been etched into the clasp. "If it wasn't you," Maria Josie had said on the day she threw Milli out, "then it was Luz. And my blood don't steal, at least not from their own."

After that, Luz and Maria Josie made do without a boarder. Maria Josie sold what little furniture Diego had left behind. Luz didn't blame her. They needed money, and in some ways, Luz was glad Diego's things were gone. His objects felt charged with a piece of him. Their mother used to say that was part of Luz's sight, her ability to sense a person in their possessions. Luz could feel Diego on anything her brother had touched, even the letters he sent.

The first letter arrived several weeks after Diego had left. Luz smiled at the sight of his beautiful cursive on the envelope.

Meeting lots of interesting folks. We're traveling in covered trucks that kinda look like the old-time wagons. They say this place is called Wyoming. Still no steady work until summer, but I've managed to make a few bucks off card tricks. The fields up north look like what I imagine the sea is like but gray winter. The cold and wind is something terrible. The money I've included should help with rent. I love you and Maria Josie very much.

The envelope included no cash, having arrived torn at the left corner. Maria Josie brought Luz with her to the post office. After they waited in a line of people like ants, the postman said there was nothing to do, especially since there was no way to prove money had been stolen.

"What's this hole for, then?" Maria Josie had said firmly and loudly, poking her index finger into the envelope, a teakettle tipped on its side, everything poured out. "You think they just peeked inside to see my nephew's excellent script?" When the siblings had first arrived in Denver, Maria Josie had gifted them penmanship workbooks. *You must learn to speak and write as they do,* she had explained, *or they'll trick you, the way it's always been.*

The postman eventually accused Maria Josie of putting the hole there herself, and it was clear that her voice, no matter how loud she hollered, wasn't going to be heard. They left the post office that day in haste, walking past one of the government buildings with marble rams and a white-worded inscription—IF THOU DESIRE REST, DESIRE NOT TOO MUCH.

Some ways down the busy street, jobless men in crinkled gray coats were lined up for free soup, the tops of their misshapen caps stretched into the horizon like stones across a river.

There came a night in early February when Luz woke up with a tingling sensation, her face and neck hardened with cold. Her hair felt frozen in place, a black broom over her pillow. Dim light trailed into the bedroom from the hall. There were sounds of iron on iron, the dings and ticks of some faraway repair. The window was cloaked in scaled ice, deepening the colors of the room. Luz groaned in an elongated yawn and her breath dissipated into fog. She reached over her body for the blankets, surprised to find an extra layer of wool. Maria Josie must have brought it in the night. Luz stood from her bed, the floorboards painfully cold beneath her sockless feet. She spun the blanket over her shoulders, a large, inconsolable moth.

Maria Josie was in the kitchen kneeling at the radiator. A kerosene lamp glowed beside her feet in work boots. She had changed from her nightclothes into blue jeans and her winter coat with a fox-lined hood. The silver radiator's side valve was unhinged and lay across the floor beside three sizes of wrenches. Maria Josie slightly bled from the topside of her left hand. It looked as though she'd been struggling in the same spot for hours. Her short hair was reddened with lamplight.

"It's broke again?" Luz asked.

Maria Josie shook her head. "The landlord never fixes a damn thing."

"I can see my breath," Luz said, the cold stiffening her fingers and joints.

Maria Josie sighed, her own breath clumped into the air. She vigorously nodded and lifted the largest wrench from the ground. She flung it out of anger into the innards of the radiator. She maneuvered herself on all fours, so that her back was arched and her hips were displayed, resilient and wide. She clunked around for several minutes until she tried another wrench, this one smaller. Maria Josie could fix anything. An automobile, a broken clock, shattered windows, crushed fences. Sure, Diego had once helped, but it was Maria Josie who guided the repairs and knew the anatomy of almost any piece of equipment. She was only thirty-five, but for a moment in that frozen kitchen, Luz worried that Maria Josie was getting old. Her tight mouth was an awful shade of blue, and she wrung her hands as though they ached.

"Goddammit." She sprang to her feet. "I'm sorry," she said, wiping the wrench with the inside of her jacket, her corded arms forceful as they circled the grip. "I don't have the right tools."

"Damn Diego," Luz cursed.

"Stop that. He couldn't charm a radiator to save his life."

Maria Josie walked to the front closet and removed her fox-lined coat and sheepskin mittens. She handed them to Luz. She then straightened a wool cap with droopy ear flaps over her niece's head. "Let's try to get some sleep. I'll find a repairman in the morning."

"It's too cold," Luz pleaded.

"We'll be all right for now." Maria Josie opened a cupboard beside the icebox. She pulled out a large porcelain bowl. From a kitchen drawer, she handed Luz several candles. "Set these up beside my bed on the floor. We'll make a heater."

"What about my side of the room?"

"Body heat, Luz."

They lay in bed side by side, shivering through layers of clothing and blankets. Her auntie's breath warmed the nape of her neck and Luz was thankful she wasn't alone. The makeshift heater glowed like paper luminarias over the oak floor. The bedroom's hanging sheet was cast in dramatic shadows and Luz lifted her hand into the cold, moving her fingers into a shadow puppet of a wolf. She opened and closed its mouth. The room creaked, as if the apartment was mocking them in its coolness, threatening frozen and burst pipes. Luz moved between hopelessness and anger. Why didn't they deserve heat? They had paid their rent, struggled for it with pawned necklaces and traded furniture and hands scrubbed raw cleaning white women's bloody clothes. Luz was red-faced, burning, and for a moment she was gratified with her temper. At the very least, it kept her warm.

That night, she dreamed of nothing—only prayed for morning.

TEN

Heat

"The name's Avel, Avel Cosme." The handyman removed his wide-brimmed Stetson as he stepped through the door. It had been several days since Maria Josie had received a note from the landlord. He would not cover the cost of heating problems, suggesting radiator issues were caused by *misuse*.

"Nope, not as far as I can tell," said Avel, crouching in his creamy cowboy boots. "General wear and tear. I see it every day."

Luz sat at the kitchen table with her knees to her chest beneath her wool blanket. Their tombstone radio rested beside the windowsill and was on Leon Jacob's afternoon hour. *Stand up*, he was shouting through the airwaves. *Don't let the governor allow your brothers and sisters to starve! Fair wages now.* Luz squinted at Avel, who walked tall with a handsome, capable stride. She couldn't remember the last time any man besides Diego and the potential boarders had entered their home. The ceiling seemed lower with him beneath it.

Avel examined the cast-iron pipes, ran his fingers over the scrollwork. "Did you bleed it?"

Maria Josie stood beside him dressed for leaving. "I can't for the life of me find a key. So, no, to answer your question, I did not."

Avel patted his pockets. "I should have one. Say," he said, "can I borrow that?" He motioned toward a plaid washcloth hanging limp from the stove.

Luz stood from her chair, reached for the washcloth, and passed it over. Avel took it from her, their hands lightly touching, a static shock. He quickly smiled, his expressive brown eyes deep with color.

"Can you fix it?" Luz asked.

"Sure can. I'm what's known as a jack-of-all-trades."

A jack-of-all-trades, Luz thought, usually had no trade.

"Oh, I can do it all," Avel said, as if he had read her mind. He dusted the radiator with a red handkerchief from his pocket, opened and closed the valves. He laid the washcloth on the warped oak floor and removed a brass key from his long chain. He pushed the key into the radiator, turning a knob until a loud hissing sound escaped. Hot water leaked onto the washcloth. Avel moved his gaze around the room, peering down the hallway into Luz and Maria Josie's bedroom, their makeshift heater visible across the floor.

"Seems like you ladies could really use a man around here."

Maria Josie sucked in her lips, as if to keep from laughing. The hissing sound stopped. "Did it work?" she asked.

Avel placed his palm against the radiator's etched metal. He waved his head. "Still cold. Seems to be a bigger issue. I'm thinking we gotta open the wall."

With a slight bounce to his step, Avel stood and walked toward the front mantel. He picked up a bronze cast of Luz's baby shoes and held them in his hands, as if to take note of their weight. Pleased, he set them down.

"That's neat," he said, gesturing with his hat down the hallway to the bedroom. "My mama has an altar just like that." Through the open door, Avel eyed Luz's dried marigolds and old photographs. "Haven't seen one since I left Califas."

Luz felt exposed. She made a scrunched face. Why was he searching about their home?

"Excuse me," said Maria Josie. "How much this gonna cost?"

"For parts and labor, maybe looking at twenty dollars. Can't know for sure until I open the wall."

"I could buy a whole new radiator for thirty," said Maria Josie.

"You could buy a new *used* radiator for thirty dollars. The new models are upwards of fifty."

"Says who?"

"Sears Roebuck, ma'am."

Maria Josie cleared her throat and, for a moment, Luz was worried she'd spit right there on the floor. "Ten dollars. That's all we can afford."

"I wouldn't normally do this, but seeing since you ladies seem to be in extenuating conditions, I can do it for fifteen."

"Fifteen?" Luz said with irritation. "We can't come up with that. It's only heat. It should be free!"

Maria Josie stood over the radiator and slammed her fist. "We'll freeze like this."

Avel turned to Luz. When she noticed him noticing her, out of instinct, Luz inched the blanket down around her shoulders, revealing the length of her long and rigid collarbones. She raised her chin into a stream of sunlight, giving full view of what she knew some considered a notable and pretty face.

"Don't you have a place you can go, somewhere you can stay?" he said tenderly.

"This is where we live," Luz hollered and Avel flinched.

Avel softened his gaze, revealing his dimples. He was hand-some, capable. Luz averted her eyes. "I'm sorry, ladies. Fifteen dollars is all I can do."

Maria Josie cussed, shook her head in anger. "We don't have that right now. It'll take some time."

Avel paused for a moment. He seemed to be thinking, his face drifting toward Luz. "I could always come back for my pay. Maybe next week?"

"Fine," Maria Josie said with irritation. "How long this gonna take? I'm due at work."

"Couple hours. Don't worry, I'll get it all patched up right."

"Get your things," Maria Josie said curtly to Luz. "You're coming with me."

Luz protested, said she never had any days off. "I just want to listen to the radio."

"Listen at the shop," Maria Josie said and stepped to Avel. She gazed upward into his face. "If you touch anything in this place besides that wall and this radiator, I'll kill you myself. Lock the door when you leave."

Avel grinned as though he appreciated the sentiment. He waved as they left.

Maria Josie had always said she found the mirror factory on an accidental turn down Larimer Street, a brick box the color of a robin's egg, a HELP WANTED sign hanging in a window. Inside, women of all ages and sizes performed duties normally reserved for men. They cut glass, carved wood, spat blue flames from high-powered torches. Even the factory's superintendent was a woman named Big Cheryl. She had hired Maria Josie on the spot, putting her near the dock, where recently completed dressers were shipped through the entire West. When Maria Josie asked Big Cheryl why no men worked at the mirror factory, she had said, "Only women can bear to look at themselves all day." The truth was, the owners were some industrial family from out East who knew they could pay women much less than men.

That afternoon, Maria Josie and Luz entered through the mirror factory's delivery entrance. Sunlight cascaded from the open garage and plunged across the concrete floor. The factory smelled of singed metal and chemical varnishes. Knives, grips, and tools hung from mounted shelves. Women in slacks and denim coverings scrambled throughout the factory, their eyes visible under black goggles, as if they were airship pilots, voyaging into space. Maria Josie walked Luz to her station and directed her to sit in an uneven chair. Mirrors were all around, stacked together on shelves, on the floor leaned against brick walls, and upright on their backs across tables and sawhorses. Maria Josie flipped on the small radio and got to work

She was finishing the edges of a square mirror, the size and length of Luz's body, resting over two sawhorses, reflecting the ceiling lights doubly into Maria Josie's face. Her hair was wild and poking up from her goggles. The mirror factory was a place of work, real work, without men. Maria Josie had described many accidents, a severed hand, a missing eye. Thumbs put on ice with no hope to be sewn back, just a good idea at the time. *You should have seen it,* she told Luz and Diego one evening over supper, *a red painted thumbnail left in a cooler, white bone showing from its stem.*

Luz tried to hear the radio, but the chaotic sounds of saws and torches tore throughout the space, the boss's high clear room overlooking it all. Luz was angry, bored. She stood and walked toward her auntie, heading past hundreds of unfinished mirrors, which spliced her reflection into endless eyes and lips, edges of nose.

Luz stopped before Maria Josie. She stood there, hands on her hips.

"Big Cheryl don't like roaming visitors, Little Light. Sit back down."

"I can't hear the radio," yelled Luz, the sound of her own voice covered by saws.

Maria Josie gestured toward her ears. She continued working before sliding off her goggles, slipping her gloves into her trouser pocket. A break bell buzzed.

"Can I just go home?" Luz asked.

"No." Maria Josie breathed. She pulled a pipe from her coat pocket and lit her tobacco with a match. The air turned sulfuric. "I'm not leaving you in the apartment with some man, a man we don't even know." She chuckled. Attractive wrinkles appeared around her eyes. "Are you crazy?"

Luz stared, unblinking. Her eyes watered. "What if he's stealing from us?"

"Well, he ain't stealing you, and you're the most valuable."

"I'm not a child," Luz said sternly, and then, under her breath, "Dammit, I hate it here."

"Don't let Big Cheryl hear that. She prides herself on keeping this place up."

"Not here," said Luz. "I mean, here. Inside myself, in this life."

"This is a gift," said Maria Josie. "It's all we have." She exhaled her tobacco smoke, considering the shapes of her breath. "You don't feel it now, but someday you'll know. You have very much, Luz."

"I want to feel in control of my own life now, not someday," said Luz. "I just want to feel safe, like I can do as I please."

Maria Josie inhaled quickly and exhaled slowly, watching her smoke turn inward on itself like time collapsing into the past. Luz watched her auntie's breath disappear into the factory lights.

"I know, Little Light," she said. "I want that, too."

ELEVEN

We Should All Be as
Happy as Kings

In the morning, Luz set out for the streetcar with her hair curled and her lips a soft pink. Her winter coat showed signs of wear in the elbows and collar, so Luz figured she'd draw attention upward, toward her face. She was going to look for work in the Eastside—where the money was. She waited on the corner for the Green Line, a streetcar she seldom took, as they didn't allow her and Lizette to ride with laundry sacks.

When the car came over the hill and juddered to a halt, Luz climbed inside, avoiding eye contact with the driver as she paid her fare. She swayed down the aisle toward the Spanish and Colored section. Sometimes, if she was alone or the car seemed particularly empty, Luz stood closer to the middle. Her skin was light enough from her father. But on this morning, the car was full, and every white-dish face stared as Luz scrambled to the back, where another girl not much older than Luz sat with a sack of colorful yarn balls in her lap. She looked up when Luz stood beside her and gripped the brass handle. The girl gently pointed at Luz's hair.

"Pretty," she said. Luz thanked her and turned toward the window for fifteen long minutes.

The neighborhood eventually eased out of the short stacks of downtown factories and office buildings. Luz rocked side to side as the streetcar climbed past the courthouse and capitol until they arrived at the vast mansions with stone balconies and widow's walks. Luz pulled the chain and exited through the rear. Against the cold wind, she walked for several sandstone blocks, arriving at the Rose Dixon Library just before noon. The building was constructed with beige bricks and red Spanish shingles while marble lions adorned the dead garden. Those lions scared Luz with their white eyes, as if warning her to stay away from their kingdom.

Inside the library, Luz stomped sleet from her boots and studied the expansive hall, the waxed floors. An orb of sunlight, constantly shifting just out of step, beamed down from the stained glass windows. The room smelled vaguely of incense, and Luz tilted her face to the high ceiling, where a mural depicted a gathering of bears with tint-black snouts and padded paws. They danced on a table piled with meats, and beneath them were the words: THE WORLD IS SO FULL OF A NUMBER OF THINGS, I'M SURE WE SHOULD ALL BE AS HAPPY AS KINGS

At the front, behind a wide oak desk, a busty librarian sat beneath the light of a lime-green lamp. She had copper hair with a pencil behind her right ear, and was reading a copy of the *Rocky Mountain News*. She shuffled sections with her arms waving like an accordion player's before settling on a page. She set the paper down and smoothed the center fold with both hands. It was a crossword puzzle, and the librarian vigorously worked the first lines as Luz, with trepidation, approached her post.

"May I help you?" the librarian asked, keeping her face to the paper.

"I'm looking for the community board," said Luz. "For jobs and such."

The librarian sighed. She dropped her pencil onto the paper and searched behind Luz. There was another librarian, an older man with a melon of a stomach. He had a thin mustache and striped suspenders. He cleaned a stack of leather-bound books with an orange cloth.

"Excuse me," Luz said, her voice louder this time and seeming to come from somewhere lower than her throat, a place closer to her heart. "The community board?"

The librarian looked straight at Luz. She had a blank face with an unflinching mouth. "Do wait here," she said, and rose from her seat, her heels click-clacking as she walked across the shining floor. Patrons glanced up from their reading materials. A white-haired woman stared at Luz. She had glasses hanging around her neck by a string of pearls. There was a dog in her lap, some sort of purebred with a ratlike face, and it looked at Luz, too. *They let dogs in here?*

The librarian approached the older man cleaning books. He stopped his task and leaned down as the librarian whispered something in his ear. The older librarian nodded, draping his orange cloth over his left shoulder. He then walked over to Luz. He had watery blue eyes with gobs of sleep in each corner. His mustache fluttered like curtains as he spoke. "I'm sorry, but we don't have a community board."

Luz felt disoriented. She looked around, keeping her body rigid. She squinted and pointed past the man's shoulder to a corkboard near the water fountain. Flyers for concerts and dances had been posted with pushpins. "What's that there?" she asked.

The man didn't turn around to look. He scratched his neck beneath his yellowing collar. "I apologize, again, but we don't have a community board for *you*."

"But that's a community board, isn't it? That's all I needed to know, thank you," Luz said, beginning to walk over.

"It's a community board for our other guests," he said, quickly holding out a hand, halting her.

"It's not in Spanish," blurted the other librarian, who now stood beside the man, fixing the thin belt around her lilac sweater. She'd spoken as if delivering a Sunday sermon.

Luz felt heat on her skin, from her face to her feet, an ugly rising fire. For a moment, she stepped outside of herself and pictured Lizette in the library, her vast personality swarming the stacks. *I'm speaking to you in English, ain't I?* Luz thought to holler.

"If you don't have any more questions," said the older librarian, "kindly be on your way."

Luz stood there for a moment. The other patrons watched, their faces beaming with something like pity or hatred or minor inconvenience. There were many places she had been told she wasn't allowed. Denver Dry Goods, Elitch Gardens, over the dead in Cheesman Park, and now, here, some rich neighborhood's library.

"I just need to look for jobs," she said.

"We have our own people who need jobs. I suggest you try your own neighborhood."

But my neighborhood doesn't have a library. Luz thought this, but didn't say it, not wanting to give them the satisfaction of knowing they had more than she did.

"I'm sick of those goddamn people," said Lizette, tearing a dinner roll to pieces in a pink booth. Though it was midwinter, she was dressed in a bright yellow dress with a fuchsia ribbon tied in a small bow around her neck. The ribbon, Luz realized, had come wrapped around a jar of jam. Large fake pearls were clipped to each of her ears and they bobbed as Lizette spoke with a full mouth. She sat alongside Alfonso. Three blocks north of the Rose Dixon Library was the Park Lane Hotel, where Alfonso worked as a waiter. Lizette usually joined him for the free employee meal. It was no problem she didn't work there herself, so long as they shared the plate. The dining room wouldn't open for another hour. They all three sat beneath crystal chandeliers as other waiters pushed in and out of the kitchen's swinging doors.

"What did you expect in this part of town?" Alfonso said, rolling knives and forks together with cloth napkins.

"To be treated like anybody else."

"But you're not anybody else. Not to them at least. You're just some poor Indian and Spanish laundry girl." Alfonso laughed and made a sarcastic sound like ay ay ay. Lizette flapped her hand across his hair. She leaned in for a kiss, but Alfonso scooted away, sitting taller to glance over the booth's wooden walls.

Luz nibbled on her thumbnail. "Laundry isn't cutting it. I need another job."

"You and the rest of the country," said Lizette.

"Look, if you need work that bad, ask Tikas," said Alfonso in a low tone.

"Tikas?" Lizette scrunched her nose. "Luz don't know a thing about grocery stores."

"Nah, not Big Tikas. Dave at the law office. He needs a girl."

Lizette cuffed Alfonso's forearm. "Good thinking, baby!"

Alfonso pushed some of the silverware and napkins toward Luz, motioning for her to roll as he shimmied out of the booth. "I'll ask around at the hotel, but get at David. And if he hires you, you can act like he does and march around with a sign that says: FAIR WAGES, FREEDOM FROM POVERTY!"

"Why you always have to make fun of him?" said Lizette. "At least he's trying to make things better."

Alfonso laughed. He looked like a poised penguin in his black button-down uniform. "David's little Communist club with that Leon Jacob is the reason why ten Negroes were nearly killed last year in Wash Park. They said take a stand, go swimming on that whites-only beach. But who do you think that white mob came for first?"

"Jeez," said Lizette, shaking her head. "Luz just needs more work. You suggested it!"

"And," Alfonso said, getting up and heading for the kitchen, "I still think David's a viable solution."

When they were alone in the booth, Lizette leaned forward, looking like a little daffodil in her ruffled dress. "Well, what do ya say?"

All around them waiters in tuxedos with long finned tails rushed about carrying silver trays. Luz wondered about the people they served, the rich, the doctors and lawyers, businessmen and silver tycoons. Though they shared the same city streets, Luz often felt she and her people were only choking on their leftover air.

"Worth a shot," she said.

TWELVE

I Heard You Need a Girl

The market smelled of pine disinfectant and chokecherry jelly and trays of baklava. The light was unusually blue as the sunshine filtered through the indigo awning above the front door. Tommy Spiegel worked the register between racks of bananas and jars of pipe tobacco. He had bad skin and wore several silver necklaces, most with different charms, a Star of David, a crucifix, even something from an Indian god named Krishna. Papa Tikas had hired the boy to unload fruit trucks in July. He came from a Jewish family, and his father was a well-respected tailor. Tommy had a habit of calling all girls *Chickadee* and *Birdy*. As Luz walked to the counter, passing through the warm smells of tortillas and sourdough bread, he said, "Look who flew the coop."

"I didn't know you're working today, Tommy," Luz said with an air of annoyance.

"Saving up for our big date, thinking Lakeside. You like roller coasters, right?"

"Where's David?" she asked.

"In back." With hooked thumbs, Tommy adjusted his white apron straps. "He's a busy man. I'm fielding visitors. What's your business with the attorney?"

"Work," said Luz.

"Work for who?"

"Please just go get him," Luz said.

Tommy picked at a pimple on his nose. He leaned over the counter and, with his chest, dusted baklava crumbs onto the linoleum floor. "Did you hear about the murder yesterday? A man got lynched over in the Points." He nodded with closed eyes. "A Negro, an entertainer. I think a horn player. They said he was working where he shouldn't. A whole gang of them got him."

"A gang of who?" asked Luz.

"Who else?" Tommy said. "The Klan. But now they got a new name and updated costumes—the Patriotic Legion, and most of them," he said, "dress like cops."

Luz frowned. "That's horrible, Tommy." She felt slightly nauseous. "Please get David."

"For sure, Chickadee." Tommy turned around and opened the back door, hollering the words *Boss Man*.

A moment later, David appeared from the back room with a stack of documents in one hand, and with the other he twirled wire-framed glasses between his lips. He held his face in a permanent smirk that coiled attractively, as though the entire world was a joke. He removed the glasses from his mouth and placed the documents on the counter, the hairs across his arms resembling etchings in wood. David patted Tommy's right shoulder, told him to take care of the shelves in back. "We don't pay you to scare away pretty girls," he said, smiling at Luz.

David briskly ran his hands through his messy hair, which looked as if he'd been napping in the back room. Since returning to Denver, most days he worked downtown in a half-subterranean office between a shoe shine and a saddlemaker. He was building his law practice, taking small cases—unpaid wages, deportations, and many, many evictions. Whenever Luz saw David and asked what he liked most about being a lawyer so far, he said the walk to and from his office. The city was aligned on a strict grid, a certainty one could count on. On Tuesdays, David still worked in the market, repaying his father for the loan to start his own practice. He oversaw the books.

"What can I do for you?" he asked.

"I wanted to check with you about something," said Luz, fingering her dress collar. "I heard you need a girl at the office."

David put his glasses on his face, widening his green eyes. "I do."

"That's great," said Luz. "You must be busy."

"I am," he said. "What's this about, Luz?"

"I was thinking, maybe, you could hire me."

"I need a typist. Girls go to school for this."

Luz smiled. "I'm a quick learner. I do laundry faster than anyone."

David looked at Luz. He turned his face to the side, balanced in sunlight. "It's not the same, now is it?"

"Fingers are fingers."

"You're too young, Luz."

"I'll be eighteen in a few months."

David said her name once more, this time longer and with the tone of pity. "Luz."

"And something else," Luz said. "I can help you. Imagine if you spoke some Spanish. You could get more clients that way."

David hesitated. He swallowed and glanced around the market.

Luz lowered her voice. "Since Diego's been gone, we're struggling. I don't want to be evicted. I don't want to come home and find our things in piles."

"I don't want that, either," he said. "But I need someone who knows what they're doing."

Luz then thought to lie, recalling a memory she had once seen in a dream, the reason he had to say yes. She was surprised and not ashamed when she actually did. "My auntie told me to ask you."

David's expression changed, cheeks twisted, jaw crunched—relent made visible across a face.

THIRTEEN

La Llorona

Denver, 1922

When Maria Josie first came to Denver, she stayed in a women-only boardinghouse on Market Street where the bed came down from a slab in the kitchenette and all night long her head was beside a hissing radiator painted gold. The room was dark without a lamp, and Maria Josie watched train lights crawl for hours across the walls. The boardinghouse had many rules, no laundry in the sinks among them. By the week's end, everything she owned was filthy—her floral dress and trousers and all her heavy underclothes.

Maria Josie stood in the fourth-floor hallway at an open window as wide as she was tall. She squinted across the city, searching for a creek. There had to be something more manageable than the Platte, where the rapids tipped white over leveled boulders. The city's grid was quilt-like with squares of slim-necked factories that coughed smog into the horizon. Some streets were paved while others were plains of dirt. Trolleys and wagons and brand-new automobiles rolled over Curtis Street. Maria Josie pointed to an area where the city almost vanished into a haze. The sky was changeable, sunlight streaking in abundant columns through gray and pewter clouds. Maria Josie made her right hand into the shape of a pistol and surprised herself as she shot. *There,* she said, a cool breeze pressing against her face.

Through sidewalks and alleys, Maria Josie walked in her black nightgown with her satchel slung behind her. Her floppy hat was pushed high on her forehead. The creek weaved through a low section of the city, toward the edge of a Westside neighborhood, in a meadow called Sunken Gardens. It reminded Maria Josie of an enormous bedded grave. Cottonwood trees grew along the banks in a solid arrangement, their leaves upturned like the hands of beggars, open to the sky and waiting for rain. The clouds blackened at the eastern edge of the city, uphill and upwind, a long way off. She'd have time. It could be hours before the storm hit.

As she neared the creek, the air thickened with moisture. Larks and magpies stepped over sticks while others flew overhead, arrowed in black. Maria Josie headed for the water, walking in tall grass. The soil moved and shifted from a heavy dirt into a fine sandy floor. She pushed through low-hanging branches, and the creek revealed its glinting and dark path. Water ran quickly, making a sound like wide-skirted ladies shuffling in rows. The creek was speckled in patches of sunlight and shadowy spots and under the rapids lay a tossed street sign and the wedge of a dismantled wooden fence. The banks were small, steep, and covered in chokecherry trees. The air smelled of motor oil and dying leaves. Maria Josie searched out an area where the water pooled. She'd need to wash her dress and underclothes first, hang them to dry, change, and then move on to her nightgown.

She came to the underbelly of a stone bridge. It looked as though it had been built at the turn of the last century, whole blocks of stone were missing like gapped teeth. The bridge had a high sloping arch and what appeared to be a flat, rail-less surface. It was a transport bridge, from one neighborhood to another. An adolescent boy and his father stood above Maria Josie on the bridge's western edge, casting their fishing lines in slow lashes. They spoke a language Maria Josie didn't know. It didn't sound like Spanish or English or the Indian languages she was used to in the Lost Territory. Since coming to Denver weeks earlier, she'd heard Italian and French. Maybe it was Greek. That could be it. Then, with further consideration, she decided it *was* Greek.

Sunlight polished grassless sand behind Maria Josie. *The best I can do,* she decided, dropping her satchel onto the ground. Beneath the bridge, foaming water lapped into an alcove of sandstone boulders while a thicket of cottonwood seeds clung together in the stream like spider eggs. Smacking the water with her floral dress, Maria Josie pushed hard into the cold liquid, pleading that the man and his son wouldn't see her washing like a pauper in a creek. Shame. She had rarely felt it before. Now shame controlled her entire life.

Maria Josie leaned over the creek and gazed at her rippled reflection in the water. She hated her curled brown hair, her full breasts and dull black eyes. She took stock of her body, the unfamiliar meaty thing it had become. The pain in her womb had eased, but her breasts ached as if they had been gutted and stuffed with stones. Her body disgusted her. Why couldn't she separate from it? Maria Josie then thought of the man she'd once loved, their last dinner together. He was a German named Hauenstein. He sat across from her at the long oak table with his knife and fork gracefully working red potatoes. He was much older than Maria Josie, and when he'd first shown interest in her at the market on Sundays, she'd brushed it off as politeness, a certain type of kindness shown by Anglo men toward pretty Mexican and Indian girls. But months stretched on, and Hauenstein cornered her with compliments, firm hands resting against her back, brushing her skin as he reached for jars of molasses, sacks of flour. He'd slipped vials of gardenia perfume into her dress pockets and rolled coins into her satchel, until, finally, she swam to him across the river dividing his section of Saguarita from hers. "He didn't want to marry me," she told a kind stranger years later, "when I told him about the baby. He put something in my food, a poison."

Above Maria Josie, on the bridge, the man and his son continued to speak their language. It seemed they were in an argument. The young man was mouthing off, smoking tobacco and allowing his legs to dangle over the bridge. His fishing line trembled. *Careful, La Llorona will get you.* As a child, Maria Josie was terrified of the Weeping Woman, who flew through moonlight along rivers and lakes, snatching naughty children and drunk, cheating men. Once, during a long summer, as she swam the river Maria Josie thought she glimpsed the water witch, all in black, a Spanish veil shielding her face. She was hunched over, climbing the side of the rock wall like a broken insect. *Impossible*, Maria Josie thought, and swam faster, so hard it seemed her heart would stop beating.

Maria Josie worked her dress with a bar of Ivory soap. Her arms hardened and deadened in the freezing water. She imagined she was a machine, thrusting water back and forth, nothing inside her to ache—only gears to rust, trivets to repair. She finished the dress, laying it flat across a sun-worked rock. The creek made an enormous sound, echoed between the banks. The water was brackish and reflected the evening sun. There were many white gnats. Maria Josie could clearly see the man and his son on the bridge. The father had gathered their tin pails and poles and carried these things to the creek's banks. The son walked sullenly behind, his chin tucked toward his chest. Leaning onto her elbows, Maria Josie pivoted her legs, one tucked behind the other, and watched. The stone lining the creek was a smooth gray-blue, pretty like shadows. The father and son were happy in the new spot, and a cottonwood tree released seeds like snow.

But the air turned. A frigid gust from the north, spitting gravel and shards of grass against Maria Josie's face and arms. Darkness curtained the sun, and the wind screeched along the creek's surface. The trees bowed and lost their leaves and weak branches. Maria Josie's hair thrashed her mouth and eyes, causing tears to roll down her face. A rumbling sound erupted upstream, a hideous gargling. In the Lost Territory, every spring, the arroyos flooded in sudden and violent ways. Entire cattle herds were swept away while work trucks floated like toy ducks. Maria Josie noted the creek's height against the bridge. She tilted her face to the left, felt the wind change in a flat, tepid way, and within seconds, the stream had swelled, bombarded by menacing muck. A flash flood, the water rushing, endless and dim until it reached the banks and pulled the man's son into the stream.

He hollered only once, something like *Papa,* before his mouth and eyes were overtaken with sludge.

Maria Josie dove into the rising water. She kicked after the young man, her legs tangling inside the long, knotted train of her nightgown. The water was so cold and so deep that Maria Josie was robbed of her breath. With stunned and paused lungs, she thrust herself toward the adolescent boy, his curly hair lowering and rising in the murky water. He was lanky and thin and they were propelled near a grouping of boulders. The boy almost seemed like an oversized doll. He floated facedown, and when Maria Josie finally reached his smooth ankle, he'd lost one shoe and a sock. With both arms, she wrapped herself around the young man's middle, trying to pull his head above water, but against the current, he was too rigid and slick. She kicked inside her black nightdress, aiming their connected bodies into the looming boulder. Their backs smacked into the surface. Maria Josie gazed at the young man. He still had his baby face, and was only fourteen or fifteen years old. He had long eyelashes and large bluing lips. Maria Josie cradled his head with her palm, hoisting his body onto shore. The boy breathed, and his back grew larger in his flannel shirt, stretched over his rib cage, but he wouldn't wake up.

"Please," Maria Josie said in Spanish. "Don't die. You don't have to. Not now, young man." She flopped him onto some grass and tried shaking and yanking on his arms and face. She crawled beside him, stared into his face. Why didn't he wake up? Maria Josie screamed and her throat burned with voice. It felt as if a loose patch of her tongue had floated into the sky like a kite. "I said you don't need to die. It's too early."

Maria Josie understood then that she wasn't yelling at the boy. She was arguing with Death. Somewhere, perched on a rock, she was certain skeletal Doña Sebastiana was waiting with her wagon of souls parked along the tree line. Her bag was already heavy. She didn't need any more. She wore a long, lacy gown, the hood pulled around her skull, her arms folded like wings. Had she been watching them all along? Maria Josie had felt her hanging around for weeks, since the day her baby had died inside her, and all she could do was weep.

"You bitch," said Maria Josie, pulling the boy close and hollering into the wind. "Give it a rest, you old hag."

She had halfway lifted the young man onto her lap, as if he

were a toddler she could carry, when his father came running down the banks. A roundish man with a kind face, he heaved and cried out for his son. "David," he said. "David. David."

The son opened his remarkably green eyes.

Weeping with gratitude over Maria Josie, the father said, "We'll never be able to repay you. What you have done, we'll never forget."

FOURTEEN

The Body Snatchers
of Bakersfield, California

Denver, 1934

L uz sat at the kitchen table, spinning the dial on her Zenith Tombstone radio. In that gray evening, Maria Josie nearby at the stove frying potatoes with heaps of salt, the radio pulsed with news and more news, detective serials, advertisements for chocolates and hard pink candies. There was a long feature on Bonnie Parker, who had been spotted in the Lost Territory with her limp. Last summer, Clyde had been speeding in north Texas and missed a warning sign of a dilapidated bridge. Their stolen V-8 smashed through a barricade at seventy miles per hour. Battery acid had poured from the crushed car, scorching Bonnie's right leg down to the bone. Luz wondered if this had made her feel less in love with Clyde.

Luz sometimes stared into the radio filament, aimlessly, as if the voices emanating from the box painted pictures in her mind. She wondered how it all worked, volts, watts, cycles, and tubes. There were shortwaves and longwaves, invisible carriers of human voice. The radio smelled of dust and minerals, and in some ways reminded Luz of reading tea leaves. They were similar, weren't they? She saw images and felt feelings delivered to her through dreams and pictures. Maybe those images rode invisible waves, too? Maybe Luz was born with her own receiver. She laughed, considering how valuable such a thing must be, a radio built into the mind.

There was a knock at the door then, muffled and polite. Maria Josie spun around from the stove. She set the burner low, telling Luz to keep watch on the blue flame as she untied her white apron strings with oily fingers. She fetched paper money from a round tin resting above the mantel and carried it to the door—opened halfway.

A tall and slim man said *Good evening* in a joyful voice, and Luz edged back on her chair, craning her neck to glimpse the handyman's features: Avel Cosme, his gentle eyes glinting above Maria Josie in the doorframe. The hallway behind him was dim, and his voice relaxed in the somber entryway. Luz turned down the radio. She tucked her hair behind her ears. His hay-colored hat was in his hands, and he was dressed nicely in a formal western shirt, roses and white stitching on black. His boots were white and clean, as if he were headed to a dance.

Maria Josie had handed him the money, but they were laughing now, and he was passing some back. "The part was actually less. I'd hate to overcharge you ladies."

"That's honest of you," said Maria Josie.

"I was raised to be a truthful man," he said.

"Well, you did good work, Avel. Haven't had any problems since."

He ran his fingers through his black hair, confident and smooth. "Thank you." He lightly bowed. "And hey," he said, "now you can bleed it yourself."

Maria Josie accepted from his hands what appeared to be a silver key, which she slipped quickly into her back pocket. She told Avel that he was too generous.

They spoke for some time longer. Their body movements widening. Maria Josie was chuckling some, bobbing her head and sliding her right hand across her waist, the way a teacher will when stopping at a student's desk for a chat. She even fully opened the door. Avel looked beyond Maria Josie and into the apartment. His eyes went straight to Luz.

Embarrassed, she looked away, turning up the radio.

"You're requested," Maria Josie called out. "And turn off the stove."

Luz felt flushed. She stood from the table, did as she was told, and checked her reflection in the nighttime window. She bit her lips to make them larger, redder, a trick she had learned from Lizette.

"Yes?" Luz said, appearing in the doorframe alongside her auntie.

Avel was smiling now, a great big smile with strong teeth. He smelled fragrant like rose, an undercurrent of groundwater. He was holding some kind of tickets, proud like a child revealing a crayon portrait. "Some old friends of mine are opening for La Chata Noloesca tonight. I thought maybe you and Maria Josie might want to come?"

"Just her and me?" asked Luz.

"I mean, me, too, if you'll have me." Avel laughed softly.

"I can't," said Maria Josie. "I have some things to take care of tonight."

"You do?" Luz asked, surprised.

"You go ahead, though. Just be back by nine."

Luz was even more shocked. "All right," she said, skeptically.

"Beautiful," Avel said, with a clap.

"But, hear me—neither of you," said Maria Josie, waving her forefinger, "do anything stupid."

Teatro Oso was dimly lit at the bottom of the Sixteenth Street clock tower, an octagonal room with sixteen bunches of curtains, the walls painted like clouds. As they entered the theater that night, a jazz singer with a purple iris pinned to her shining hair swayed with a smoke-lined view of a piano player behind her. The barroom floor was thick with the smell of liquor and musky perfumes. Glasses clinked and patrons laughed. Conversation roared. Red lanterns on circular tables illuminated black hair, warm skin, that rich combination of people from all neighborhoods having fun. At Teatro Oso, anyone was allowed, the clock's bell raining down on all.

"The next act," Avel said, warm and loud into Luz's ear. "They're my old band, Los Soñadores."

They had taken a seat up front, stage right. The jazz singer dazzled in her spotlight, her dress shimmering with thousands of small white beads. Her black skin appeared a gorgeous blue.

"You like it here?" Avel asked, flagging a waitress with their numbered card.

"I love Oso," Luz said. "My brother used to perform here."

"He's a musician?"

"No," Luz said, finding his enthusiasm charming. "He works with snakes."

"He must be one brave son of a bitch."

"Or crazy as hell."

They ordered ginger ales and watched the singer finish her set with a folding curtsy. Avel kept his hay-colored hat calmly in his lap like a sleeping kitten. Luz appreciated his attention to detail, his eye for beautiful clothes. Avel had grinned when he saw Luz had changed into her yellow McCall's dress with the square neckline. She and Lizette had saved up for months to buy themselves enough fabric for the pattern. The inspiration came from a more expensive version they had seen, crumpled and stained, at the bottom of their dirty clothes sack.

The lights brightened to an eerie green, and Los Soñadores, a five-piece with two violins, a trumpeter, a guitarist, and a woman in a black veil, took the stage. The woman walked to the silver microphone, cupping its neck in her hand like Eve's apple. She opened her mouth. She said, "Good evening, Denver," and then howled in a pleasurable piercing note. The band kicked off behind and beside her, the theater filling with music.

"That's Leonora Mondragon," said Avel. "She's real good. Back home in Califas, she's famous. Sings like an angel, but dresses like death."

Luz gazed at Leonora, her face shielded in thin netting. The song she sang was heartfelt and cruel, a tale of lovers destined for destruction, the woman wailing from the ground, holding her man's ankles, pleading with him to carry her into their home by the sea. Luz had never seen the ocean in person, and she listened intently, imagining the sea.

"It's true love," said Avel, and Luz laughed, searching the audience, still anxious from Diego's attack, uneasy with her back to a crowd.

In Teatro Oso, there were Westside girls with older fiancés. Some of Maria Josie's former *friends* with their unattractive husbands. A couple of Diego's old girls, too, but whenever Luz looked their way, they averted their eyes and drank from glasses of champagne. Luz regretted her wandering gaze when she locked eyes with Mrs. Montoya from three tables down. She immediately waved and stood from her table. "Oh, good gracious," Luz said to Avel, who watched with amusement as the middle-aged woman waddled toward their table in a garish purple dress. Her lipstick was smeared just past her lips, and one of her false eyelashes hung lazily like a half-opened cocoon.

"Luz Lopez! I haven't seen you in ages, and I have some questions for you, jita." Mrs. Montoya scrunched her brow into a forking path, causing her upper lip to recede. She turned to Avel. "Well, aren't you handsome." She winked at Luz. "Lucky."

Luz introduced Mrs. Montoya to Avel as one of her clients. She then rested her arms across the table in a way to show that, no, there was no room for her there, but Avel drank the last of his ginger ale, pulled out an empty chair, and waved to the waitress. "Have a seat, Mrs. Montoya. What kind of client of Luz's?"

"Oh, she hasn't told you? She's quite the fortune-teller, this one." Mrs. Montoya plopped into her chair. She tossed her purse over the table's glass covering. "Tea leaves."

Avel patted Luz's hand, and that side of her body tingled like with pins.

"To think," he said, "Luz hasn't told me how our date ends."

A date, Luz thought, *an actual date*.

Mrs. Montoya snickered. "She does see it all. Now, Luz, I've been having the worst trouble with my joints again, and just recently after I helped Pa salt the walk, my left ankle had a pain, like a twinge, a needle of sorts, and it just wouldn't go away for hours and you know how important it is that I get outside at least once a day. Pa isn't in the best shape anymore, either, and I just need to know if this is a passing thing or if I should be prepared for something worse."

Avel looked bemused as Mrs. Montoya went on, but the band

started up again before anyone could say more, and Mrs. Montoya sighed in her purple dress.

Luz hollered across the table. "I can read for you, but maybe another time?"

"Yes, yes," Mrs. Montoya shouted back, clearly disappointed.

When Los Soñadores finished their set, Avel and Luz left their table to greet the band in a rear booth. As the stage was readied for La Chata, the room hissed with the high frequency of a crowd waiting. Leonora was gathering her long black dress in her hands, sliding into the shiny red booth. After taking her seat, she reached for a glass of water resting on the table. She removed her veil, and Luz saw that she was beautiful and vibrant with a black mole above the left side of her mouth, one front tooth jagged and chipped, the imperfection inviting.

"You made it," she said in a voice gone hoarse, glancing at Avel. "And who's this lovely little dove?"

Avel grinned and moved toward Leonora, embracing her with a long handshake that included much of her thin right arm. "This is Luz," he said. "And I see you're still covering yourself when you sing."

Leonora tilted her face to the side. She laughed. "Hoarding my resources." She turned to Luz, looking at her with up and down eyes. "Avel's quite the horn player, Luz," she said, gazing at him now, focused.

Luz stood awkwardly at Avel's side, as if she were intruding on a private conversation. "I'll have to hear you play," she said.

Leonora lit a slim cigarette. Her face bones glowed in firelight. "You ever need to run away again, you're always welcome back home with us."

Avel chuckled. He knocked on the table with his knuckles. "Who doesn't appreciate an open door?"

Luz felt the pains of jealousy, a bad feeling she rarely experienced.

They left Teatro Oso a little after eight and walked slowly down Nineteenth Avenue. Despite the night's industrial amber haze, the air felt mountainous and cool. The streets were lined with dirty snow, and steam rose from the gutters, highlighting the silhouettes of drunks as they staggered from one bar to another. Luz and Avel turned a corner and he reached for her arm, guiding her away from black ice. The couple headed toward a Greek diner on Colfax, walking in silence for some time, until they passed beneath a faulty streetlamp. The lights blinked on, then off.

Luz said, "I always think it's a bad sign, when they go out like that."

"It could be worse. They could be dead entirely."

Luz told Avel that was very true. "What kind of music do you like to play?"

"Mariachi mostly," he said.

"You have a suit and all that? A big hat?"

"I had the biggest hat in the group."

"You'll have to find a band here in Denver."

"First things first," Avel said, opening the diner door. "Let's get you fed."

The diner smelled of baked pies and steaming coffee, grilled hamburger meat. Luz removed her gloves and fluffed the cold from her hair as they took their seats near the front window. Beyond the glass, the road was a stretch of black. Headlights flickered whenever an automobile passed by. They ordered coffee and fried baloney sandwiches and Avel looked on, observant with deep eyes. There was something steady beneath his surface, an unfamiliar trait for Luz. He seemed a calm man without much to hide.

"What about you?" he said, sipping his coffee. "What're your people like? Your folks? Maria Josie is your tía, right?"

Luz glanced around the diner, at the tables and booths filled with other young couples, men about to begin their night shifts and eating solo dinners at the long counter, the overworked waitresses who were happy to endure aching backs for small tips. "Yes, she's my mama's younger sister."

"What about your mama and papa then?"

"They're in another place now."

"Oh, shoot," said Avel. "I didn't know. I'm sorry for your loss."

Luz smiled, staring at the square napkin in her lap. She found it odd how people sometimes said they had *lost* a person, as if death was some kind of misplacement of the soul, like an absent sock or an errant hairpin. "No," she said, sweetly. "Papa left a long time ago, and Mama stayed down below in the Lost Territory when my brother and me come north. She didn't take his leaving well." Luz scooped sugar into her coffee. She stirred with a long spoon. "She isn't well. It hurt her mind."

Avel nodded, as if he understood it was time to change the subject. "How'd you like the show?"

Luz giggled. She told him La Chata was a hoot, and that Leonora, what an entertainer. "Do you want to travel again and play music with her?"

Avel said, "No, I don't think I do. Say," he said, "how did you know you're a fortune-teller? My abuelita was one, too. You read palms and all that?"

Luz shook her head. "Only tea leaves."

"What about coffee grounds?"

"Haven't tried. Suppose I could."

Avel rose from the table and walked toward the counter of men eating solo dinners. He leaned over the pie case, the light pressing against the mother-of-pearl buttons on his western shirt. He spoke to an older waitress with her gray hair in a bun. She laughed first but then nodded and called into the kitchen. She handed Avel a small white bowl.

At the table, he poured the contents of the bowl into his coffee mug. "Fresh coffee grounds," he said, taking a few sips before passing the cup to Luz.

She laughed and brushed her upper lip with her index finger. "You've given yourself a mustache," she said.

He made a kissy face and wiped his mouth on his sleeve. "Distinguished."

Avel shimmied into his seat, bumping Luz's legs beneath the table. "Now, I'm sure you have your own way of doing readings, a process. But I'd like to see you in action. That Mrs. Montoya wasn't disappointed."

Luz feigned an overworked sigh. "I can give it a shake."

Somewhere jazz played, a sonorous saxophone, a gullet of notes. As a joke, Luz told Avel not to watch her as she read his cup. "I'm a shy reader." Avel smirked. She liked that he was casual and light. Luz smiled and sat up straight, smoothed the paper napkin in her lap, and stared into the mug. Warmth moved into Luz from the floor, through her pumps, along her legs, and into her center. The coffee grounds were like tea leaves, only darker, a little like blood.

"There's a man running," she said, turning the cup like a dial. "He's marveling at tents. An enormous citrus orchard is now a shantytown. There are orange trees." Luz paused and beamed with joy. "How pretty. I've never seen orange trees before."

Avel slowly turned to face her as she spoke, a stunned look on his face.

"*Star people*," said Luz, with awe. "My mama used to talk about them visiting the Lost Territory, but those snatchers came from the sky. These ones, they're Anglos."

"You see all that?"

"Is it wrong?"

"It's happened. I mean, it's happening."

"Really? Then I'm on track?"

Avel nodded and leaned across the table to Luz, as if to listen to a storyteller who had fallen to a whisper.

"At night, dogs are barking. There are lanterns behind curtains. Strangers are pulling men from their beds, taking them as they sleep. They are putting them on packed trains." Luz wound a string of her hair around her finger. She pulled it tightly as she continued to read. She had never seen anything like this before, such defined images in the cup. There were square homes with their windows illuminated in chaos. She heard men shouting, their wet-lined lungs coughing commands in both English and Spanish. Women wept as their husbands' feet were dragged over damp grass. Inside wooden boxcars, the smell of urine. Luz felt sickness rising in her heart. She looked at Avel across the table, and his face was gentle in its surprise.

"They're calling it repatriation," he said, flatly. "They're deporting us to Mexico to make room for white men without jobs. Doesn't matter a lot of us were born right here in the USA."

"That's why you're in Denver?"

"In a sense."

Two policemen entered the diner then, their badges shiny and their thick batons swinging like dead snakes at their sides. With broad, authoritative gaits, they walked to the counter, taking two stools beside the jukebox. One removed his cap, ran his fingers through his hair, and pointed to the jukebox with an irritable look on his chinless face. The second officer stood, deposited coins into the machine. The music shifted from jazz. An abrupt cut into fox-trot. No couples looked up from their tables and booths. Every-one, it seemed, lowered their eyes.

"We should get you back home," Avel said softly. "I'd hate for Maria Josie to worry."

FIFTEEN

The Red Streets

On her first day at the law office, Luz wore a church dress, not sure what office girls wore. She stood on the busy corner of Seventeenth and Tremont where the triangular Brown Palace Hotel pointed like a ship's bow. City wind fought against Luz as she crossed the packed street, walking to the row of underground businesses where David's office nestled in the middle. Opening the slim glass door with his name and the word ESQUIRE stenciled in black, Luz was embarrassed by her hands, her filthy fingernails, her callused palms.

"Right on time," David said, sipping coffee in shirtsleeves and black slacks. He leaned against a massive bookshelf facing a windowless eastern wall.

Luz lowered her head. She spoke quietly with her hands folded behind her back. "It's a short walk."

He approached her, asking for her coat, which Luz removed from her shoulders in a rigid, nervous way. "You can keep your things here," he said, pointing to a metal hook between two book-shelves. Luz had only seen that many books before in a library. She didn't know people kept as many themselves, and she won-dered who had time to read a wall's worth of words.

"To begin," said David, hanging her coat from the rack, "I'll need help keeping the office organized, papers straightened, books dusted, that sort of thing."

There were traffic sounds outside, and the floorboards above them creaked. Luz nodded as David led her around the front room, long and narrow, ending at his office door. The room smelled of dust and the burnt stench of the saddlemaker's labor one busi-ness down. In the tiny green bathroom, David pointed to dishes drying on a rack, the cabinet filled with hand towels and unused bars of Ivory soap. In the main room, he patted his pockets and dropped a set of keys into Luz's hand. "Keep these for the desk and front door."

Luz placed the keys in her dress pocket and trailed David as he pointed out various filing cabinets, brown husks beneath sash-barred windows.

"These should be locked every evening." He gestured toward a file drawer marked A–C. Beyond his left shoulder, Luz peered at his diplomas on the wall, the elegant inked calligraphy, the seal of Columbia University. Luz marveled at the small articulated throne.

"Today you'll straighten paperwork, and next week, from your first wages, I'll put you into some kind of class for typing at the Opportunity School." At a dark metal desk, David swiped an olive-colored typewriter's keys. This, Luz realized, was to be her seat.

"I like the noise," she said. "Sounds like rain."

"Good. You'll hear it a lot."

In the far corner, David reached into a crate resting on the hardwood floor and removed a stack of papers. He pushed them into Luz's hands, and she was surprised by their heaviness. "You'll need to put these in alphabetical order. They're simple documents, assessors' notes from various neighborhoods. When you see a neighborhood that starts with B, such as Baker, it goes here." David opened the first filing drawer and lifted a folder. "And so on and so forth. Any questions?"

Luz shook her head.

"Now if anyone should stop by, you'll greet them. Say, 'Good afternoon, sir or madam, the attorney will see you in a moment.' I'll teach you how to take appointments soon, but for now, check everyone into the ledger, but wait five minutes before knocking on my door. If I'm in a meeting already, never interrupt."

Luz said she understood.

David paused his instructions for a moment and glared at Luz's blue dress. He smiled, his perfect teeth glinting against the office lights. "Do you own anything black or gray?"

"I have a navy blue dress. It almost looks black."

"That won't do," David said with a warm smile. "You'll still look too pretty."

Luz blushed.

"I'll give you an advance for some new dresses. They should be modest yet chic."

The front door opened then and a tall and commanding white man with a black cane entered from the street. The hissing sounds of trolleys and automobiles rose and fell in volume as he opened and closed the door.

"Good afternoon, sir," Luz said. "The attorney will see you in a moment."

David grinned. He said, "It's fine, Luz. I'm right here."

Wiping his patent leather shoes on the doormat, the man removed his gloves, and without so much as looking at Luz, handed her his cap and jacket.

"Let's get on with it," he said, pegging the wooden floor with his cane as they stepped into David's office.

When she was alone, Luz sifted through the paperwork, documents she decided were insurance notes on various Denver neighborhoods. In the top corner, neighborhoods were listed, and all along the middle sections the percentage of foreign-born residents, homeowners, and Negroes were tallied, along with other notes concerning the area's makeup. Trying to decipher the papers reminded Luz of learning to read tea leaves. There was a language, a set of rules, a particular style laid out by generations before her. Sure, these papers were stamped and notarized, but with their watermarks and fading ink, all of it could have been alchemy. When she came upon the Westside, Luz was surprised by what she read.

In this old area, flanked by industrial sections, there are many terraces containing approximately 1,000 living units. Bordering the industrial district is a Mexican concentration. Structures near the railroad yards are cheap, having deteriorated considerably since 1929. Detrimental influences include unpaved streets and the stench from packing plants. Some of these ramshackle terraces have been picked up by speculators.

It was the last part that gave her pause. How could any speculators take interest in the Westside?

When the man with the cane eventually exited David's office, he walked toward Luz and crunched his hands like flippers. Luz handed him his hat and jacket.

"Consider what I've said about this latest manslaughter," said the man. "It gives you an idea of the prosecutor, to go for such a lenient charge."

"What else can we expect with the current governor?" said David.

"Human decency," the man said, stomping past Luz, slamming the front door.

After some time, when all the papers were filed, the bookshelves dusted, and the windows washed, David called Luz into his office, where he was hunched over his desk. Behind him, sprawling over the wall, was an enormous map of the city, Colfax a central stream. Each neighborhood was displayed in a different color, the Westside in red. Along the edges, David had pinned photographs to the wall. Luz shivered at the images of crosses burning over Table Mountain, Klansmen in white hoods marching down Seventeenth Street, the stark photo of a man's torso flopped over gravel, a group of burned shops, and many empty storefronts like poked-out eyes.

"All finished?" David asked, without looking up from his desk.

"Yes, it wasn't so bad at all."

"Very good. You can leave early today to find a new dress." He reached into the drawer at his side and rummaged around for a moment before handing Luz a five-dollar bill.

"I appreciate it very much."

David set down his pencil. He glanced up, showing off his comely face and curly hair. "You'll learn quick."

"If you don't mind me asking," Luz pointed to the picture of the man's beaten face, the trail of blood, "who's that man?"

David turned in his leather chair to an untidy pile of publications on his left. He scrambled papers around for a moment before handing Luz a copy of *The Colorado Call*, the socialist newspaper published on the Northside. Maria Josie never allowed it in the apartment. She said the government people kept track of who read that sort of thing. The article was dated the previous December. "One of my cases, a civil suit, wrongful death. He's from your cousin's neighborhood. Familiar?"

Luz lifted the paper into the light, a tiny block of text. Twenty-three-year-old Estevan Ruiz had been loading scrap iron into a flatcar at the Union Pacific freight house when his shift supervisor claimed he had stolen another man's lunch. It was three o'clock in the afternoon. The responding officers claimed the young man took off on foot and was found dead after falling from a rail bridge into an empty freight car. Luz stared at the man's photograph. His face concave, a black pit.

"No," Luz said, shaking her head. "He fell?"

"Yeah," said David. "Right onto a policeman's club."

SIXTEEN

Three Sisters

The Opportunity School was a tall sophisticated building with amber-colored bricks and grimy windows. A row of fruitless crabapple trees lined the entrance's sandstone walk. Luz stepped inside, heavy with nervousness, and remembered the last time she'd had any schooling. That was in Huerfano, the one-room schoolhouse with Diego. There she learned to read and write, add and subtract. She also learned that speaking anything but English was impermissible. Once, Diego, in his perfect Spanish, told their classmate that he'd rescued a bull snake locked and left for dead inside a dilapidated outhouse. The teacher, who was the color of soapy water, heard the tale and moved away from the green chalk-board, directing her body toward Diego like a shotgun blast in a black dress. Before the class, with a metal ruler, she struck Diego's knuckles so hard and so many times that at first his skin opened and bled, later scabbed, and eventually scarred. The beating sounded like bones garbled in a sack. After that, Diego hardly spoke Spanish outside of their home, and eventually he even forgot certain words.

"Have a seat," said the teacher, an older Anglo woman in a purple hat with an oversized feather and a bushel of a dress, as she entered Room 121. She was turned to the chalkboard, where her name, Mrs. Fenwick, was written in steady script alongside a diagram of a typewriter's keys. Three long wooden tables were behind her, sporadically filled with two dozen or so students, all of them girls around Luz's age. The room was chilly and smelled of talcum powder and Chanel perfume. Conversations pooled in murmuring pockets.

Luz dropped herself into a nearby chair, sliding her hands out of her gloves.

"Not there," said Mrs. Fenwick without turning around. *"There."* With a stub of white chalk, she pointed to the far left corner.

There Luz found three girls with hair as black as hers. Each was arched over the table. The girls wore similar dresses, the same maroon color but different cuts. They had matching leather notebooks, and the table beneath them had been scratched in long swirling streaks, as if a tiny ice-skater had run her blades over the wood. Above one of the girls, hanging from the wall, was a simple pendulum clock with a lengthy lance and a brass bob. The clock ticked and seemed out of place in the otherwise bare room. Luz immediately felt uneasy around the girls. They were like mirrors of one another, but distorted and pieced apart.

"Don't worry," said the girl beneath the clock. "We ain't vultures."

"Or crows," said one with strikingly large front teeth.

"Both of you quiet now," said the third in a lace-collared dress. "I prefer ravens."

Luz smiled lightly and sat among them at an empty chair.

The lace-collared girl flicked her wrist, as if to say, *Don't mention it.* She had a strong face with a sharp jaw. Her nose, though attractive, jutted out and shadowed her broad lips. She motioned to herself with an open palm. "I'm Isabella, that's Marcella, and this one, well, she's Anita. We're sisters."

Anita grinned with her big teeth, and her eyes seemed to sink into her small face.

"Hi," Luz said, and told them her name.

Marcella whispered in a singsong voice, "Santa Lucia."

Mrs. Fenwick then appeared at the head of their table, distributing papers that came around like empty, square plates. Each one had a typewriter's diagram and a mock set of keys. "This is called the QWERTY layout," she said. "Follow along as I show you on the board."

Luz and the sisters placed their diagrams down, a dinner party of paper. At the chalkboard, Mrs. Fenwick used a lacquered black stick to slap her drawn keys. Thumb, *smack.* Space bar, *smack.* Q, *smack.* Ring finger, *smack.* After some time, she stepped away from the chalkboard and rummaged through her knapsack. Her face was rippled in forehead lines as she sifted through the bag. She pulled out a coverless book and flipped to a middle page. In a droning voice, Mrs. Fenwick read: "The 1910 Cuba hurricane was said to be one of the worst tropical cyclones that has ever hit Cuba. The storm formed in the Caribbean Sea on October ninth." Luz didn't understand, but Mrs. Fenwick explained to the class. "These sentences contain nearly every letter in the alphabet for your striking."

"But, really," said Marcella beneath the clock. "It was a horrid hurricane. It threw around cows."

"How do you even know that?" Isabella stammered.

"I heard about it on the radio. It was a history special."

"What about horses?" Anita asked. "Are they heavier than cows?"

Luz soundlessly scooted her chair away from the sisters. She tried to concentrate on the lesson. It was useless. She still had no interest in the sentences about cyclones. Instead, she found herself studying Mrs. Fenwick, who either couldn't hear the sisters talking or didn't care. "Are you secretaries, too?" Luz asked after some time.

The girls shook their heads.

Anita said, "We don't want husbands and so our father is making us learn a trade."

"Why don't you want husbands?"

"Come to the Northside, you'll see."

"Why are *you* here?" asked Marcella.

"My boss wanted me to come. He's an attorney."

"A Mexican lawyer?"

"No, he's Greek."

"We shouldn't be talking, you know," Isabella said.

"Why's that?"

"You're a spic and we're wops."

Luz couldn't tell if she was kidding, but the sisters eased into a kind chuckle and she decided it was a joke. "You're Italians?"

"No, we're Americans, like you. But our father's from Naples. Italia!"

Luz laughed. She had never been called American before. That was a word she and Diego used to be nicer about Anglos, but Isabella was right. They were Americans.

Mrs. Fenwick reappeared at their table. She held up her black stick as if she had a great thought, but her face froze with half-opened eyes. She sneezed and then blew her nose into a blue hankie. "Pardon me," she said, dabbing inside her nostrils with the handkerchief. "Will you girls please demonstrate the correct finger positions."

"Certainly," the sisters said almost as one.

Luz and the sisters began methodically tapping away on their flattened paper keys. Mrs. Fenwick watched for half a minute with a drizzly nose and reddish eyes. When she seemed satisfied with their progress, she blew her nose once more and pushed the hankie deeper inside her nostrils before stepping away.

Isabella smoothed her piece of paper. "Whatever you do, don't fall in love with him."

"With who?" Luz asked.

"Your boss, silly. Those things never end well."

"Show me the back," said Lizette, propped up on her elbows as she lay on her side on Luz's bed. It was late afternoon, and the green shades were drawn. The cousins drank peppermint schnapps mixed with lemonade from a thermos, the radio up loud, Cab Calloway howling throughout the apartment. Luz twirled in her new work dress. They weren't quite drunk, but they were on their way.

"You look like a million bucks, I swear it," said Lizette. "Where's it from again?"

Luz's new black dress had a white sailor collar, white sleeve cuffs, and silver ribbons along her neck and down her back. "LaVerna's."

"What a smart dress," said Lizette, resting the thermos between her thighs. She reached out, smoothing the fabric along Luz's hips, dissecting the pattern in her mind. "That stitching should last you a while." She then pretended a typewriter was before her and, with perfect posture, clacked away into the air. "So, how was school?"

"Fine, just learning about typing," Luz said, thinking back to the lesson and the abundance of distraction. "I did meet these three sisters. They looked like triplets."

"Oh yeah?" Lizette hiccupped.

"Yeah, and they said something about David."

"Like what?"

"Not to fall in love with him."

Lizette shot upright. She said, "Did he make a pass at you?"

"No, no," Luz said. "Nothing like that."

"I mean . . ." Lizette pointed at Luz's body, her dress. "He is buying you fancy things."

"It wasn't free. He's taking it out of my wages. Maria Josie and I barely had enough for rent last month."

"Apply for relief. There's no shame."

Luz gave Lizette a serious look. "Maria Josie would never. The relief people make you sell everything you own, the clothes off your back."

"The naked deserve release!" Lizette hiccupped into a laugh. "I mean relief. Well, what about that Avel you've been seeing? Can't he help you? And does he know David's buying you fancy dresses?"

Luz faced the oval mirror hanging near her altar. She considered the dark ponds of her eyes. She looked mature in the fitted dress, elegant even. "He is not buying me dresses," Luz said a little louder than intended. She adjusted her white collar, and then said quietly, "And Avel's like us, not a dime to his name."

"Well," said Lizette, raising her skinny eyebrows. "It's love that counts, right?" She hiccupped again, and the cousins laughed.

SEVENTEEN

Words into Words

Within a month, Luz had time to do laundry with Lizette only on weekends. She had attended three more classes at the Opportunity School, but was disappointed by the absence of the Northside sisters, who seemed to have materialized and then vanished like morning frost. David appeared impressed by the speed at which Luz was acquiring new skills. He'd swiftly walk toward her with a prideful expression, resting his arms around her shoulders and onto her desk as she typed. With David above her, Luz would grow self-conscious, carefully noticing how quickly her fingers struck each key. It didn't help that Luz could smell him whenever he was near her, the ripe currant of his aftershave, a plum-like ghost briefly overpowering the scent of acrid ink.

"You're quick," David said one afternoon. He was rummaging through a file cabinet with his shoulders to Luz as he spoke. Outside, the sun was shielded by a coal-fueled cloud, darkening the office a shade more than usual. "Much faster than I expected."

"Thank you, David," Luz said, feeling her head bow out of reaction. But she wasn't *that* thankful. After all, she knew that she was a fast learner.

"Have you ever had any schooling? I mean, besides the Opportunity School." David moved on to another filing cabinet. He stepped with ease, but his face pulled with a look of agitation, as if he wasn't finding what he was looking for.

Luz said, "Just to grade four at the schoolhouse in the Lost Territory."

"It's a shame there isn't a greater drive for smart girls like you to go on in school."

Luz moved her index finger along her forehead, as if to scratch an itch. She didn't agree with David. Luz knew she had spent her life learning. All the women she knew had. Lizette could sew an entire dress from a pattern she'd glimpsed only once. Teresita could heal someone as good as any doctor. And Maria Josie's physical strength mirrored her abundant and steady mind. David had no idea what Luz had taught herself in the time since she and Diego had arrived in Denver. A whole new city, a map in her mind. Luz could speak two languages, and sometimes, without knowing how or why, she dreamed and understood another language, too, something older. When she first learned to read tea leaves, Luz's mother told her that there was one every generation, a seer who keeps the stories. She had learned that, too, and still was.

Luz only said, "Maybe I'll go back someday. To school."

David repeated this word *maybe,* like his voice was a dinner bell. He had turned around and grinned at her over a stack of papers in his arms. He had pulled documents from a bottom drawer, which he plopped onto Luz's desk, the stack shifting into a wayward tower. "This statement in Spanish," David said, tapping the top slip of paper, "can you please transcribe it into English? It's

not very lóng. I understand some of it, but not all." He then explained that he needed to leave early for a community meeting.
"Don't work too hard," he said, swinging his coat over his shoulders.

Luz spent the afternoon typing documents on client meetings,
billing notifications, and other scraps of casework. As she worked
her way through the ledger, she saw Eleanor Anne's name, and she
made a note to ask him about it later. She then studied the slip of
paper she was to translate. It was written in fine cursive, a steady
hand, delicate black ink with the letters *CR* at the signature. Luz
was used to moving words into words. She had been doing it since
she was a little girl, but there was something about the way the
writing made her feel, as if the letters themselves were weeping.
As she typed, Luz found herself crying. Quiet at first, then building into staccato sobs. At one point, Luz dripped tears onto the
page and had to blow it dry. It was a letter written by Celia Ruiz,
the older sister of Estevan Ruiz, the young man found dead in the
freight car.

Since my brother's life was so viciously taken, Mama does
nothing but sleep. Our father is gone and has been for many
years—killed in a mining explosion where they only recovered
his left hand, the simple wedding ring intact. It goes without
saying that Estevan provided for our family. I am not yet married, and I fear the things I will be forced to do in order to
feed myself and Mama. And if they ever read this, the men
who murdered my brother, officers of the law, those who claim
to protect us, I have a message for you. My brother Estevan
was not a worthless body to discard as trash. He was a man, a
big brother, a son. His heart was gentle and good. He made
coffee every morning, a little extra for Mama and me. He

learned to bake cakes for our birthdays, and he was a beautiful artist, a real talent with his pictures of mountains and faces. This pain, the absence of his life, it is unnatural, it goes against God's will. I am embarrassed that I have prayed for the dead to come back to life. Please God, I have begged, give me back my brother, let me visit my father, give me a moment of their joy. But my prayers are never answered and I am so angry with God that I am ashamed of myself. And you, the men who murdered my brother? You face nothing, no judgment, no consequences for killing. I wonder if you even can feel the sickness in your souls?

When she finished, Luz read the statement aloud and squeezed her eyes shut, trying not to see the pool of blood spreading from the pictures in her mind into the room before her.

That night after work, Luz met Avel at the Emerald Room for Tuesday Night Open Mic. Avel hoped some of the local musicians might hear him play and invite him into their bands. Luz liked the idea because she could read leaves there. The owner was a flighty older woman from the Midwest named Lady Red who encouraged audience participation and, during late-night shows, varying levels of public nudity. Of course, the Emerald Room was often cited by police, and several times a month, without warning, was closed until Lady Red paid the bribe.

The club's ceiling was a vast atrium, a sky of glass. Luz had been offered a corner booth where Avel sat beside her, shining his trumpet with his red handkerchief. He looked handsome in a yellow shirt. He smelled good, too, a scent like autumn when some of the leaves are scattered around the streets.

"Are you nervous?" she asked, and Avel shook his head, moved close.

"I only get nervous when I have to speak. But play music? I can do that all night."

A young woman approached the booth then, a nickel between her forefinger and thumb.

"A customer," Avel shouted and sprang from his seat, kissing Luz on the forehead. "I'll leave you to your work."

Luz smiled at the young woman and began fixing her tea. Avel's name was called, and Luz watched as he confidently walked to the stage, next in line, his trumpet glinting with bluish light. They had been on several dates since their time at Teatro Oso—a picnic in the mountains, a picture at the Santa Fe, walks alongside the river at sunset. The first time Avel had kissed Luz, a rainbow trout leapt from the water and smacked against a boulder before flopping into the foam line. Luz gasped and Avel figured the breathlessness was for him, or at least that's what she let him believe.

A singing ensemble finished their set as Avel waited in the darkness to the left. Luz read tea leaves for the young woman, then three sisters, and quickly for a husband who was certainly lying to himself and his wife about his bedroom needs. Luz stared into the atrium. String lights crisscrossed the room, as if God had wrangled the stars inside. Avel was called to play as Luz made herself a cup of tea.

"I said 'Don't work too hard.'" It was David, standing before her. "And here you are, working some more."

"I didn't know you come here," said Luz coolly, masking her surprise.

"I don't," said David. "My date does, who has currently been in the ladies' a very long time." He edged back in his shiny shoes, searching the barroom.

"Maybe she skipped out," Luz said.

"Occupational hazard." David winked. "My yaya used to do this." He pointed to her tea leaves and kettle. "She read spoons, too."

Luz smiled and looked past David, where Avel was taking his position center stage beneath a blue light. He made eye contact with her through the crowd, beamed as he held his horn. There was an angel's halo of light inside the instrument's bell.

"My name's Avel," he said, "and I've just come here from California." The first notes of his breath moaned like the trumpet itself was crying.

"David," Luz said, glancing upward slowly.

"No," he said, "I don't want a fortune reading."

Luz shot him a bored look. She took the opportunity to bring up what had been gnawing at her. "Today in the ledger, I saw that girl named Eleanor Anne visited you, but you didn't charge her anything. Why?"

David peered downward, scratched his head. His curly hair fell into his eyes. "Luz. Sweet Luz. I can't tell you that."

Luz looked to Avel then, his cheeks inflated like balloons. She couldn't hear his song very well and with David standing beside her, Luz felt torn for her attention. "Does it have to do with Diego?"

The vacant echoes of Avel's horn moved around, distant and low. There was a moment between them where nothing was said. David smiled in an ineffectual way. He asked if he could sip her tea, and Luz considered saying no before sliding over the cup. David drank once and set the porcelain cup down. She wondered about his mouth, and where it had been.

"I helped her with an arrangement, housing," he said. "You should pity her, really."

"Pity her?" Luz said. "My brother isn't here anymore because of that girl."

"There's more to it."

"They attacked Diego."

"Imagine the worst men in the world," he said. "Men who hate anyone different from themselves. Now imagine that's your whole family."

"Then I imagine I'd be just like them."

Avel returned to the booth then, and Luz hadn't realized his song had ended. He was wiping sweat from his face with the same cloth he had used to shine his horn. He stepped beside David and asked Luz what she thought of his song. Ashamed of herself, Luz had barely heard a thing. "Beautiful," she said, breathless in her lie.

"Wonderful job," said David, removing a dime from his pocket and leaving it on the table. He waved across the room, seemingly to his date. "Thank you for the reading, Luz. You always have such clear sight."

After David walked away, Luz watched as the room swelled with movement, the chatter of a silver tray, a drunk woman's laugh, the bartender's shout. More than once, musicians approached Avel. "Take my name," said a few. "We can always use another horn player."

Avel talked and music blared and the Emerald Room faded into blackness between acts. Luz looked through the dark until in the distance of her mind she saw a figure slowly coming into view, skin smoothed over bone, eyes shadowed by a felt hat, a face she knew anywhere. A pristine moon, Luz realized, floated in her cup.

EIGHTEEN

The Love Story of Eleanor Anne

Denver, Summer 1933

Diego waited in the courtyard of the Immaculate Conception Cathedral. It was summertime at night. Streetlamps shined honey-hued between cottonwood trees, their long yellow lines falling at his feet. The air smelled of jasmine. Cicadas pulsated. A warm breeze brushed through his hair, raised his skin. As Eleanor Anne approached on her silver bicycle, the wheels churning a rusted rhythm, Diego finished his cigarette and hung his head in grief. He stood to greet her and she kicked off the bike, her legs long under a pink-lace dress, her strawberry hair newly bobbed and framing her green eyes.

"Are you ready?" She stepped toward him, her cheeks flushed, as though she'd been crying.

Diego placed his palm along her damp neck, kissed her forehead, inhaled her rosy scent. Sometimes, when he looked at Eleanor Anne, Diego felt like an old man traveling along a seemingly endless mountain road, one eventually ending in her, a warm winter cabin, a smoking chimney, a pretty wildflower yard. He said,

"We don't have to do it, you know. We can go away tonight. Never come back here."

Eleanor Anne shook herself free of his arms. With her right foot, she tucked away the kickstand on her bicycle and guided the handlebars as they walked. "You know my family won't let that happen. Let's get it over with."

The curanderas lived in a crumbling violet house with a lop-sided spiked fence. Against the night, the home seemed like an extension of the clouds. Diego opened the front gate and followed Eleanor Anne as she pushed her bike to an empty area on the lawn. They shared a look before a Virgen de Guadalupe shrine. *I love you,* Diego mouthed and Eleanor Anne smiled, swiping her hands along his shoulders.

Inside was a dollhouse of rooms, filled with those in need of healing. They walked past a young couple in the kitchen seeking counseling on how to conceive, a day laborer in the sitting room, speaking to a young curandera about his foot warts. A rumored prostitute, Diego noted, was in the hallway, discussing something in hushed tones. The curandera Eleanor Anne had somehow found was an abuela, white-haired and patient. The home smelled of menudo, burnt cedar, incense, and church. A heavy woman of middle age with sparkling skin that looked very soft seated the young couple in a dim bedroom with a connected bathroom. She wore a huipil, the flowers embroidered in purples and golds.

"How far along?" she asked in Spanish. She bit a piece of copal between her lips, placed the amber chunk into a sahumador. Sprinkling dried cedar over charcoal, she lit the pile with a skinny match. The room blossomed in smoke. Diego translated for Eleanor Anne, who said, "Just a month or two."

"Sí," said the curandera. Her teeth glinted with gold caps. Along her wrists, bracelets of shells pushed into her flesh. From a high shelf, beside white votives and a San Miguel candle, she pulled down a stone metate and placed it on the ground, between her clean, round feet. The woman removed several packets of herbs from a leather pouch around her neck. Like the copal, she bit these into pieces, placing them on the stone's flat surface. She ground the leaves into a fine brown dust. The woman stepped into the other room. Diego looked to Eleanor Anne, who seemed very scared.

When the woman returned, she had a steaming blue cup and a slim spoon. "A scoop for every missed moon."

Diego translated for Eleanor Anne. She nodded, said she understood. She told him this twice. With a slight tremble, she poured three spoonfuls into the cup. The curandera made a drinking motion with both hands, gliding her fingers down her own throat and over her belly. When they had finished, Diego offered the woman cigarettes, two gold necklaces, and rose quartz.

Diego walked with Eleanor Anne to the border of her neighborhood at the edge of Park Hill. Her bicycle made turning, rickety sounds as they passed the stone mansions and vast library, the roads of Park Hill illuminated by streetlamps. They were quiet for some time. Bats flickered above them, cascaded through the air, dropped from the sky to eat mosquitoes. Reina and Corporal, Diego thought, would have enjoyed the sight. In the stark nighttime, Eleanor Anne allowed her hands to touch Diego's side. When they rounded the corner from one block to the next, she leaned in and kissed his ear, the sound a starburst of lips. "Don't be sad," she whispered. "It was all we could do."

Diego wanted to say that no, it wasn't. He was willing to marry her, to raise their child and live in another city, a bigger town, go west to California where he'd make money from his show, could quit the factory, buy a little bungalow, and teach their daughter to dance with snakes. It was a little girl—he was sure of it. Diego was shocked at how he was already speaking of the baby as something that once was. How he wished that Eleanor Anne didn't come from such a hateful and bigoted people. How he wished they could have their life together in the light instead of like this, alone, side by side, in the night.

"Diego," Eleanor Anne said, "I feel strange."

"You probably just need rest," he said, guiding her by the small of her back.

"No," she said, shaking her head, pausing with the bicycle handlebars in each hand. "Something's wrong." She let out a cry, touched her lower stomach, and bent over.

Diego took the bike from her hands, kicked up its stand. He reached for Eleanor Anne and asked was what wrong.

"My insides hurt."

"Baby," he said cringing at the sight of her pain. "It's supposed to hurt. I'm sorry, baby."

"I think I took too much. I took extra, to make sure it worked."

Eleanor Anne shook her head with her red bob. She started to cry, thrusting herself forward from Diego's grip, falling over the sidewalk and onto the wet grass. Diego kneeled beside her and grabbed her face with his hands. She had fainted, her eyelids fluttering between the waking world and the place she had gone. Diego called her name and lightly slapped her cheek. He hollered louder, pleaded with her to wake up, shook her arms and legs. It was then that he noticed the blood at her center. Diego lifted her dress and saw that she was bleeding badly between her legs. He wiped her blood on the grass. He lifted her head and pulled her torso up from the ground. As he began to hoist her body over his shoulder, Diego turned and saw a line of three Anglo men on the sidewalk two houses away. They were dressed nicely in black suits, drunkenly holding conversation, headed for a parked automobile. When they reached the Ford, jostled the engine, and turned on the headlights, Diego's heart sank. It was all over.

"What are you doing over there?" they hollered. "My god," said another one. "Look at her dress. What have you done to her?"

Diego eased Eleanor Anne down from his shoulder, sliding her body onto the grass. "I'm so sorry, mi sirena," he said and kissed her mouth before running toward the alley, lightless and long, back to Hornet Moon.

NINETEEN

Justice Cannot See, but Can She Hear?

Denver, 1934

Sometimes Luz thought about when they first came to the city—how she didn't understand the layout of the world. She was only little. Before, when they had lived in the Lost Territory, she was surrounded by mountains from Huerfano to Trinidad and all the mining camps in between. The mountains were permanent yet shifting, ancient though young, their white peaks reminding Luz of gray hairs while their aspen groves resembled veins. Luz felt partly made of mountains, as if the land was family.

But the city was different. Smog and concrete. Morning light spilling between stone squeezes, landing on the worn hoods of Model Ts resting on Curtis Street. In the evenings, the sun slipped behind the mountains, sinking away with long tentacles of light reaching over the brickwork city for another chance at brilliance. Maria Josie insisted Diego and Luz must *learn the map*, as she called it, and she showed them around first on foot and later by streetcar. She wore good walking shoes, and dressed herself and the children in many layers. *It tends to heat up*, she had said, *another moment, it might hail.* The siblings learned to be cautious. It was dangerous to stroll through mostly Anglo neighborhoods, their streetcar routes equally unsafe. There were Klan picnics, car races, cross burnings on the edge of the foothills, flames like tongues licking the canyon walls, hatred reaching into the stars.

Luz and Diego were once walking downtown when a man yelled, "Go back to your own country!" and spat at them from a truck window. They were supposed to be learning the map. It was the first time Maria Josie had sent them off alone. Luz had cried, wiping the stranger's hot phlegm from her tiny face. Diego cursed, held up both arms. But he lowered them cautiously and told Luz he finally recognized where they were. He pulled his little sister by the sleeve of her oversized dress into the market, a place called Tikas, a ringing of bells.

"What happened to the little one?" a voice called, and Luz saw it was the older boy, David, the shopkeeper's son, watchful behind the counter.

Diego pointed to Luz's wet cheek and asked if she could please use the sink. She was only eight years old, and everything in the market's storeroom was unlike anything Luz had ever seen before. Shelves of canned food, sacks of flour, heaps of wooden crates. They must be rich, she thought, scrubbing her face nearly raw with a clean white towel.

"Where'd it happen?" David was asking when Luz returned.

She pointed to the front door.

"What color was the truck?" David said, stepping down from the counter. He was carrying a baseball bat. He gently took Luz's left hand and walked her to the door, opening it with a sweeping gesture. "Which direction?"

Luz shook her head. She was done crying now. Embarrassed, she held the towel to her face, trying to hide herself from David.

"I don't know any directions yet. We got lost today. We're trying to learn the map."

David softly pulled the towel away from Luz's face. He smiled when she looked at him. He wasn't a grown-up, but he wasn't a child and he was tall and slim-shouldered, a warmth in his gaze. He motioned down the wide avenue, between the brick buildings and wire-filled sky. "See that?" he said. "Those are the mountains. They'll always be west."

Luz looked to the horizon, allowing the line of sunlight to bathe her eyes.

"And over there," he said, "it's flat. That's the prairie land. East." David pointed to the mountains once more. "Which direction?"

"West," said Luz.

David gestured right.

"East," said Luz.

"Good work," he said. "Now say, *This is my city!*"

Luz didn't say anything, and David nudged her to go on.

"This is my city," she said quietly.

"This," David spoke louder, "is my city!"

Luz giggled before she sucked in another breath. "This is my city!"

"All right," said David. "Now once more like you mean it."

"THIS IS MY CITY!" they yelled together until their voices boomed, high and arching, rattling streetcar cables and smoggy windows, soaring between stone tenements and factory tufts. *This,* she repeated, *is ours.*

The courthouse sat on a sloping grid of patchwork grass pocked with snow. Luz followed David as he climbed the stone steps in his black suit and glistening shoes, a briefcase at his side. It was a

Wednesday morning. The sun shined over his shoulders, absorbed into his curly hair. The majestic building of many floors curved inward as if embracing the city. The windows were blank, reflective, the doors massive and brass. David turned around as they reached the walkway's peak.

"This is a hearing," he said, outside the front doors. "For the Ruiz case. I'll normally go to court alone, but sometimes I'll ask you along. This is to show you how things work. Should be quick."

Luz said she understood and tried to ignore the gnawing feeling of nervousness inside her stomach. She had never been in a courtroom before, though Diego had once been arrested for loitering when he was doing nothing more than charming snakes across from the train station. He'd spent the weekend in jail and was later made to pay a fine by a surly old judge who looked upon him with disdain from behind tiny circular glasses. It was bullshit, Diego had told Luz. Never enter the courts, he had said, if you can avoid it.

The revolving brass doors fanned Luz and David until they landed in an impressive marble hallway flush with morning. There were Anglo women in red lipstick, their hair held to their scalps with pins, folders in their arms, their feet sounding with the tap dance of work. David said hello to a man dressed like himself in the same black suit and shiny shoes. They walked deeper into the hallway, a tunnel of cream, stone benches, and unused water fountains. On the walls, murals depicted covered wagons, miners panning for gold, an abundance of white men coming to the land. The doors were wood-framed with frosted glass, words printed in black lettering, CITY COUNCIL CHAMBERS, COUNTY CLERK. David guided Luz with his hand at her hip until they reached the doors of COURTROOM 108.

"Take a seat," he whispered, pointing to what looked to Luz like a church pew.

The courtroom was smaller than Luz had anticipated, nearly empty, an American flag, a high bench with two smaller desks before it, one on either side, everything made of wood and stone. There was an officer that David had explained was called a bailiff, a woman perched over a typewriter, a court reporter, and another attorney, a man with white hair and speckles of dandruff across the shoulders of his thick woolen suit. He worked for the city, David had mentioned on their walk over, a real dinosaur.

"All rise," said the bailiff. "The Second Judicial District Court for the City and County of Denver is now in session, the Honorable Judge Roberts presiding."

Luz watched as the ancient judge appeared from behind a wood panel as if emerging from a secret passage, stepping quickly in a black robe.

"Thank you," he said, taking his seat above them. "Please be seated. This record is being made for Ruiz versus Carmichael and the City and County of Denver. Present for the proceeding is Attorney Tikas on behalf of plaintiff Celia Ruiz and Attorney Johnston on behalf of defendant Officer Mitchell Carmichael and the City and County of Denver."

Luz listened intently but found it difficult to follow the judge's words. She had the familiar sensation of being in church, half expecting a priest and altar boys to appear with incense and the Eucharist at any moment. The proceedings in the frigid courtroom felt like a ritual, a ceremony Luz didn't recognize, but she was convinced that she could learn. She sat a little higher, leaned forward on the bench. The judge first called upon the city attorney, who stood and cleared his throat with a wet hacking sound. He was asking for something to be dismissed, a motion he called it.

"They have no claim here," said the city attorney. "We could go on at length about the stated facts in this case. Yes, Mr. Ruiz is dead. Yes, his death occurred during an altercation with Officer Carmichael. The defense accepts those facts, but we reject the nature of the suit. The fact remains, the City and County of Denver cannot be held liable under sovereign immunity. You cannot," he said, "sue the king."

The city attorney continued before he was interrupted by his own cough, his voice wilting under the sounds. When he finished, the judge called David, who stood elegantly, buttoning the bottom of his suit and sliding his hands through his hair.

"Your Honor," he said, "on behalf of Plaintiff Ruiz, we reject the basis of this motion. The defense claims the city cannot be held responsible, but with all due respect what will suing some drunk cop do? We all know Mr. Carmichael has nothing to his name but a lengthy record of excessive beatings, an abhorrence that the city knows of and has done nothing about. Mr. Carmichael chased my client's brother, clubbed him unconscious, and threw his body from a metal bridge into an empty freight car. In the killing of Estevan Ruiz, Mr. Carmichael has denied an entire family food and shelter, for they relied upon the young man's wages to care for them all. When an officer decides to murder a member of the community, it is not one life snuffed out. It is a web of consequences— one killing damages a thousand lives."

Luz had never heard David's voice used in such a way. He was turned slightly and Luz could see the outline of his face, a calmness over his jaw, illuminated like that of a performer onstage.

"Counselor," said the judge, "as impassioned as your plea is, the simple fact remains, there is no claim to be settled here. I'll make my ruling in a written statement by the week's end. Court adjourned."

David spun around slowly, an almost visible halo of anger rising around him. He neatly pushed his papers into his briefcase and looked to Luz. "We have another stop," he said, ushering her out of the courtroom.

The streets were packed with midday crowds, young men selling newspapers, factory workers moving through lunch counters, bankers stepping into automobiles. David walked briskly along Seventeenth Street, his jaw clenched as he glanced at Luz, his coat and shoes the same gray as the clouds. It was cold. Their breath formed fog. The air smelled of manure and dead cattle.

David's eyes seemed heavy with consideration. Luz hadn't learned to read his expressions the way she could with Lizette and Diego. With Maria Josie, she never fully learned. Some people were like that.

"As you might have guessed," said David, stopping at an intersection, "that did not go well." He pointed across the street to a slanted building that resembled a public gym, only smaller. Above the entrance, as if impaled on iron rods, were the letters KQEZ glowing in pink. "I have a small favor to ask."

The radio station was down a set of crunched granite stairs capped in metal, through a dim hallway, past a bathroom with the door open to the toilet, and in an oblong room with a smaller room of glass built into a corner. As they stepped forward, Luz realized a man was sitting inside the glass room, a single lamp beside him on a wide green desk with an enormous radio with many nobs and wires and lights. The man wore headphones over his frizzy hair. He was seated cross-legged, calmly grasping a chrome microphone in his left hand. From where Luz stood, it almost looked as though the man was arching a bow, sending arrows into the air. It was only upon hearing him that Luz realized it was Leon Jacob, a man whose voice she'd heard a hundred times but whose face she'd never seen.

The papers are calling it a hero snake. You hear me right, ladies and gentlemen. The snake is not a sandwich but a Hercules, our very own FDR in a reptile no less. And for those citizens of Denver who say "But where are our Baby Face Nelsons and John Dillingers and pretty Bonnies and poor Clydes?" Well we have 'em in the fallen of this story. An unlucky bank robber with an unremarkable name, stopped in the act by a vigilante rattlesnake. Someone come get your pet.

David knocked on the glass. Leon ignored him for several seconds until David fished from his briefcase a piece of paper, which he held to the glass and knocked once more. Leon looked, this time removing his headphones. He stood and opened the door.

"Don't tease me," he said. "Thought she was afraid to read it on the air."

"She is, but remember Celia said we could always get someone else." David waved to Luz. "Now we have someone else."

Leon gazed at her. "Comrade?"

David said, "My new secretary, Luz."

"Lightbringer," said Leon. "How do you do?"

Luz shook his hand. He was shorter than she had expected, and when she glanced down Luz realized that Leon had only one leg, the other ending below the knee, his dark green trousers tied in a knot. Everyone knew Leon had been a radioman in the war. He was blasted with machine-gun fire emerging from the trenches. "Injustice is suffering," Leon sometimes said on the radio, and Luz figured he knew a lot about that.

"When do you want to do it?" he asked David.

"Now, on the three o'clock. Encourage people to show up to the next protest, outside the capitol."

Leon clicked his tongue. He removed his circular glasses from his face and blew on them before wiping the lenses on his woolen shirt. "All right," he said. "That might work." He returned to the glass room, letting Luz and David know he'd signal them when he was ready for her.

Luz took a seat beside David in the larger room on an old sofa with several red wine stains. The subterranean windows were small squares close to the ceiling, a slice of afternoon light falling into the basement. Lizette and Alfonso sometimes made fun of Leon, said he was an idealist, out of touch with reality, but a lot of people from a lot of different neighborhoods had started listening. To people like Leon, a new world was possible, a city where the poor weren't evicted or made to line up for hours for cold soup, where women weren't forced to sell their bodies for cow's milk and men weren't killed on factory floors. Maybe, in some ways, Luz agreed with people like Leon. Still, she was nervous to read the note on the radio, but David assured her they wouldn't use her name or mention anything about her at all.

"Like borrowing," he said. "We are borrowing your voice to help people."

Luz nodded, gripping the statement from Celia in her hands, both the original and the version she had typed in English.

"Think of him like Diego," said David.

Leon waved from inside the glass room, signaling for Luz. David patted the top of her hand before Luz entered the chilly space. Leon was perched beside the radio knobs, lights glistening over his glasses. He showed Luz how to flip on the mic, turn down the sound in her headphones, where she should speak and how loudly. Leon examined the document, turned it over from Spanish to English, reading through each side.

"After you finish reading the statement in English," he said, "I'll let listeners know where to march tomorrow, and when I'm done I'll bring you back on to read the note again, but this time in Spanish. Can you do that?"

"Yes," said Luz. "I can, but I think I'll need some practice."

"Practice on the air," said Leon with a smile, and handed her a glass of water. "Don't drink it when we go live—it'll pick up your gulps."

Luz grimaced and looked over the note, silently moving her lips as she practiced reading aloud. Leon flipped on the radio receiver. A red light blinked in the booth. Leon announced that he had a very important message, a statement read by an individual like themselves, a girl of their background, from a neighborhood just like theirs. He gazed at Luz and with his index finger motioned for her to go.

Luz inhaled, the microphone catching hints of fear before she steadied herself, dashing into speech. As she read, the statement seemed to slip away from the page, Celia's words pushing into the air and forming a blanket of weight. Luz imagined her voice and Celia's riding together through the wind, landing in living rooms and workstations, Estevan's life entering the minds of all who listened. Luz read and spoke and thought of Diego in the fields, his body arched over crops, his face badly scarred. How close had he been to being murdered like Estevan? How close was Luz to having no men left in her family at all?

As she finished the statement, this time in Spanish, Leon held up his fingers—*one, two, three*. He clicked off the mic. He threw off his headphones and pulled Luz close for a hug. He smelled of machine oil and nice pomade, and he shouted humidly into Luz's ear. "You're natural, a natural!" Luz thanked him with an anxious laugh, and when she cupped her mouth, she felt tears along her cheeks. The radio room went quiet then and Luz looked through the glass at David. He was standing very still with a tender expression, his eyes dazzling in low light. Good work, he mouthed, placing his hat slowly on his head.

Luz wouldn't see Leon Jacob again for several months, and by that time she will have nearly forgotten his face. The neighbors' power will have been shut off for days, and one night Luz will walk by candlelight to the shared bathtub down the hall. Glancing out the window, she will spot a man dressed in black, single legged, carrying copper wire from one building to another, siphoning power from the city offices down the street and pumping it freely into the tenements strangled by the dark.

TWENTY

The Dressmaker

The city was changing from the bleak winter into new life struggling to be born. Though the nights still dipped into deep cold, in the April mornings on her walk to work, Luz saw signs of spring's early arrival. Daffodils poked their yellow faces up from thin, snowy blankets. Pines existed in two tones, their bases made of hardened, dark needles while their edges were tipped in a soft, radiant green. The Platte, snake-like in icy scales, broke free of itself, rushing with crystal snowmelt that flowed all the way down from the Continental Divide. Diego had been gone a little over six months, and Luz and Maria Josie felt his absence like a fire that had slowly burned down, the embers still red and flickering, but the heat mostly gone.

David paid Luz as much as other beginning secretaries, but with the cost of her Opportunity School classes and her new wardrobe, there wasn't enough to keep her and Maria Josie comfortable. They ate stale tortillas with butter and salt. Meat was a rarity. They saved coffee grounds and old tea bags in worn tins, reusing their remains throughout the week. Luz's winter stockings had begun to run, the soles coated black. Lizette taught her how to draw a line with a kohl pencil down the backs of her legs, making it appear as if she were wearing a pair of crisp, new hose. But nearly everyone was hurting. Most days, Luz walked through the neighborhood, avoiding eviction piles like shoveled snow. People's things were scattered about street corners, their travel trunks, immigration papers, worn leather shoes, horse bridles, white wedding quilts, clay mugs, chipped porcelain chamber pots. Their things were more sorrowful than they were, neglected, humming with an orphaned sadness. Objects were left behind as their people moved on, picked themselves up, gathered what they could in handkerchiefs, and set out for the beet fields, north into Wyoming or farther west, into the land of sunshine and once-fabled gold.

Luz wrote Diego weekly, though his letters were much more infrequent. She described the change of seasons, Lizette's focus on and determination to have an extravagant wedding that might never come. *Money is always short,* she explained. *But her and Alfonso, they keep planning, keep hoping.* She told Diego about her new job with David, and kept the details to a minimum. Diego had never liked David, said he was a real asshole, born with a particularly long silver spoon. Luz focused instead on brief passages about Avel. *He's very tall, and has a goodness to him. He's a performer like you, a musician.* Luz thought to mention Avel's coffee reading, but she hesitated, worried that by warning her brother about the raids, she'd force something into fruition.

Do you think, she wrote in one of her letters, *that if the men who hurt you were arrested, you could come back home? Do you think we'll ever be completely safe?* But Luz understood more and more that this was merely a fantasy of justice. Now, working for David, she heard of crimes that no Anglo newspaper mentioned. A colored drifter named James Batas had recently been murdered by a white mob when he dared fall asleep on the streetcar, riding the Green Line until it became the Red, where only whites were welcome. Rather than ask Mr. Batas to leave, a horde of Anglos beat him within an inch of his life with a broken fence post, tied him to a Chevy, and then slowly killed him as they dragged his body through a junk-lined dirt lot at sunset. These crimes were frequent, and Luz saw confirmation of what she always sensed, that her country believed only certain Anglo lives were something other than cheap.

In any case, Luz wrote in one of her letters to Diego, *the family goes on like it always has, it's just a little harder than usual. Still, sometimes we get lucky.*

On a Sunday, Luz arrived at Lizette's house at noon. Together, with Tía Teresita, they were to visit the dressmaker, a woman Lizette had heard was the best and most affordable wedding gown seamstress in Denver. The cousins would have gone earlier in the day, but Lizette still washed and ironed laundry, the task now taking twice as long without Luz's help. Luz felt guilty over this, but if Lizette was angry with or envious of her cousin for finding another kind of work, she hid those emotions somewhere deep within herself, revealing only happiness for her cousin. This, Luz thought, was what she saw in Lizette that so many others didn't—an instinct for kindness.

Luz ventured to the front door. The boy cousins were making a ruckus that could be heard from the street, caterwauling like sickly cats. Luz laughed as she opened the chain-link gate and walked the cement pathway to the door. She knocked, hard.

Teresita opened the door in a white dress with a ruffled collar, holding a diapered baby. She promptly handed the baby to Luz before spinning around and hollering for Lizette to come downstairs. Her hair had slipped away from its braid like a frayed rope. "Next weekend," she said, dabbing sweat from her brow, "we're having a card party. Saturday night. We'll have cake for you."

"For me?" Luz asked, rocking the baby in her arms.

"Yeah, isn't your birthday that Monday?"

Luz nodded and held the baby slightly into the air. "Who does it belong to?"

Teresita laughed. "*It* belongs to Priscilla next door. I'm watching him while she's at Tikas."

Before Luz could answer, one of the boy cousins, Antonio, ran by in cowboy boots, a dress shirt, and underpants. No trousers. He forcefully hugged Luz around her waist and then aimed a gun-shaped stick at her face. "Bang. Bang, Lucy Luz." Another boy cousin, Miguelito, this one younger and less loud, came chasing after Antonio with alligator tears rolling down his cheeks. "He took my stick!"

"Did you take your brother's stick?" Teresita shouted. "Give him back his stick."

"Bang. Bang," Antonio said with a sadistic giggle as he darted into the kitchen in a blur of brown boots.

Teresita looked at Luz. "I'm gonna beat that little shit."

Lizette appeared at the top of the stairs, her eyes done up with blue shadow and her lips in red. She wore one of her best dresses, blue-finned with capelet sleeves and gray floral details along the hem. She smiled like a pageant queen as she came down the stairs, but paused, scowling, when she saw the baby in Luz's arms.

"Where'd you get that?" she asked.

Luz shook her head. "He isn't mine."

"Well, of course not," said Teresita, taking the baby from Luz. "I'm watching him."

Lizette redirected her confusion toward her mother. "But aren't you coming with us?"

"Sorry, jita. Can't. These kids are running wild and Priscilla isn't back yet."

Lizette's face dipped into disappointment. She resembled a sad clown as she continued down the staircase. Another one of her brothers, this one named Jesús, came running from behind, pushing Lizette to the side and snickering. "Hope you find a good dress!"

Teresita took off after him, the baby balanced on her left hip, slobbering shiny pools across his arms. "What have I told you about the stairs? Careful, careful," she said.

Lizette raised her eyebrows at Luz. "Let's get out of here."

The dressmaker wasn't far from Tikas Market. The narrow storefront was nestled between a bakery and a shoe repair. When they walked in that afternoon, Luz felt like she was inside a closet that stretched into an infinite darkness. The shop wasn't busy, but it was designed as if it could handle a high volume of orders. There were three stations with the newest Singer pedal machines and one four-paneled mirror where Luz imagined brides-to-be stood before their reflections and pictured themselves walking down the aisle, gallantly crying as their fathers gave them away.

Lizette approached the glass counter and hastily rang the silver bell. "Hello, hello," she said, and after no one answered for a while, she became impatient. "You want our business or not?"

The cousins took seats along the front windows, slumping into lazy postures as they waited. The shop had a stale stench, as if mold grew behind the walls. The lighting was dim and gave the room the sensation of being covered in moss. It was cold near the window, and Luz could feel the fine baby hairs along her neck rise whenever a truck lumbered down the street.

She whispered, "Where did you find this woman?"

Lizette shrugged. She bit at a hangnail on her left pinkie. Droplets of blood appeared on her skin. "The dancers all know about her. She makes their gowns."

"What dancers?" Luz asked, with suspicion.

"The flamenco dancers. I know people other than you, Luz."

"I know," Luz said affectionately. "But what would you do without me?"

Lizette rested her head on Luz's left shoulder. "Why? Are you running away, joining the circus? I can see the show now. The great Madame Luz, clairvoyant nightingale."

The dressmaker appeared from a door carrying an oversized spindle of white fabric. She walked with a slight limp, as if sidestepping over a roped bridge. Her red hair was pulled away from her round face with metal butterfly barrettes, and she wore an unattractive sack dress with brown printed flowers. She told them she was Natalya, and she spoke with a thick and musical Russian accent.

"What can I help with, girls?" she said, keeping her eyes lowered to the white fabric.

Lizette stood at the front counter and tapped her fingers on the glass. "I'm getting married, and I'd like you to sew my gown."

Natalya placed the fabric on a low table behind her, and opened her palm to Lizette. "You have idea? Or pattern? What you have?"

"Here," said Lizette, pulling the folded pattern from her purse.

Natalya cleared her throat as she took the piece of paper. She maneuvered the chained spectacles up from around her neck and placed them on her face. She moved to examine the pattern in the natural light streaming in through the front windows. "Modified from McCall's?"

"Vogue," said Lizette. "I like their recent designs better."

Luz glanced at the pattern. She was surprised at how well it had come together. Lizette often talked about the dress, a gilded gown, as she called it. She had incorporated the usual style, a slim silk or rayon bodice, but she'd added notes for gold taffeta along the sleeves and collar, accented by pearl buttons. And she'd made a note for a hidden zipper beneath the left sleeve, rather than a more usual placement at the dress's back.

Natalya returned the pattern to Lizette. She walked in her sidelong way behind the counter and retrieved a leather-bound ledger. She flipped several pages, and then ran her index finger over the sheet. She stopped. "I'll order the taffeta special from my supplier. It won't be cheap, and will take two months to arrive. You still want?"

"How much?" Lizette said.

"Hard to say. Five or ten dollars."

Lizette sighed, and Luz thought of something that Diego once told her. Every sigh is a breath stolen from life. She handed the pattern to Luz. "Honest opinion?"

"It's a lot of money," Luz whispered, but then she considered the pattern once more. In her mind, she saw Lizette from behind, wearing a crown of red roses. She saw her turn her chin over her left shoulder, her dark eyelashes fanning downward toward the collar of her exceptional golden gown. Luz could see the dress clearly, fully made and sparkling over her cousin on her wedding day. "But I think you'll have the dress you want."

Lizette smiled in a sad way. "I can't afford it, but thank you for checking."

Natalya raised her gaze, and for the first time since they had entered the shop, the dressmaker really looked at Lizette. "Who made dress you're wearing?"

"I did," said Lizette.

"Where you first see it?"

"I made it up from nothing. Not even a pattern."

"You know to sew like that?"

"Oh," said Lizette. "Yes. But it's nothing like a gown. I'm not that good."

Natalya walked around Lizette, examining the dress's woolen fabric, the closed seams and delicate brass buttons. She gently guided Lizette by the left wrist into a column of warm sunlight. She told her to spin around. "A princess seam? That's very tricky. Who taught you?"

"My mother."

"She's a dressmaker?"

"No, but she sews up all kinds of things. Dresses, people." Lizette laughed and nudged Luz.

Natalya removed the spectacles from her face. She wiped under her eyes, and pinched the bridge of her nose. "Come back next Saturday. I need help around here, a girl with good hands." She reached out and grazed Lizette's right sleeve. "If I were a young, pretty girl, I'd want dress like yours. Maybe we can work trade."

"You mean, you want me to help around here?" Lizette spoke with genuine disbelief.

Natalya returned to her ledger. "I said that, yes."

Lizette looked to Luz and the two girls shrieked. Lizette came around the counter and startled Natalya, offering her a large, warm hug. "Thank you!"

"What about you?" Natalya said, pointing at Luz. "You have wedding coming? Need dress?"

"No," said Luz, laughing and shaking her head.

Lizette took Luz by the arm, stuck out her tongue, and danced them toward the door. "We're working on it."

That night when Luz left Lizette's, Avel was waiting for her out front beneath two crabapple trees. He was holding a white lily. His skin blended into night while his eyes and Stetson hat beamed with light. Luz grinned at his presence, the peaceful way he stepped out of the trees in his burly coat, moving with one hand in his pocket and the other presenting the flower. The wind had died, though the night still throbbed with a brisk undercurrent.

"Why, thank you," Luz said, taking the lily from his hand. She gave it a good whiff and noted that the scent of lilies always reminded her of death.

"What's your favorite flower?" Avel asked.

"Marigolds," she said.

"Sweet but bitter. Ma always had an altar covered in marigolds." Avel hooked Luz by the elbow and guided her away from the Westside. "They grow great big in Califas. Like you wouldn't believe."

"I'd like to see that," she said with her chin lifted upward, her face absorbing the moonlight as if it were the sun.

The city felt dreamy. Parked automobiles and road signs were cast in stretched shadows. They walked arm in arm, Luz breathing the scent of Avel's sandalwood cologne and his horn's valve oil. Luz enjoyed the sounds of Avel's bootheels clomping over pavement. She liked the way he made her feel. Safe, mostly, like she could walk the city at night without fear of being mugged or worse. She tried not to imagine what was worse. Mama had once told Luz that being raped was worse than being murdered, and Luz wondered how that could be. To be raped and to live seemed more desirable than to no longer exist. Luz did not want to find out. The fact that the protection she craved from men was mostly to ward off incidents with other men frightened her.

The couple soon came to a street corner beside the capitol where a smattering of people were leaving the front lawn. They carried hand-painted signs, WE DEMAND A LIVING WAGE, FIGHT POLICE BRUTALITY, STAND UP OR STARVE. An iceman's horse carriage was parked nearby. The ice delivery man was high on his post, sleeping with his head falling downward, arms folded over his belly. The horses were fine and black, handsome though their eyes were shielded by blinders. Avel stepped forward first, spooking the horse beside the sidewalk. It jerked its veined neck, breathed fog into the dark. Startled, Luz accidentally dropped her lily in the gutter. She didn't care for horses. Their size alone was intimidating, but more than that, she didn't like how they seemed both intelligent and senseless at the same time.

"Easy, easy," said Avel to the horse, gliding his hand along its glimmering neck, patting around its jaw for good measure. "Come here," he said to Luz.

She shook her head, told him no. "Oh, stop."

Avel kept one hand on the horse and with the other pointed to a spot on the ground for Luz to stand.

"People get kicked to death," said Luz. "They call them brutes for a reason."

Avel closed his eyes, chuckled. "No, no."

"What if the driver wakes up?"

Avel pointed at an emptied liquor bottle, turned over and resting beneath the driver's carriage steps. "He's drunk as piss. I'd be surprised if he wakes up with the sun."

Luz examined the bottle. She gazed at the driver. "Fine," she said, and took a step forward. Avel grasped her right hand and moved it along the horse's jaw. The cold dark pelt felt coarse though silken. If night had a feeling, she thought, this was it. The animal had calmed and seemed pleased with the strangers' attention. "Hi, pretty girl," Luz whispered, peering into the animal's wet eye.

Luz was blooming with a smile when Avel leaned in and kissed her short and dry on the mouth. She moved away, studied Avel's face, the serenity in his heavy eyes, the sheen of his shaven cheeks. Luz tilted forward, this time kissing Avel with more pressure and the tiniest slip of tongue. He tasted pleasant like salt water, and Luz imagined Avel was an endless blue sea. After a short while, they continued their walk and Luz said, "I like you very much."

TWENTY-ONE

Invitation Only

That Thursday evening, as Luz was finishing her tasks for the day, David emerged from his office carrying a newspaper. He took a seat across from her desk and fastened his cuff sleeves. He stared at his gold watch, moving the face along his wrist. He groaned and stretched his arms above his head, cracking his knuckles in the air. "You did a very brave thing."

Luz nodded, secretly hoping that David wasn't there to assign her more work.

"They've covering Estevan's murder in the big papers now." David held up the *Rocky Mountain News* and gave it a good shake. "The protests are growing."

"They are?" Luz asked with wonderment.

"Yes," he said. David grinned and looked up, staring at Luz for a long second. "I like when you wear your hair down. I like that it's longer than other girls'."

Luz blushed. Sometimes David acted as if she hardly existed at all, but other times, his attention was drawn away from himself and directed fully at Luz.

"You must be starving," he said. "It's nearly dinnertime."

"Well, as a matter of fact," said Luz, "I was going to get supper with a friend, but he can't now. He's playing a last-minute show."

David stood up. "A friend? A boyfriend?"

"A friend," Luz repeated, sheepishly.

David stepped around to Luz's side of the desk. He put his hands over her papers. His fingernails were delicate, pearlescent white, as if he had them buffed and shined. "Come with me tonight, for dinner."

Luz laughed and shook her head. "No, thank you." She looked away from David and toward the long front windows. Outside it was dark. A fire truck ambled by, churning the walls with its screeching gears.

"Come on, Luz. Don't make me beg."

There was something in the way that David said *beg* that Luz enjoyed, the long, sharp way he carried the word out until it sounded boxed somewhere in the air. David would never beg. The idea was laughable. He wasn't a man who needed to—anything he wanted came to him without pleading. That was how it worked, Luz decided. Those with money and an education rarely weakened their dignity. Luz shook her head once more, and her hair fell into her face.

"I'm serious, Luz. Just come." David reached out and smoothed away her hair, clearing her face. He looked handsome with a slight mist above his upper lip and his long lashes fanned over his eyes.

She softened. "Fine."

David said, "Go on, get your coat."

—

David drove Luz to a private supper club called Suville's. It was on the edge of City Park in a white stone mansion that resembled a castle with balconies and block-like towers. Luz had seen the manor on her laundry trips, but she had figured the house was vacant, for the windows didn't show signs of life during those early mornings, and the city was now scattered with empty mansions abandoned by silver barons and bankers gone broke. Never had Luz imagined that in the evenings, behind those decadent stone walls, rich men played billiards, smoked cigars, and ate hearty portions of cheeses and meats. At a side entrance, beneath a green awning, David told the doorman a password ("mustard gas"), and they were ushered inside through a red corridor that led into a reading room and eventually into a dining hall. The ceiling was a stained glass Noah's ark, a strange depiction of paired animals one might see painted in a baby's nursery, their images blurred behind thick plumes of smoke. The tables fanned around an elevated stage, where a smallish white woman sang in a crystal gown the same color as her flesh. She appeared naked at first glance, and Luz had to look twice to confirm that she wasn't. Luz couldn't tell if she was any good. Her singing was covered by the cackles of men, their full-bellied laughter, some cursing, some jeers.

A hostess in a striped gown sauntered to their table with menus as David and Luz followed her, but a large and wide bald man stood from his booth and blocked their path. He was someone important, Luz noted, because David stopped, shook his hand, and embraced the man like an old friend. As the man spoke, spittle flew from his mouth, some landing warm and wet on Luz's cheek.

"You'll sit here," the man said, his head shining like polished granite. "We have plenty of room. Don't we, doll?" He gestured with his whole left arm toward the table at a woman half his age with brilliant brown hair and a diamond brooch. She wore black eye makeup and was so thin that her chest was notched. Luz imagined that beneath her skin, the woman's bones resembled an animal's spinal column she had once seen bleached by sunlight on the prairie. The woman's dress was a blazing silver color with delicate glass beads. Surely, wearing a gown like that, a girl could also afford to eat.

"Steelman, we couldn't possibly intrude," said David.

"Nonsense," Steelman said. "Dining alone is for degenerates and old maids."

How was he alone? Luz thought, she was right beside him.

"And tell your father we thank him for the latest contribution to the club. They bought a damn fountain with it!" Steelman motioned with his butter knife to a statue in the corner of the room, coughing water from its mouth into a marble basin. "Sometimes I think you Tikases are all right—for damn near commies, at least." He chuckled, the boom reverberating.

"I'll tell him," David said with a shrug, and motioned with his right hand for Luz to slide into the booth. The tabletop surrounded them like a pink half shell, and across the white cloth Luz eyed the man's plate. Ribs, a rack of lamb, corn, and beside it a glass of brandy. He continued speaking to David without so much as looking at Luz. When the waitress appeared, the man placed his enormous arms casually around her waist and ordered cocktails for the table. "I hope you like martinis, doll," he said to Luz, finally glancing at her with a wink.

All women, she realized, were his dolls.

"How 'bout yous," said the waitress. "Whadyas want to eat?"

"My god, girl. With English like that, I'm surprised you aren't headed straight for DU." Steelman laughed and hooked his arms tighter around the waitress's hips.

The waitress let out a trained giggle, though she squirmed.

David smiled and looked up from the menu. He told the waitress he'd have the prime rib. He then ordered Luz the top sirloin.

"How'dya want it?" the waitress said.

"She'll have it medium," said David, pointing at Luz.

"What side?" said the waitress.

"Mashed potatoes," David said. "With gravy."

Luz didn't want mashed potatoes at all, and said so. "Actually, I'll have green beans. Thank you."

Steelman laughed a short, disapproving laugh.

After listening to the conversation for some time, Luz understood that Steelman was an important attorney and the thin woman beside him wasn't his wife and wasn't his daughter. She didn't engage in conversation with anyone at the table, only smoked cigarette after cigarette and gazed around the room as if searching for an exit. When the martinis came, the woman drank one quickly, then ordered another.

"So now you're telling me unless we open a grand jury," said Steelman between bites of sloppy ribs, "the damn niggers and spics won't stop their looting and riots. At this rate, they'll burn down half of downtown."

David said, "To be fair, most of the protesters aren't Negroes or Mexicans, Steelman. There are a fair number of demands coming from white men and women like yourself."

"I wouldn't liken myself to radical Jews and Communists!" said Steelman with a sonorous, rupturing laugh. Luz half expected him to froth at the mouth with stomach bile.

Steelman then pointed across the table at Luz. "Now, David, where'd this delicate doll come from?"

"She's my secretary," he said. "Recently hired."

"This one's quite pretty."

Steelman studied Luz and she shifted in her seat, knocking into David on purpose. Steelman shoveled a cut of lamb onto his fork and then spoke through a mouthful of meat. "You know what they say about Mexican girls," he said, raising his fork with emphasis. "Insatiable."

At that moment, their food arrived. Luz watched as the white tablecloth disappeared beneath white plates, piled high with steak and prime rib. Then came more martinis, spilling over, clear gin knobbed with green olives stuffed with blue cheese. She was trapped by a feast of food and alcohol, this man directing the waiters like his own personal chorus. The room was chaotic, boisterous. Luz's stomach turned, and she felt lightheaded. The thin woman tipped her head and swallowed nearly half her drink in one swig, then set down the glass and asked Steelman if he could find the waitress for another. She had the hiccups, and when she spoke to him, Steelman became enraged, told her to handle her liquor better. "You sound like a goddamn hillbilly," he said.

As the two bickered, David scooted next to Luz. His leg was against hers under the table. He walked his fingers over her thigh, and moved his face along her hair. Luz could hear him sniff.

"Don't pay attention to him," he whispered. "He's an old bat, a crazy old bat. And the district attorney."

Luz stiffened in her seat. She turned her face toward David and forced a smile. "I need to use the ladies'."

"Of course," said David. "Downstairs to the left."

Luz slipped out of the booth. She zigzagged around the tables spattered about the dining room. Glasses chinked, silverware scraped plates, liquor flowed into seemingly bottomless cups. The singer had finished her set, and the stage stood barren beneath red lights. Wherever Luz walked, she caught the eyes of men, menacing like owls in three-piece suits and gold pocket watches. Their dates were Anglo women in rose-gold satin and silk bell-sleeved dresses, their thin necks flanked by diamond earrings and spiral clumps of blond hair.

"Are you his latest?" said the waitress from earlier. She had stopped Luz as she exited the dining hall.

"I don't know what you mean," Luz said.

"His latest girl?" She was carrying a tray of pink glasses. "Do yourself a favor, honey, and don't get your hopes up." The waitress moved her eyes toward David, who was laughing with Steelman at the table. "A good Greek boy like that? He wants in, and girls like you aren't allowed in. Ever."

"In where?" said Luz.

The waitress rolled her eyes. "Look around you," she said. The entire room, it seemed, laughed as one, their mouths open like dark wet pits. "White women only."

"That's strange," Luz said and breathed heavy. "Because I'm here now. Excuse me." She tempered her anger as she hurried past the waitress and down a narrow hallway, a cave with throated walls.

Luz tried the first door on her left, searching for the staircase, and found, instead, a broom closet. She tried the next door and found an empty lounge. On her third try, Luz was startled by the sight. A small shooting range. Men without suit jackets stood in their shirtsleeves, flushed faces gleaming with sweat, their large bellies covered in suspenders as they aimed handguns down three long lanes. They blasted their guns at black targets drawn on white paper. Gunshot after gunshot, metal bullets cascaded upon the floor, clinking, clinking, like copper rain. Luz looked on, frozen in horror, for the men's rhythmic and forceful movements, the quick bursts of sound, the smell—of gunpowder, alcohol, and sweat— hit her with a familiarity she couldn't place. Luz was too over- whelmed by the sight of the guns to continue her search and she found herself back at the table, uncomfortably waiting with a full bladder for David to finish his meal.

David soon drove Luz home with the radio crackling in the background, a low murmur of a detective serial. Outside it was dark. The streetlamps dropped light over red stone sidewalk. Luz breathed heavy. The windows fogged.

"Did you like your steak?" David asked, keeping his eyes on the road.

Luz told him that of course she did, but looked out the window, instead of at him. "Thank you for dinner," she added, remember- ing her manners.

"It's my pleasure, Luz."

David made a left turn and looked over his right shoulder, catching Luz's gaze. "Are you sad you didn't get to have dinner with your friend?"

Luz softly forced a laugh. "No," she said.

David turned the knobs on the radio until the Chevrolet fell silent. "What's he like?"

"He's a horn player," said Luz. "He moved here from Califor- nia."

"Ah, a musician. Be careful." David reached across and patted Luz's thigh over her work dress. "You ever been with a boy before, Luz?"

Luz was shocked at the question, the boldness of it. She couldn't decide if it was disrespectful or true curiosity, acted on by liquid courage. Was that any of his business, and how could he think that she had been with a man? She was seventeen, eighteen in a week, and she wasn't even engaged to anyone. Though she knew of plenty of girls who had been with men—Lizette with Alfonso, the long line of girls who'd been with Diego—Luz was almost afraid at the idea of it. It seemed it could hurt her in ways she wasn't capable of understanding. But most of all, Luz was afraid that she'd enjoy it, maybe too much, and if she had learned anything from what happened to Diego, it was that pleasure is dangerous.

"David," she said in a whisper.

He laughed, and pulled up outside Hornet Moon. Smog from the meatpacking plant huffed a great amber halo into the sky. "Ignore me," he said.

TWENTY-TWO

A Game of Cards

"Hel-lo, birthday girl," Lizette said as she swung open the front door. She leaned to the right, edging against the doorframe, one leg kicked up through the fringe of a white dress. Ranchera music fell into the street. The house was lit in scarlet tones, the colors bleeding from the doorway into the yard, where bagged luminarias lighted the sandstone pathway.

Luz and Maria Josie stood on the stoop. Maria Josie held a warm dish of cheese enchiladas.

"You didn't need to bring anything," said Lizette as she ushered them inside.

"And what kind of people show up empty-handed?" Maria Josie said.

"Alfonso did," she said, pointing to her left, where he came through the narrow foyer and swooped Lizette off the ground with both arms, placed his Stetson on her head, and swished her around, like a rock-a-bye baby, before setting her on the ground and retrieving his hat from her head.

"I may be empty-handed, but not for long." Alfonso reached over and squeezed Lizette's ass before taking the enchiladas from Maria Josie, tucking the platter beneath one arm while he made his other arm as straight as a tree branch. He asked for their coats, and they shook out of their jackets, delicately placing them across his right forearm. Alfonso carried the enchiladas and coats in the same way he often stacked dinner dishes at the Park Lane. He dashed out of sight, into the kitchen.

"Why, don't you two look strikin'," said Lizette.

Maria Josie was dressed in a dapper men's suit with her hair slicked against her scalp with citrusy pomade. Luz wore an emerald dress that had once been left on Diego's bedroom floor. What the girl had worn home, Luz had no idea.

"Nearly everyone's here," Lizette said, slurring her words a bit, guiding them deeper into the small house. The smell of tequila floated around the air, mingling with the scent of cologne and perfume and green chile. The narrow hallway was lined with couples, some married, some courting. Men cloaked their women in their arms. When they neared the downstairs bathroom, Maria Josie cut away from the cousins, fiddling with the belt loop on her slacks as she walked toward a tall, slender woman with delicate pale skin and black hair. Luz hadn't seen the woman before, and she admired her floral silk dress. It seemed Maria Josie knew her well, for when they met, she cupped both of the woman's hands in her own and tippy-toed upward, as if to lay a kiss on the woman.

"Food's on the stove. Mama made her famous mole, and I made the green chile." Lizette didn't look back as she walked. She only raised her hand as she spoke, as if putting emphasis on certain sounds and certain foods. "There's *fried* chicken, too. DeeDee from Five Points made it. And the Greeks brought a *rack* of lamb."

Though she hadn't been consciously aware of it, Luz was searching the house. "What about Avel? Is he here?"

Lizette paused before rounding the corner into the kitchen. She laughed, biting her bottom lip. "Yeah, Avel's here," she said. And, then, softer: "And David."

The men were in the kitchen seated about a large round table covered in a purple cloth. The wooden sounds of poker chips clinked beneath their rumbling laughs. The room was blurry in lines of smoke. Tío Eduardo was the dealer, shuffling a red deck of cards with short, nimble fingers. Several men Luz didn't recognize sat around him. Avel was seated against the window, the reflection of his neck on the glass. David was across from Avel, and Luz could see some of his cards. A red queen, a black spade, a red diamond seven. If she knew anything about poker, she might be inclined to think he was winning. The room moved with a mysterious language that was circular yet pointed, the language of men.

When Avel looked up from his hand, he glimpsed Luz with such anticipation that he immediately stood and almost knocked over the table. The others groaned and heckled him as he walked across the kitchen. He took Luz by the hand, kissing her gently on each cheek. "What a dress," he said.

"She bought it special for you," Lizette lied, and Luz jabbed her with her left elbow.

"Here," Avel said, rummaging through his blue jeans pockets. "I have a present for you."

David said over his shoulder, "Can't it wait? We're playing a card game here."

"Jeez Louise," Avel said. He shook his head and smiled, in a goofy way. "Forgive me, Luz. I have prior obligations, but you're next. Well, you're first. Always first."

Luz swiped Avel's right shoulder. She enjoyed his enthusiasm for her, the rabid way he focused solely on her. No one had ever treated Luz like that. "It's not my birthday yet. A couple more days."

Avel had gone back to his seat, and he looked up at Luz once more. "You deserve more than one day. A whole week. A whole month." And then he was back to his cards, and Lizette was fixing a plate, which she thrust into Luz's hands before dragging her into the parlor where the radio music was heavy and sumptuous.

Luz sat on a pink sofa and ate a pork tamale with her plate balanced on her knees. Lizette and Maria Josie were on the floor in the corner, going through a stack of records beneath a long-necked lamp. Maria Josie usually would have been in the kitchen with the men, had she any extra money to gamble away. A blond Anglo girl stood by herself, swaying to the music with closed eyes. She had on an expensive store-bought dress that was too tight around the middle and the buttons bunched and pulled away from her substantial breasts. Naturally, Luz thought, she was David's date. She rolled her eyes at his predictability. Tía Teresita was standing with two of her sisters, both visibly pregnant. They all ate bizcochitos, spilling crumbs over their dresses and onto the rug. The little cousins were outside in the yard, tumbling in the cold grass and narrowly avoiding the lighted paper bags. Luz grinned at their joy. It amused her how children at adult parties celebrated in their own way. Not necessarily with their parents and aunties and uncles, but alongside them in their own smaller and happier world. Every now and then, Teresita would open the front door and scream for them to put on their coats. The children would disperse like geese being chased by a dog.

Luz had finished her plate when Lizette came over and set a warm cup of atole in her hands. "See that girl over there?" Lizette said, making eye contact with Luz and then dropping her gaze to her knee, jutted to the left. Near the fireplace, a young woman in a light blue dress stood with her face turned up, as if she were studying the ceiling. "She's Avel's singer."

"That's funny," Luz said. "He didn't mention he found a singer."

"Yeah, supposedly she's real good."

Luz studied the girl. She was pretty, though somewhat plain. "Who is she? Why haven't I seen her before?"

"Dunno," said Lizette. Then, with a whistle, she called to the girl.

The girl lowered her gaze from the ceiling and widened her eyes as if she had won a prize. She first mouthed *Me?*, and after Lizette nodded, the girl cheerfully stepped across the room.

"Thanks for having me here," the girl said. "And happy birthday, Luz. Wow. Eighteen. I guess that means you'll be looking to start a family soon."

Luz said, "Thank you, I suppose."

"What's your name?" Lizette asked.

"Monica."

"And who are your people, Monica?"

"Oh, I'm a Pacheco. I'm from Delta. My husband and me just moved here."

It was settled. She was a Western Slope girl. And a husband, too. "I heard you're Avel's new singer," Luz said. "Does your husband mind you singing?"

Monica nervously giggled. "He doesn't mind me making money. He's working the night shift at the UP now, or he'd be here to see our show tonight."

"What show?" Luz asked.

"Tonight. When Avel performs for you. We've been practicing for weeks."

"Dammit," said Lizette, who popped up from her seat and

walked the girl back toward the fireplace. "Have you ever heard of a surprise?"

Just as soon as Monica left, two girls approached Luz with heavy, sorrowful expressions. One had a cherubic face. The other was nearly her opposite, flagpole skinny. They asked, almost simultaneously, if she had heard anything from Diego.

"What do you mean?" Luz asked.

The skinny one spoke up. She fanned herself against the room's party heat. "I mean, is he okay? We've been dying to know."

Luz stared at the white moon of her plate. She couldn't talk about Diego without getting upset, and so she said, "He's fine. Don't worry about *my* brother." Luz stood from the sofa and headed toward the kitchen.

She stopped in the hallway and looked at the card table. She was in the dark, against the edge of their light. The men had just finished their game, and Avel was seated before a stack of chips. Luz grinned with pride. It wasn't that she didn't expect him to win, but she was genuinely excited to see the jubilant way he studied his chips. The others were congratulating him, shaking his hand and laughing. David had poured a large glass of ouzo, which he glided across the table to Avel.

"Have another," he said. "You've done good."

Avel shook his head. He held up his hand, signaling no more.

"Come on," David said. "Just have another. It's tradition."

"I'm not much of a drinker," said Avel, taking off his hat and smoothing his blue-black hair underneath.

David said, with seriousness, "It's a card game. Drink."

Luz watched them from the hallway, at first smiling at their exchange, but the mood shifted and she soon felt worry enter the room, as if it had taken a seat beside the men and joined their game. Avel, she realized, was already drunk. Very drunk.

"You insult me," David said. "You don't drink what I've poured for you, and you insult me."

"Come now," said Alfonso. "Leave the boy alone. Good hand, Avel. You did good."

Avel appeared to study the clear liquid resting before him. He reached for the glass, as full as a coffee mug, and guzzled the entire thing. A moment later, he was up from his seat, both hands to his mouth. He knocked the table, spilling his chips to the floor as he leaned over the sink and began to retch. The men laughed and hollered at him to leave the kitchen. "Get the hell out of here," they said. "Did your mother teach you to drink?" Only Alfonso showed any kindness in the ugliest way. "Come on now, Avel. Take yourself out before you ruin the night for us all." No one helped, and despite how much she knew it'd embarrass him later, Luz rushed in and pulled Avel away by his shirtsleeve, the vomit stench of his lips and hands rubbing into her skin.

She tried the nearest escape, the laundry closet with its large sink, but the little cousins had barricaded themselves inside and were shouting and giggling behind the door. She pulled Avel upstairs only to find that bathroom occupied by one of the pregnant aunts. And, so, she tugged Avel into the front yard, where she bent him over the juniper and told him to get sick.

"Go on," she said, the night around them like a curtain. She rubbed his back, her fingers sliding down his spine. "Let it out. You'll feel better."

Avel got sicker than anyone else Luz had ever seen from drinking. He was bent over, hands on his knees, retching in forceful waves. Just when she thought he'd emptied the contents of his entire stomach, more came up, bitter and violent. She comforted him, told him it was fine and smoothed his back and shoulders. They were outside for a long time, Avel slurring his words, apolo-

gizing, crying out *Forgive me,* as he rounded into a standing fetal
position.

"I have a present for you," Avel slurred, moving his hands dully
to his pockets. When he finally pulled the small envelope from his
blue jeans, it fell directly into the bush. He reached for it, but Luz
eyed his vomit webbed over the shrubbery and told him they
could get it later.

"It's a good present." He was drifting now, his world going
black.

The front door opened then and Luz pushed Avel farther into
the darkness of the juniper. She heard two voices, laughing and
carrying on. Walking bodies passed in front of the lanterns, causing shadows to shift over Luz's face. It was David and his date,
snickering and holding hands, strolling to his Chevy. *I thought
there was going to be some music,* the woman said. David's engine
soon started and the headlights beamed on, passing over Luz as
she comforted Avel alone in the dark.

TWENTY-THREE

A New Vision

The morning of her eighteenth birthday, Luz awoke to the sounds of Maria Josie in their small kitchen fixing breakfast, a clanging spoon, an opened and closed cabinet, a screeching kettle. Luz wrapped herself in her thin cotton robe and entered the kitchen with sockless feet. The floorboards were cool, and the room was blisteringly white with morning. Maria Josie stood at the sink, her shoulder blades jutting up and down as she worked an avocado's brown seed from its green bed. The vibrancy of the green startled Luz as she took a seat at the table. Maria Josie presented her with a plate of fried potatoes, flour tortillas, pinto beans, and thick, sugary bacon. She set the avocado down separately, cut into half-moon strips. Luz's mouth filled with saliva at the sight.

"Happy birthday, Little Light. I love you very much," Maria Josie said, embracing her niece warmly.

She took the seat across from Luz and motioned with both

hands for her to *Go on, eat.* Luz felt her face crease in an enormous smile. She hadn't seen food like this in their home for years. She began to eat, using a tortilla to scoop up beans, heavy with lard, topped with an avocado slice.

"It's delicious, Auntie," said Luz between bites. "Thank you so much."

Maria Josie patted Luz on the left forearm. She smiled with her eyes. "Today is a significant day for you. You're further from childhood than you've ever been, and I'm proud of the woman you have become." At that, Maria Josie reached to the floor and pulled up a small package wrapped in white paper. "For you, jita."

Luz opened the package carefully, sliding her index finger beneath the seams, and pulled the wrapping away from the small wooden box. Inside, she was surprised to see the quartz rosary. Maria Josie's face beamed with pride as she told Luz to pull it out and hold it in her hands. Cool, weighty nodules of prayer. Luz squealed as she draped it around her wrist.

"I thought Milli had stolen it?" Luz asked, thinking back to when Diego first left and they had cycled through a string of renters. Looking at her wrist, Luz was stunned at the sight. The rosary shined pink and silver, with beads carved into flowers. And for just a moment, Luz smelled roses.

"I got it back," said Maria Josie. "A pawnshop had it on Broadway. It belonged to your grandma."

"Simodecea," said Luz, knowingly.

Maria Josie nodded in a sorrowful way. "You remind me of her. She was very independent, very strong. I know I don't speak of her much. Did your mama?"

"Almost never."

"Sometimes we go through things in life that are so hard and ugly, we'd rather forget than remember, but now I can't remember very much at all. I regret that now."

Luz didn't know why, but she began to cry. Maria Josie pulled her close. "Don't do that," she said. "She would be happy for you to have it."

"Thank you, Auntie." Luz wiped her face with her hands. "I want to wear it as a bracelet. I know I'm not supposed to. Do you think that'd be all right?"

Maria Josie smiled. "Wear it any way you want. Let everyone in Denver see it."

In her bedroom, before readying herself for work, Luz took in her birthday. She lay across her bed clutching her grandmother's rosary and considering Diego's envelope with dirty fingerprints and frayed edges. The stamp, an illustration of bundled lavender, had faded, as if bleached by the sun.

Little Light,

I've seen the ocean. It's like nothing you'd believe. It goes forever and the waves collapse on each other all filled with fish and shells. The smell is like some salty stew and the sounds are roars. Oh, it's something. There's more work here, but the Anglos are unhappy, think there isn't enough to go around. You got to be careful. There are raids. Police come and ship men to Mexico, some who've never been. I've got my wits about me, though, and I've got lots of time to think. We ride trucks and trains, go from town to town, and work until night. I miss you and Maria Josie. Happy early

birthday, Little Light. p.s. I got a new snake. Her name is
Sirena.

D

Luz missed Diego more every day, and sometimes she wondered if she'd ever see him again. She pictured a red thread, tied
from her wrist to his waist, yanking her in his direction, allowing
her to never lose sight of his broad back. She read the letter several
more times, kicking her feet against her bed's frame with a dull
rhythm. But the sounds of her feet were interrupted by the distant
echoes of a barking dog, as if its growl were trapped inside her
bedroom, inside her throat. Songbirds came next, and soon the
room was filled with the sounds of swaying grass. The air smelled
fresh, alive, flooded with rich soil. Luz closed her eyes and saw in
her mind a sunset sky above a great green basin divided into long
leafy rows. Farmworkers in wide brim hats hunched down, exposed their backs to the sky, hobbled forward as if they were their
own kind of human crops, bending in motion, as if moving
through green waters with wooden oars. Like a bird flying from
treetop to fence post, Luz searched the rows until she came upon
Diego, his face marked in dirt, his skin beautifully darker from the
sun. He wore a red kerchief around over his nose and mouth, his
eyes black and purposeful as they searched the earth. A basket of
lettuce, harvested and pulled from the soil, fanned out from behind him like a peacock's dazzling feathers. A cowbell rang then.
Diego raised his face to the sky. Another day done. As the other
workers positioned their baskets heavy with greenery to their left
side and staggered toward the water truck, Diego held his gaze,
inhaling the heavens, as if giving himself just a moment of rest.

From his front pocket, Luz saw the vibrant, yellow slit eyes of a girl snake. She poked herself up and nuzzled against Diego's kerchief-covered neck.

When Luz opened her own eyes, she was in her white bedroom, lying across her bed, beside her altar with its dried marigolds, beneath her ceiling, so still in its blankness.

Was it possible? Yes, Luz decided, it was.

Her visions were changing, growing into something larger, something greater than pictures in the leaves.

PART 3

TWENTY-FOUR

The Sharpshooter Simodecea
Salazar-Smith

The Lost Territory, 1895–1905

Simodecea was in her spacious trailer when Pidre and the photographer knocked. She looked at her reflection in the hanging mirror, straightened her black braid woven with colorful ribbons, fiddled with her ruffled vestido, white and lavender lace all down her chest. She applied one last dab of rouge before reaching for her fringed gloves, the deerskin delicate and malleable against her hands. She considered her collection of guns before reaching for her Remington shotgun, hoisting the familiar weightiness of its Damascus double barrel, the engraving of her own name etched into the receiver. She stepped out of the trailer into the Animas sun.

The mustached photographer had traveled by railcar from that northern city, Denver, and he stood sweating beside Pidre outside the trailer with his accordion-like camera, a white backdrop, and a wooden chair centered in the landscape. Pidre offered Simodecea his hand, but she ignored the gesture and stepped down from her trailer in a wave of drapery, her skirt sweeping red soil. Simodecea lifted the fabric from the ground, shotgun and lace filling her palms.

"Here?" she asked, stepping beside the wooden chair, turning her chin until she felt the white backdrop bouncing sunlight over her face.

The photographer wiped his wet brow with a dirty kerchief from his breast pocket. He squinted. He wore a two-piece suit and he hunched over the camera to see Simodecea upside down in the glass plate. He twirled his jacket over himself and his camera, where he remained for a long moment. He then reemerged and twisted his mustache. He consulted with Pidre. "Standing or seated?"

Pidre made his fingers into a square. He peered between his own frame and shook his head. He wore a deep purple tunic and wide cotton trousers, and his clothes trembled with mountainous wind as he walked toward Simodecea. The air was fragrant with juniper and sandstone, the constant perfume of gunpowder.

Simodecea smiled. "What say you, boss?"

Pidre held his fingers to his mouth. His hair was violet black in the sunlight, longish to his shoulders. He took a seat on the chair, and Simodecea could see the lightness of his scalp. He then stood and pointed to the ground. "One leg on the chair," he said. "They'll see more of the dress that way."

"And the gun. Hold it high," the photographer said.

Pidre flashed her a tender smile and retreated from the camera's eye.

Simodecea watched as the cloudless sky grew crowded with two hawks that soared toward the red theater. There was a meadow marked with wildflowers. The other performers' trailers sat in various areas, some lower, some higher in the grassy land. Simodecea hoisted her shotgun and prepared herself to hold its substantial weight for the duration of the photograph. Images were important promotion, Pidre had explained. Keeps them telling stories about us.

"My goodness," the photographer said, as he peered at the glass plate. "Wow. You make for a striking image. *One, two, three.*" He stepped aside and pressed the shutter. *"Hold, hold, hold."*

He took three photos in that pose, and each time Simodecea imagined that her gaze spoke for her. What did she have to say? She laughed inside her mind. *I'm a damned good shot,* her eyes told the world.

As they finished, Simodecea breathed and dabbed her face with rice paper, absorbing the oil and sweat she was accumulating.

"Now," the photographer said, checking his brass pocket watch. "Why don't we get one with the two of you? After all, it's Pidre's Extravaganza."

Pidre had stepped through the meadow and was turning a blade of grass between his index finger and thumb. He spun the blade and smiled. He held the grass to his mouth. He blew. There was a sound like a quacking duck. Simodecea laughed.

"I thought you'd never ask," he hollered, knee-deep in purple flowers. He walked swiftly through the tall grass as if he were wading in the river. Pidre bowed slightly upon entering Simodecea's space before the white backdrop and wooden chair. He smelled of the morning cook fire. He was several inches shorter than Simodecea, and she offered to sit in the wooden chair.

"No, I like you standing," said Pidre. "It shows your stature."

Simodecea smiled and caught herself wanting to once again check that the Remington wasn't loaded. It wasn't and she knew it, but it made her nervous to stand with a gun beside a man. Sometimes she wondered why her gift had given her so much when it had gutted her life just the same. Pidre reached up and rested his elbow against Simodecea's shoulder, the pose of business associates.

The photographer retreated beneath the cloak of his jacket, checking his focus once more. Simodecea looked straight ahead. She could smell spearmint leaves on Pidre's breath. She couldn't remember the last time she had been this close to anyone, let alone someone who smelled so sweet, and this thought made her sad.

"Look this way, you two," the photographer said. "Wonderful. Perfect. Hold, hold, hold."

As the camera clicked, Simodecea relaxed, loosened her joints. Pidre glided his arm briskly off her shoulder. He looked into her eyes, an unpredictable softening warmth.

Animas grew by the day. There were more mines, more farms, more trains. Within several months of opening, Pidre's Extravaganza had sold out weekend shows. Pidre had hired performers from across the region, some he'd convinced to leave other shows, and others who had auditioned for the first time. There were snake charmers, tea leaf readers, dancers and acrobats. Simodecea at first didn't enjoy being rooted in place. She had always traveled, but Pidre was a gifted businessman, and she and the other performers respected him and counted their earnings. Sometimes when they didn't have a show, if the moon was full, Pidre made a great feast with the hornos and bonfires and an underground barbecue pit. He welcomed undertaking the traditional chores of women. He baked the breads and served his compadres hearty plates of beans and bowls of brisket stew, all while wearing a dusty leather apron.

There was a summer night when they all sat together in the meadow on woven rugs, their bedrolls and sheepskin, tin plates of food. The fire dancers were beautiful and moved their bodies like serpents. Simodecea had become friendly with two of the younger girls, and they brought her clay pitchers of mezcal. They had both had a recent night with a Greek miner. I've never felt anything like it, the prettier one said. She was named Sabina and had a beaklike nose that was handsome in its uniqueness.

"What did he do?" asked Simodecea amid the crackling of fire and pulsating crickets.

"It wasn't what he did," chimed in the other. "It's what we did to each other."

They all three laughed, and Simodecea noted the musical sounds of their throats. She excused herself from the ground and stood with her tin cup in search of the water bucket.

The bonfires were blazing against the night. There were sounds of crackling cedar. Simodecea stepped near conversations, the lumped bodies speaking softly in the dark. The stars were heavy though hidden by firelight. The cottonwood trees along the center ditch stood in fashionable poses, limbs elegantly resting this way or that. Through the grayish air a far ways off, Pidre stepped away from the party. He cut across the meadow, continuing beyond his temporary cabin adjacent to the adobe home he was in the midst of building. Simodecea stood in the grass and told herself no but then told herself yes.

Pidre was turning the corner of his cabin, returning to the group with an armful of firewood, when Simodecea stepped before him.

"Evening to you," she said, and raised her chin. "Beautiful moon."

Pidre glanced up. A silver glow bathed his serene features. "Guards the people at night."

Simodecea waved her hands through the chilled air. Her skin was pale under moonlight. "It's cold out here," she said.

Pidre held the firewood a little higher in his arms.

"I was thinking," said Simodecea, "we could go in there?" She made eyes toward his cabin.

Pidre shook his head. "Just as cold in there, colder without a fire."

"We can heat it."

Pidre was silent. A log of firewood fell from his arms, hitting the dirt with a thud.

"Pidre," Simodecea said.

"Yes."

"I want to go into your cabin with you."

Pidre peered at Simodecea. He squinted under moonlight. "Oh," he said. "Wow, señora." He repeated wow as she took him by the hand. "I mean, I'm honored."

Once they started, they couldn't stop. They plummeted into each other, fitted together as earth and sky. Simodecea spent nights in Pidre's cabin and rushed home under starlight to her wooden trailer, lush with her satin and velvet curtains. She'd close the door and silently run her hands beneath her cotton nightdress, amazed at how good she was still able to feel. She hadn't been with a lover since Wiley, and the first time she revealed in candlelight the notches of her scars to Pidre, he reached his soft hand to her skin and asked with sorrow, "Do you hurt?"

"Sometimes," said Simodecea, standing from bed and lifting her skirt from the ground and fitting it around her waist. "For some time after it happened, I felt the pain all over again, like a phantom. I remember when it was happening, how I couldn't believe my body could take that much hurt." She let out a hoarse laugh, turned her face to the scanty window above their pillows.

"How could God let us feel such pain? And that's when I thought about the devil and hell and how surely they are real."

Once at dawn, as she was walking through the saturated meadow with her hair blowing like a blade, she was stopped by Mickey. He stepped out from the storage shed, a toothpick in his mouth, his misshapen hat low on his forehead. Simodecea stopped walking. She instinctually laid her right arm over her breasts in the flimsy nightgown. Mickey was Pidre's bookkeeper, and other than drinking away nearly all of his earnings each month, he didn't seem to contribute much to the family of performers. Simodecea spoke to him as if a coyote had crossed her path. "Yes?"

"I've been watching you," he said. "Pidre's a good man, my closest friend."

"I also enjoy him," said Simodecea.

"Then why you sneaking around at night like some owl?"

Simodecea lifted her face to the spreading dawn. She removed her arm from across her chest and stepped past Mickey.

He turned around on his boots. "I see you. You've kept his name. You'll never love anyone else."

As she walked away, Simodecea stopped some ways off from Mickey and removed her nighttime moccasins. She strolled barefoot over the earth, felt the cool soil and harsh grasses etch into the balls of her feet, the fat of her heel. She moved her face to the sky, the morning animating the world, birds and trembling trees, the sweet smell of water and stone. "You know who else was jealous," she called over her shoulder.

Mickey said nothing. He started in the opposite direction.

"The fallen angel," said Simodecea. "Be careful who you model yourself after."

———

Simodecea sensed it all along. They were destined to make life. This didn't mean she was prepared for it or wasn't beside herself when it happened. Admittedly, it was difficult when her belly began to limit the downward movements of her arms. She was more fatigued than usual, and there were some cancellations of her evening shows. Still, she was able to shoot from an upholstered yellow lounger, the crowd dazzled at seeing a woman so full with child shooting clay disks from the sky.

Some weeks before the baby was born, Pidre and Simodecea had a ceremony to ensure the newborn's safe passage between realms. During the blessing, a curandero named Raúl wrapped Pidre and Simodecea in a woven blanket, blue lightning and red mountains across their backs. Inside the blanket's cave, through pinpricks of glowing light, Pidre gazed upward and cradled Simodecea's face in his hands. He smelled of summertime at night, the sweetness after rain. Her cheeks balled with happiness. Pidre placed his palms on her belly and smoothed the lacy fabric. Simodecea didn't tell Pidre, but in that moment she felt as if they had married, and she thought to herself that if Wiley were to meet her again in the afterlife, she hoped he wouldn't feel betrayed.

The first child was Sara. She was a small baby with large black eyes like seeds and a full, grown-looking mouth. She showed a talent for clairvoyance, a gift Pidre suspected came from his Grandma Desiderya. "Bird in the house," Sara once uttered, and a crow, enormous and black, squeezed its plump body through the adobe fireplace, landing on its talons, as if Sara had called the animal to her side. Sara was a compliant infant, and at first this thrilled Simodecea, who could hike some ways off from the theater with her infant and her Remington or Winchester strapped to her back in a wicker basket. She'd practice her show with the infant nestled behind her warmly in the sweetgrass.

Maria Josefina was born a little over a year later. She had an adventurous spirit and was much more assertive than baby Sara. Maria Josefina seemed like Sara's protector, sent from another place to shepherd and watch. She showed an interest in building, and whenever Pidre's Ute compañeros from the south visited the theater, she closely eyed how they hoisted their cedar lodgepoles into the endless sky.

The girls loved spending time with their father—they assisted him with collecting firewood, drawing water from the river and well, harvesting modest handfuls of yucca and osha, piñon and juniper. They accompanied him on trips into Animas, where their father purchased bulk ammunition, barrels of pinto beans and rice, and thick stacks of dried venison. The Anglos of the town, especially the women, the schoolteachers and wives, they adored the girls. They often complimented Pidre on his *mixed-breeds,* to which he would not reply. On their way home from town, Pidre would stop a little ways from the theater's ridge. He'd place his strong hands under each girl's arms, removing them one at a time from the cart and setting them face out on the mesa, the earth below like a windswept moon, a moon whose soil had created them. "Listen to the land," Pidre told his daughters. He taught them to say a prayer thanking Creator, acknowledging the mood and feel of the earth, their life among the animals.

For a time, they were happy.

In the late spring of 1905, Simodecea noticed canvas tents lining the upper ridge beyond the theater. She used the iron binoculars Pidre kept beneath the bed and peered across the countryside. Her eyes moved over sagebrush and thistle until they worked into the bark of the trees and landed in a thickly webbed patch of yellow aspens. There were several Anglos, some kind of prospectors, portentous in dark hats. Simodecea showed the men and their tents to

Pidre, who shrugged and told her that Mickey was taking care of it. Besides, Pidre believed they could share the ridge. "There's plenty of room, and remember, Simo, we did not come from here first."

While Simodecea respected his viewpoint, she was fearful of the encroachment, of whether or not *those men* believed there to be plenty of room. She approached Mickey one afternoon in his stale smoke-filled office. He was seated before topsy-turvy paper piles, banknotes, and empty jars of preserved peaches from the Animas mercantile. When she opened the office door, he was startled into an upright position. He began fiddling with the ledger, as if he had been hard at work all along.

"While I respect my husband's ideology, that doesn't mean this isn't the Lost Territory. The word *lost* is in the name for a reason."

"I can't say I have the slightest clue as to what you're referencing, Mrs. Salazar-Smith."

Simodecea examined the room. In the years since Mickey had stopped her at dawn, her mistrust had grown. He was older now and his age showed in his smoke-stained fingers, his rocky face and pallid skin. "I'd like to see the land deed."

Mickey laughed. "You're not legally wed, don't forget that. What is his is, well, not yours."

"My husband may trust you, but I'm not nearly as kindhearted as he is. Show me the deed, Mickey."

He cleared his throat, tapped his dirty fingers together. He shuffled papers to the left of his desk. He looked up through longish black and now silver hair, green eyes bright as a cat's. "Would ya look at that? Can't seem to locate it."

"You know how I make a living, right?" Simodecea said as she exited the office and before slamming the door. "I shoot things."

———

During her long siestas on show days, stark sun shining through-out their new adobe home, Simodecea sometimes dreamed of her late husband, Wiley. The dreams were always in daylight, them walking over a mountain trail, Wiley opening a wooden gate, him pointing beyond the horizon to a flying hawk full of itself in a wind shaft, dancing or falling. Whenever Simodecea woke up from these dreams, she was groggy with transition from one real-ity to another. Once, as she and dreamtime Wiley laughed to-gether, changing bedsheets, Simodecea thought Pidre might be upset with her for spending time with her late husband, even if in her dreams. She told Wiley so, flicking the sheet into the air. *You have to remember something else,* he told her. *Besides your last view of me.*

Simodecea swallowed hard, nodded and agreed.

She was wide awake the morning Pidre rushed home with a map that he unraveled over their pine table. It was of the newest routes of the Union Pacific, and Pidre laughed with a giddy smile as he smacked the page lightly with his right hand, using his pretty turquoise rings and handsome nails to iron the contours. "They've opened a line near Pardona," he said, "where I come from."

He smelled of tree sap and white sage, and Simodecea inhaled deeply, pleasurably reaching for her husband's hand. She studied the map, the corridor between the mountains and the arroyo where Pidre's village was located. She had asked him many times before if they could visit his people, but Pidre said he had been told not to return, at least not for a long while. He had heard sto-ries of other men who had left their Pueblos, only to return with sickness they didn't know they carried, infecting everyone they loved. Now it wouldn't be like that. Now with the railroad, many people must have passed through Pardona. It would be common-place, the village would be prepared.

Simodecea said, "We must take the girls."

Pidre kissed his wife. He told her they would leave right away.

She let her gaze linger on the map, the yellow and red lines, the starburst compass. Her husband, she knew, was not able to read in the traditional sense, but he recognized patterns of letters and different symbols. Along the railroad route, there were illustrations of mineral deposits, stacks of ore, bars of silver. Simodecea pointed near the Red Theater on the map. There were several drawings of what appeared to be miniature suns.

She asked, "What's this here?"

"Where?" said Pidre, looking intently.

Simodecea tapped the map with loud nails.

Pidre squinted. "A scientist, a woman. Her name is Curie. She found it all the way in Paris. Mickey was telling me all about it. They're saying it'll save people."

"And it's here?"

"Those men in tents seem to think so. Radium, they call it."

Simodecea's breath shortened in her throat. She turned to the window, eyed the ridge. More white tents had appeared in the last few months. They perched there like vultures drying their wings.

It was a cool-wind summer day when they arrived in La Tierra Perdida, their eyes burned from fragments of coal ash that had floated from the train's engine into their faces through open windows. Pidre had closed the theater for the summer, his performers either visiting their families in cities like Santa Fe or Denver or touring with other shows for the season. When the train pulled into the station, Simodecea made sure to take both daughters by the arm, carting them away from the railroad tracks as if they were tied to her wrists with rope. The depot building was bustling with passengers elbowing their way on and off trains. The girls and their mother carried lace parasols and spread out in a line. Across the depot's white-painted façade was a large and incorrect clock.

"Someone," said Simodecea, pointing to the clock's drooping big hand, "ought to fix that."

Pidre approached a merchant in a booth, a heavily bearded man in a striped cap with both thumbs tucked beneath his leather suspenders. A single line of perspiration ran over his sooty skin, clearing a wet path of flesh. Pidre pointed east, motioning to his heart and then outward, as if releasing an injured dove into the clouds. The man shook his head. His beard did not move.

"We need a horse and cart to get to Pardona," Pidre said.

"It's not on the map," the man said, his voice muffled with beard.

"It's very close, not even a half day's journey."

The bearded man guffawed with skeptical eyes. All around him were the voices of workingmen, miners and vaqueros, the scream of a train's whistle. After some time, Pidre sifted through his satchel and presented the man with a handful of silver dollars. Money was money. "A cart, compañero, and two horses."

And that, as they say, was that.

During the ride, Pidre recited energetic stories of his village. He spoke quickly and passionately about chokecherries, thistle, bellflowers, and bergamot. He went on about his grandma, the Sleepy Prophet. Though she had left this world when he was only a little boy, he told them he often felt her spirit, especially within the gaze of his daughters.

They had been traveling with the horses and cart for a long while, the sky turning from an orange blush to mellow evening, those colors of lilacs and dust. The earth smelled of burnt sage and the lushness of Rio Lucero. Wind carried the ashen taste of clay.

The babies were little girls by now, seven and eight, and in the cart they were seated politely on either side of Simodecea, bundled in itchy wool blankets. The sun was setting and the land had grown colder, mosquitoes and crickets whispering to one another, as if to raise the hairs on the earth's neck. They went on like that, the horses' hooves pounding over the worn trail with an unevenness from those wagon ruts plowed into the earth by Anglos pushing west.

After the sun had nearly set, Pidre glanced back from his perch, bridle in hands. "The Land of Early Sky," he said, pointing with his hat to a low brown flatland, clasped by an arroyo, the stars reflecting over running water. "Pardona."

Simodecea stepped down from the cart, gripping the length of her dress with her shooting arm, motioning for the girls with the other. They moved to the edge of the cart—first Maria Josefina, who told her mother that she didn't need help and hopped down in an athletic feat of red booties and dirt. Then it was Sara, who stood at the edge of the cart and stared across the land. Her eyes scanned with uneasiness, an expression Simodecea recognized in herself. A clenched mouth, flared nostrils, a distorted mirror.

Sara said, "But there's no one here, Mama. Everyone's gone."

It was only then that Simodecea peered deeper through twilight. The land was sleeping in muted green and blue tones, no firelight, no sweet sting of smoke. In the vast grounds far off and slumped sat a complex of clay homes and an adobe church. They were hollow, empty, the blue doors and windows blank. The wind rippled the sands beneath their feet. Simodecea told her girls to keep at her side.

Pidre had stepped away from the horses and cart. He walked forward, centered by generous mountains and empty dwellings. A skimp black dog crossed his path. He whistled and the animal came near, nudged its glistening nose into his palm before skirting away. Pidre walked faster, the clinking sounds of coins in his trouser pockets mixed with the crunch of his boots on rocky soil. It wasn't long before he was running, moving smaller and smaller away from his wife. He ran toward the cemetery under red willows as if being chased by oblivion itself. He began yelling in Tiwa, asking for anyone, someone, then changing dialects, begging for a response. Simodecea reached down and held her daughters' cool shoulders against her waist. She watched in anguish as her husband leaned over a grave, crossed himself before touching the faded white marker.

"Grandma," he said, "we are here. I've brought my daughters. I've brought my wife. We've come to see our Early Sky." He told Desiderya how much he missed her and loved her, pushed his hands through the dirt. He made a fist and tossed soil into the night. Pidre wept then, low and quiet, dripping onto the ground.

Maria Josefina tugged on her mother's dress. "Where did everyone go, Mama?" she asked, looking upward with sorrowful eyes.

"I don't know, my baby," said Simodecea, who stared beyond the deserted Pueblo at the bluish mountain, railroad tracks like scars etched into its back.

Pidre stood from Desiderya's grave. He wiped his face with quick hands. He called out to his daughters and wife to come near. "Your great-grandma," he said. "This is her grave. This is her resting place, and her village. I will take you to the river where I was baptized, where she found me."

Simodecea stepped forward. She hung her head. With certainty in her heart, she knew bad days were to come.

TWENTY-FIVE

A Life of Her Own

Denver, 1934

The booming shouts and footsteps of Lizette's brothers ricocheted throughout their Fox Street home. Not even the inviting smells of warming tortillas and beans, fried eggs and potatoes, could offset the stomping of boy feet over hard oak, the barks of *Where's my sock? My turn in the washroom. Who left the icebox open? We need more milk.* Having her own room was Lizette's only luxury, but she suspected that had to do more with being in a woman's body than anything else.

From the moment she opened her eyes in the still-dark mornings until she closed them at night, Lizette worked. It had always been this way. She had stopped attending school in the fifth grade to work in a candy factory downtown, where she rolled turquoise-colored sweets at a large metal table with a dozen other girls from the Westside and elsewhere. The owner was a cowboy named Rickson who had gotten one of the elsewhere girls pregnant, a fourteen-year-old named Marilou. He didn't claim the baby, and Marilou grew huge with what she suspected was a little boy. Lizette never found out what happened to Marilou and her baby, because by her second year in the factory, her mother made Lizette stay home with her youngest brother, Marcelo, while Teresita rode on a truck bed three days a week to Eaton, Colorado, where she picked beets with other mothers from their block, one hundred pounds for a dollar a day.

"Wake up, Lizzy!" shouted her brother Antonio, who had strode into her bedroom in cowboy boots and a bandito mask. From the end of her brass bed, he let out a huge belch and giggled frantically. He gripped the bed frame and shook it with all his might. Lizette groaned and told him to get the hell out of her room. She said *Goddammit, Antonio!* and stood from her bed.

"Don't forget," said Teresita as Lizette stepped into the kitchen and grabbed an apple from the table. "Lucrecia is dropping off her twins this afternoon. You're watching them."

Lizette opened her mouth full of mealy fruit. "No, I'm not."

Teresita shot her daughter a merciless look. She whacked one of her son's hands away from the stove, where she was flipping tortillas over the black comal. "Yes, you are, and you don't have a choice."

Lizette took another bite. She was used to her mother forgetting that she had her own obligations. Not everything, she thought, revolved around family. "Mama, in case you've forgotten, I'm at the dressmaker's all day today. I'm not going to be here."

Teresita shrugged. She tied her white apron strings around her waist. "So? Tell her you're busy."

At that moment, Lizette's father walked into the kitchen with a pastry in each hand. He smiled at his family through sugar-powdered cheeks.

"Papa," said Lizette. "I can't watch no stinking twins today. I have work."

"Okay, mija," her father said, and reached for his work boots beside the door.

Teresita began shouting at Eduardo, telling him he was always a pushover. Lizette imagined she was somewhere else, a big white house that was all her own, a quiet place to keep her fine dresses and fur coats and books filled with facts, all the things she wanted and deserved in life. At the very least, she thought, lifting her brother Miguelito from the floor and moving him away from the back door, she had Alfonso. Once they were married, he would take her away from this life of endless chores and little brothers. Once they were married, she'd finally know what it was like to have a life of her own.

In a bad mood and rushed, Lizette arrived fifteen minutes late for her shift after missing the streetcar when her mother made her change a diaper before leaving. Natalya was behind the counter at the edge of the dress shop, glasses on and a cigarette burning.

"You come late today, like every other day," she said, without looking up. "I hire you to help, and this is how you repay me?"

Lizette wanted to yell out that it wasn't her damn fault, but if there was one thing she had learned about Natalya—she didn't like excuses. "It won't happen again. I'm very sorry." Since she had started working for Natalya, Lizette had given most of her laundry route to a woman down the block named Sensionita, who at nineteen had three babies and a husband who had been fired from the smelter after a long bout with flu.

Lizette spotted a brown parcel, wrapped in burlap string. "What's that?" she asked.

"When you come late, you miss out," said Natalya, lifting the box into the air.

That was when she knew. "No!" said Lizette running to the rear counter, nearly tripping on the uneven floor. "Is that what I think it is?"

Natalya looked up. She had kind, translucent blue eyes, fine wrinkles about her face surrounded by red hair. She puffed on her cigarette. "No smoking when open it." She winked.

"It is!" Lizette shouted. "My wedding dress fabric." She was dancing now, snapping her fingers, swinging her hips. With a happy laugh, she reached out, as if asking for a slice of cake.

"Not so fast," Natalya said. "I need drop-off today. Then we open your package."

Lizette wilted like a frostbitten rose. "Natalya," she whined, but it was clear the dressmaker didn't care.

"The address here," she said, handing Lizette a piece of paper and a wrapped bundle of cotton slips that they had sewn the week before. The slips had expandable waists and were to be delivered to the Saint Agnes Home, on some street in Capitol Hill Lizette had never heard of. Lizette crunched her face as she grabbed the bundle.

Natalya dashed out her cigarette on a white dish. "Hurry back," she called as Lizette exited the shop.

The Queen Anne mansion looked like any other from outside. Red brick, flamboyant windows, a large encapsulating iron gate with murderous spikes, either to keep people out or to keep them in. As she walked the sandstone footpath, Lizette hardly thought of anything else besides delivering the damn slips, collecting payment, and getting the hell out of there. For months, she had been perfecting her wedding dress pattern, imagining the pull and grainy texture of the taffeta, the satin train, and her face proudly unhidden by a veil. Whatever the hell this place was, it was keeping her from her happiness.

Lizette knocked and waited, then with no response yelled out, *Delivery, open up.* She was startled when a young nun in a white veil opened the door.

"Right this way," she said, ushering Lizette into the mansion of dark wood and marble stairs. The young nun's habit skirt was loosely cinched at her broad waist with three knots, signifying her three vows—poverty, chastity, and obedience. Lizette shuddered.

"I got some slips for you," she said. "Just need payment."

"Of course," said the young nun, motioning with her draped arm toward an airy hallway with floral wallpaper, reddish like scabbed knees.

As they walked the hallway, Lizette eyed framed photographs of Anglo girls with distant, somber expressions, as if the camera had captured their ghosts. They were seated on the lawn during some kind of festival, balloons and streamers on the sides. Lizette was nervous and felt her heartbeat charging into something quick, preparing her to flee.

"What kind of place is this?" she asked as they reached a dining room with an oversized table and deep mahogany chairs. There were water glasses stacked on a hutch with a bell-shaped pitcher, fogged in condensation.

"It is a home," said the young nun, opening a side door and directing Lizette into an office.

"You don't say," said Lizette.

"Please have a seat," the young nun said. "Sister Florence will see you soon."

Lizette sat down in front of the metal desk, a single piece of

paper and a cup of dull pencils before her. In rich-people hand-
writing, curly and thin, someone had written the Apostles' Creed.

I believe in God, the Father almighty, creator of heaven and
earth. I believe in Jesus Christ, his only Son, our Lord, who was
conceived by the Holy Spirit, born of the Virgin Mary, suffered
under Pontius Pilate, was crucified, died, and was buried; he
descended to the dead. On the third day he rose again.

Lizette laughed, imagining this was some kind of punishment
room. *Well*, she thought, *money is money.* Beyond the desk was a
latticed window cloaked in lace curtains. Outside on the lawn,
young women with yellow and brown hair were gathered in a
circle. Lizette walked to the window for a better look, but as she
got closer the office door opened and an older nun entered the
room in a shuffle of fabric, her wrinkled pale face squeezed by the
black veil of her habit. She cleared her throat, a wetness in her
lungs. The room suddenly smelled of chalk and milk.

"May I help you?" she asked.

Lizette waved. "Yes!" she said overly enthusiastic. "Can you pay
me for these?" She handed over the bundle of slips. "Please."

The old nun pulled a long set of rusted scissors from inside the
desk. She cut the strings, unwrapped the burlap. She pulled the first
slip from the set, held it thinly into the air, and inspected the seams.
She then reached her veiny hand inside the slip through the neck
hole, grabbing around as if gutting a chicken. "There isn't enough
room on the front end," she said.

Lizette smiled, showy and fake. "Oh my, how can that possibly
be? We followed your directions to a T, Sister."

The old nun looked at Lizette, marionette lines along her
mouth.

Go on, Lizette thought, *try me*.

The old nun softened her gaze. "I asked for more inches. You can always take in with pins, but you can't let out."

Lizette held up her right index finger, energizing her posture. "May I?" she said, and waited for the nun to hand over the slip before she revealed the hidden network of ties at the top left.

"It's really quite ingenious," Lizette said. "It's simple yet effective. Saves me and you both money and time, or," she said, "whoever wears these."

Through a stone-like face, the old nun nodded. She told Lizette one moment and turned around, clearly trying to hide that she was opening a chest of drawers and turning the combination of an iron safe. Lizette wished that old bat knew she could read those numbers if she wanted to, but she didn't want to and instead looked once more through the window. The group of young women had dispersed—the lawn was as green and empty as it had ever been.

The old nun stepped from behind the desk, handing Lizette an envelope containing a single paper bill. She placed her hand on the small of Lizette's back, guiding her out of the office and into the cavernous dining room as a bell rang throughout the mansion. At the far end of the airy house a door opened, daylight cascading onto blond floors covered in red rugs. A dozen or more Anglo girls with flushed pink faces and large pregnant bellies walked single file in felt slippers, filling the room with their bodies like a flash flood of white women. They stepped to the stacked glasses at the hutch and waited while perhaps the most pregnant of all poured each of them water. Lizette was dizzy with the unpleasantness of the whole situation, and she turned to leave without so much as saying goodbye to the old nun, but as she stepped toward the front door, someone caught her eye.

A redhead stood in the parlor, slowly making her way toward the dining room, waddling from the fullness of developing life.

Lizette stepped back, as if pushed by a cold wind.

Eleanor Anne stood between the open French doors. She slowly frowned as if the sight of Lizette had harmed her like a blow.

They looked at each other straight.

Lizette felt sad all over, her skin, her mouth. She knew exactly what this place was, and in that moment, surrounded by those young Anglo women alone without their families and only in the company of one another and bitter nuns, Lizette was grateful that she didn't come from a people so unbearable as to hide their own women away when they believed them full of unfavorable babies.

"Alice Jean," called the old nun from the dining room.

Tears rolled over Eleanor Anne's cheeks. "One moment, Sister," she said through silent sobs. *Please,* she mouthed to Lizette, *don't tell.*

And with only the look on her face, Lizette promised she never would. She had no reason to. Besides, she needed to get back to work. There was a new dress to make, and this delivery had already taken too much of her time.

TWENTY-SIX

Shelter from the Storm

"**S**eems strange, don't you think?" David said to Luz as he opened the office door to the street. It was late afternoon, the end of April. Luz was almost done with her shift. Sunlight moved around David's shoulders and curly hair and pressed into the lobby.

"The thunder?" Luz asked.

"No, it's too consistent," David said, and stepped outside onto the sidewalk.

Luz stood from her desk and followed him into the warmish spring air. "What do you mean?" she called.

The sounds grew into a roaring pitch, a mass of jeers, their source concealed by the great gray city. The air turned. The sky was laced with a stinging cold. Several passersby had also noticed the unusual sounds, and they slowed to a stroll, faces turning toward the rumbling.

Luz stayed on the sidewalk and watched as David walked through the eerily traffic-less street, down the thin median surrounded by parked automobiles and dated brown carriages. He looked upon the horizon, where the sight of the road ended in the train station, nestled between brick offices and the backdrop of the mountains. Luz watched as David walked in his black suit. He moved gradually, but as the sounds grew, he sprinted until he reached what Luz suspected was a higher vantage point, the place he could see the source of all the commotion.

At once David turned and, with both arms waving, yelled for Luz to get inside. "Now," he hollered, sprinting back in her direction. "Right now. Inside."

Hairs rose along her neck. A darkness swirled overhead, dizzyingly strange, as if the city was about to be engulfed by a tornado.

"Now, Luz!" David ran to catch up to her on the sidewalk.

As David rushed toward her, Luz searched over his shoulders and scanned the long road once more. At the blurred edge of Seventeenth Street, in the space reserved for sky, Luz saw the unrelenting beginnings of a long white parade, men and women cloaked in robes, their pointed hoods bobbing along the horizon, an American flag displayed among the first row, a pine cross held high into the air. Luz hadn't seen a Klan march with such numbers since her childhood, and the longer she stared, the more the parade revealed itself like a flopping white serpent emerging from the ground. A hateful moving body. In those fleeting moments as she stood on the sidewalk before David yanked her by the left wrist and guided them both inside the office, Luz stared at hundreds of Klan members. There was a section of women, their white faces rosy in the chilly afternoon, their small children, some no more than three or four years old, pulled along in red wagons. How could they bring their babies?

Once David pulled Luz into the office with him, she hunched forward, feeling as if she had swallowed stones. She coughed and sputtered in horror, half expecting herself to vomit rocks. David locked the door behind them. He directed Luz to close the curtains as he shut off the lights. He retrieved a wooden board from a cabinet and secured it across the front entrance, barricading them inside.

"Why are they marching now?" Luz asked as she fumbled with the blinds, her hands shaking. "There was no warning. I heard nothing, saw no flyers, nothing. I haven't seen them out like this in years."

"Into my office," David whispered.

"How will we get home?"

Once they were inside his office, David locked and bolted the door. "You can't leave, Luz. Neither of us can. Not until whatever it is they have planned comes to an end."

Luz considered this and looked around the office, wondering what she could use as protection. All she had was the knife in her purse. "There's so many more of them," she said.

David asked her to take a seat in one of the black leather chairs for clients. He sat across from her at his desk and dropped his head between both hands. He sighed many times. "They're considering opening a grand jury investigation into Estevan's murder. Next month or so, likely. I just got the call."

Luz leaned forward over the desk. She asked David what he meant.

"I was about to tell you. We could be celebrating right now."

There was a sound like a hammer on the front door. Luz scooted away from the noise.

David looked at his papers, exhaled. "I don't know what to say. But they're not going to intimidate us." He removed his suit jacket, laying it across his chair. He walked to the door, pressing his ear against the frosted glass. Luz could make out screams. David's office had only three half windows toward the ceiling. The afternoon was fading into dusk. Luz focused on the dwindling sunlight as she listened for familiarity in any of the screams. She hoped no one she knew was being hurt.

David sat back down and was tinkering with an electric kettle atop his desk. From a wooden box with the words FINEST EMPIRE TEA, he scooped out tea leaves and with them filled two ball-like metal strainers. He gazed at Luz as he waited for water to boil.

"I'm sorry I have no food in here. They say it brings rats from the sewers."

"Oh," Luz said. "I couldn't possibly eat with this going on outside anyway."

"Fair enough."

When David finished making tea, he stood and wheeled the metal tray beside Luz. He took a seat in the second black leather chair across from his desk, so that his knee was slightly touching the edge of Luz's thigh. He handed her a cup on a plain saucer, steam rising into her face and hair. It was good tea, expensive, full-bodied black.

"How long do you think . . . until it's over?" Luz asked.

"No idea," David said in between sips. "If they're doing a cross burning, this could go on until midnight or so."

They both jerked as glass shattered in the front office, as if a brick had been thrown through the windows. David held his finger to his mouth. *Shhhh*, he mouthed and motioned for Luz to get under the desk. *In case anyone should make it into the office*, he whispered. Luz slinked from her chair and crawled over the rugs until she reached David's desk, retreating deep into its walnut undercarriage. She pressed her body against the wood and looked out at her knees. Night had fallen, and beneath the desk it was dark, though just beyond, where David now crawled on his hands and knees, the room was a bluish gray.

When David entered the space, he pressed himself beside Luz. He smelled strongly of Ivory soap, his breath opulent with the aroma of black tea. Their bodies remained strict and silent—only the sounds of their heavy breathing passed between them. Luz prayed inside her mind that no one would enter the office, drag them out, beat them in the street—she imagined the horde, their jeers at the Greek lawyer and his *spic* clerk, lawing for the rights of the underclasses. Luz clenched her jaw to keep herself from crying out in fear. Then, from far off, they heard car horns and hollering, an indication that the march, the parade, the hate-fueled mob, was nowhere near finished. How long were they to stay there, packaged together like canned meat?

David faced Luz in the dark. "Are you okay?" he whispered.

Terrified to speak, she nodded.

"Good," David said, and placed his palm on her right knee, cupping inward along her thigh. "Luz," David said quietly. He then put his mouth on her neck, sending a pleasant shock from his lips all the way to her thighs, where his hand moved gradually beneath her dress, underneath her panties, and inside her body. Luz's breathing changed, quickened and deepened. It happened so quickly. She had never experienced such a heavy want, and it pulsated through her entire body until a murmur of a moan fell from her lips. David covered her mouth with one hand and Luz found herself opening her lips to taste his palm. When he removed his hand, he pushed the whole fat worm of his tongue into her mouth. He began to remove her dress, working the zipper with such knowledge of women's fashion that it was alarming. He moved his hands around her body, squeezed hard along her breasts.

Luz was jolted into dread. If she let him, David would take her virginity right there on his office floor, in the middle of a Klan march. "Stop," Luz said. "We have to stop."

"I understand," David said, and slowly moved forward, biting down on her lip before moving out from under the desk and briskly standing up. It appeared the hollering outside had quieted.

"It seems to have cleared up," he said. "I imagine we can go home now."

TWENTY-SEVEN

A Day Without Work

It was Sunday and Luz had gotten up early and had a fried-eggs breakfast with Maria Josie before her auntie had gathered picnic supplies and fishing poles, heading out the door to meet her new friend, a woman named Ethel who drove a shiny Standard car. They were going to the mountains, to a blue lake. Ethel seemed to work as much as Maria Josie, and Luz rarely got to spend time with them, but she had taken a liking to the woman, a physician with a steadfast gaze behind dark-framed glasses. She had a wave of chestnut hair, and Maria Josie always came home from Ethel's smelling of her gardenia perfume. Though Luz would never admit it to Maria Josie, she worried that Ethel could take her auntie away from her. Ethel lived in an Eastside bungalow, a far cry from the ramshackle Hornet Moon. It was only a matter of time, Luz feared, before Maria Josie packed her bags and left for good. Then where would Luz go?

At a little past eleven o'clock, Luz was startled by banging on the front door. She was shocked to find Lizette standing in the hallway, holding a garment sack, as if she had lugged a bagged corpse all the way from the Westside to Curtis Street.

"What's that?" Luz asked.

Lizette was out of breath and sweating through her light blue dress, wet spots seeping around her underarms and in a line beneath her breasts. "It's ready," she said, and pushed her way past Luz. "Let's open it in the kitchen, where the light is best."

Luz figured inside the garment bag was another one of Lizette's creations. Since she had gone to work for Natalya, the dressmaker had given Lizette the freedom to design several dresses and blouses and bring them to life, straight from her mind. In some ways, this seemed nothing short of a miracle—to be able to think something up, labor away, until one day that piece of clothing existed in the physical world.

Lizette scanned the kitchen with a critical eye. "Oh, that awful smell," she said. "I don't know how you get used to it."

"Like the Westside smells any better with the train yards."

"For one thing," Lizette said, "it *does* smell better than carcasses. Most things do." Lizette got to work shutting the kitchen window.

"What're you doing?" Luz asked. "It's hotter than hell!"

"I don't want the smell seeping into my dress."

"What dress?" Luz asked.

Lizette smiled in a mischievous and beautiful way. She returned to the garment bag and slowly lifted the bottom. A honey-colored wedding dress spilled forth.

"My goodness," said Luz, stunned. "You made this?"

"Natalya taught me how to do some of the trickier stitches. We worked on it together."

"And the cost of the fabric?" Luz couldn't take her eyes off the dress. It was as if a piece of liquid gold floated through the air of her sweltering kitchen.

"She gave me an advance, said I've been doing good work at the shop."

Luz asked if she could touch the fabric, and Lizette motioned *of course*. Luz wiped her hands across her cotton blouse and then moved her fingertips along the wedding dress's buttons and seams. It was exactly as Lizette had planned. A simple satin silhouette with hidden clasp buttons along the left side, a fine grouping of lace around the bodice, and capelet sleeves. "Wow. You'll be a beautiful bride," Luz said, frankly.

"Are you kidding me?" Lizette puffed out her hair. "I'm gonna be a dime. Everybody is gonna be mad they ain't marrying me."

"I'm so happy. You made the dress you wanted." Luz stepped toward Lizette and they embraced, their sweaty faces smearing saltiness across each other.

"Let's get it back in the bag and open up these windows. It's hotter than fresh dog shit in here."

"Lizette . . ." said Luz with a frown.

The cousins hugged once more and stood together with their joy. Sometimes, when Luz looked at Lizette, it was as if she were peering into a speckled mirror at pieces of herself rearranged in another person. It was her shyness distorted into assertiveness and her delicate features pulled into the beauty of a masculine femininity. Luz reached up and moved her hands through Lizette's black curls, and they were cooler than the air between them. Luz thought of when she first came to Denver at eight years old and how Lizette seemed to instinctively understand the heartbreak Luz had experienced in losing both her mother and father to something different than death. She remembered how Lizette noticed that Luz's clothes were stained and ragged when Maria Josie first brought her and Diego over to Tía Teresita and Tío Eduardo's Fox Street home. Lizette, in a sly manner, brought an embroidered dress from her own closest to the front room, wrapped in a white washcloth, which she passed discreetly to her newfound cousin.

Once a date was set, things happened quickly. Alfonso found a small two-bedroom home to rent on Inca Street that had a square yard and a blossoming peach tree. The landlord had given him a special deal for being Pinoy, or so Alfonso claimed. He was a man named Buck Valdez, originally from the Lost Territory, a village called Antonito. He took great interest in Alfonso's collection of ten-gallon hats and bolo ties and said that once in his youth, when he traveled as far as California, he worked the fields alongside Filipinos, enjoying their humor and taste in clothing and women.

After he paid the deposit, Alfonso brought Luz and Avel along for a tour, each of them whistling with echoes throughout the empty stucco rooms.

"Do you think she'll like it?" Alfonso asked as he stood in the blue kitchen. The stove was a new gas-range model with two ovens and Luz thought if Lizette ever learned to embrace housework, that stove alone was enough to make a girl's dream house.

"The question is," said Luz, walking under the low archway into the front room, "will she be able to throw her parties here?"

"Yes, ma'am," said Alfonso with pride. "You'll be here so often, Lucy Luz, we'll have to charge you rent." He chuckled some and nudged Avel, who laughed and stepped away, examining the light fixtures and windowsills, a true handyman always.

"I wouldn't say that," said Avel and turned around on his boot heels, grabbing Luz by the left wrist. "Lucy Luz might have her own place someday soon."

The men seemed to share a knowing look, and Luz frowned. "I don't see it in the leaves."

———

At work, David pretended nothing had happened between him and Luz. The office was in disarray. The vandals had pushed their way into the front room, rummaging through Luz's desk, taking with them several notarized documents and signed paperwork for the Ruiz case. A grand jury investigation still hadn't been announced. Whenever Luz thought to ask David about what had happened under the desk, she'd open her mouth to speak but could only picture white moths fluttering from her lips. Maybe it wasn't her place. Maybe it was something she'd have to wait on David to bring up, and Luz wondered why she was always waiting on men to act.

Luz occupied her evenings and weekends with Avel, going from dance hall to dance hall, Benny's, the Emerald Room, Teatro Oso. She watched his new band move the crowds each night. Occasionally Lizette and Alfonso would tag along, and there were times when even Maria Josie and Ethel appeared at the edge of the dance floor, fingers touching delicately at their sides. While Avel never gave Luz that warm giddy rush of her insides twisted like rain clouds, he did make her feel valued, wanted, cared for— qualities she had never received consistently from any man. In her letters to her brother, Luz announced Lizette's wedding date and Maria Josie's new friend, but for some reason she didn't dare mention anything new about Avel. In her latest letter, she begged Diego to consider coming home for the wedding. He wrote back a few weeks later.

So, they really did it, huh? They saved up and found a Catholic church that would marry those two. (Can you imagine Lizette in confession?—ha!) I wish I could be there. She'll make a beautiful bride, and Alfonso is a lucky man. But I don't think I can come home for the wedding, Little Light. It won't be safe for me or the rest of the family, but as more time passes, I keep hoping that I can stop moving from town to town, following the beets, or lettuce, or garlic and just come home. The fields are as endless as the landowner's pockets. With Sirena in tow, we make extra money on weekends, when we usually find a festival or fair and I can perform. How I've missed the crowds, their open happy faces. I miss you and Maria Josie. I had a dream about Mama the other day, and I woke up crying. Here's a few dollars to help with your dress for the wedding, and here's a few more for Lizette and Alfonso.

In mid-May, there was a rare occurrence when everyone dear to Luz had a day without work. Maria Josie and Ethel planned a picnic near the famed Jack Wesley's grave atop Lookout Mountain. Lizette jumped at the opportunity—for weeks she had been gathering pine cones for her wedding decorations. Alfonso and Lizette drove in the Chevy while Luz and Avel rode with Maria Josie and Ethel and her little white dog named Marcus. As the days grew longer and warmer weather greeted the mountains, snow melted and filled the creeks and rivers, increasing their size and velocity until the waters broke free of their banks, matting down grasses and expanding into mud. Luz watched the roadway as Ethel's Standard car chugged along Coal Creek, hugging granite cliffs and rising past mountain goats and the occasional lone deer.

"Ethel," said Avel, as they neared the peak of Lookout Mountain, "who taught ya how to drive? You're the best woman driver I've ever known."

Maria Josie snorted beside her in the passenger seat, and Ethel moved her gaze from the road ahead to the rearview mirror, making eye contact with Avel and then Luz in the backseat. "I taught myself after medical school, Avel. I figured, if I can deliver a baby, I can drive a damn automobile."

Everyone chirped with laughter and Maria Josie scooted closer to Ethel. Luz admired the easy way they seemed to care for each other. Since they met, Maria Josie had stopped running around with her other friends and devoted every moment of her spare time to Ethel. It was almost enough to make Luz jealous. And the little dog up front on Maria Josie's wide lap seemed to like her just as much.

"How did you become a doctor?" Luz asked, turning her face away from the window. "I've never known a doctor before."

"Many years of studying, Luz. But I always wanted to mend people. It was my calling, I suppose." She drove with perfect posture and both hands firmly along the shiny steering wheel.

"I took classes once," said Luz. "At the Opportunity School. David sent me, but I don't think I'm a very good student. You must be very intelligent." She smiled and looked outside at a group of bighorn sheep with their devilish horns.

"School doesn't make you smart, Luz," said Ethel. "It's just a type of training. Real intelligence—that comes from our grit, our ability to read the world around us."

"Like reading tea leaves," said Maria Josie, moving her arm along the front seat and turning to wink at Luz. "You have an old kind of intelligence, Little Light."

Luz glanced modestly at her lap as Avel, beside her, reached over and cupped his hands over hers. *An old kind of intelligence,* she thought, repeating the words in her mind as they topped the mountain, Denver a haze below.

———

They parked the cars some ways off from the designated picnic area. Experience had taught them that they would be run off by Anglo families and park rangers if they stayed near the tables, so it was best to keep to themselves in a small meadow on the mountain's eastern side. They hobbled with picnic supplies from the cars in a bright bursting row of family. Everyone was dressed beautifully in spring colors. Under their cowboy hats, both Alfonso and Avel wore white trousers and light-colored suspenders while Lizette stepped out of the Chevy in a gauzy yellow dress that lifted behind her in the wind. Maria Josie was striking in men's denim, her short black hair tied with a red kerchief and Ethel in a modest floral dress in the style of farmgirls on the eastern plains. Luz, in blue, watched as her people carried wicker baskets, tin pails, bundles of tortillas wrapped in cloth to hold their long-gone warmth, and, of course, Lizette with a secret bottle of homemade hooch poking out from her armload of blankets.

They picked out a spot in a grassy expanse surrounded by wildflowers—black-eyed Susans, columbines, chicory, daisies, fire wheels—all the names that Mama had taught Luz as a little girl in both English and Spanish. All around them they were enclosed with towering ponderosa pines and blue spruce, the smells of sagebrush and pine sap riding the light mountain breeze, rushing over their skin and into their hair. The blue sky sagged with low-hanging clouds clinging to the midsections of far-off mountain peaks. Songbirds dazzled, their chirping in leveled whistles. The air felt good to breathe.

They ate fried baloney sandwiches and tortillas spread with butter and cinnamon, red apples and still-green bananas. Lizette leaned into Alfonso, using his torso and legs as a chair, stealing sips from her bottle of booze and then conspicuously passing it to either Avel or Luz. Ethel's little dog, Marcus, sniffed about the rocks covered in hardened turquoise moss. Maria Josie told a long joke involving a broomstick in a broken coal shaft that left Luz bewildered, but she still laughed and draped herself over Avel's shoulders. He smelled wonderfully fresh, cottony and clean, and his black hair absorbed heat from the sun, moving warmth across Luz's face as she pressed into him. It had been a long time, maybe forever, since they could all be together without work.

When everyone had devoured the picnic, Lizette stood up and dusted her hands off across her dress. "All right," she said, "I want everyone to get five pine cones. Big ones. The best pine cones God has ever made."

Alfonso was propped up on his right side, leaning on his elbow, flicking a blade of grass between his fingers. "Five? Why not ten?" He threw the grass into the air, and it floated to the ground. He stood with a jolt, grabbing Lizette around the waist with both arms, laughing. "Everyone, come on, help my girl get her pine cones."

Avel stood then and reached out to help Luz up. Maria Josie and Ethel followed. Even little Marcus seemed to get in on the hunt. They started out from the blanket, moving in a bouncing racing line, tumbling over one another, taking huge strides over the rocky earth, hollering and laughing together in the sunlight.

Lizette disappeared beyond the tree line and Alfonso cut away by a clearing of aspen trees. Ethel and Maria Josie stayed arms locked as they laughed and searched the ground. Luz and Avel sprinted near an enormous ponderosa with reddish pine needles, dry and brittle at the top. Luz spotted a grouping of fallen pine cones and bent over, handing the fine specimens to Avel, who gathered them in a pile.

Luz stepped away now, searching a few yards off. "There," she shouted to Avel, and went to walk toward him, but when she turned around, he was there on the ground, one knee pressed into the dirt. "What're you doing? There aren't any more over here."

"Luz Lopez," he said, inhaling deeply and opening his right hand to reveal a white box with a delicate gold ring. "I want to be with you forever."

Luz felt dizzy, confused. "What do you mean?" she whispered, ducking to make sure her family wouldn't see.

"Can't you tell?" he said. "I love you, Luz. I want us to have a life together."

"Like get married?"

Avel nodded.

"I just, I don't think Maria Josie will go for that. We've only known each other a short time."

"This is between us," said Avel.

In that moment, she heard a cricket's tune begin to play and the trees shivered at their tops, as if telling secrets to one another, passing along the news about the humans below.

"How are you going to live in Hornet Moon forever? Huh? You can't live like this. You barely have anything, and it could all be taken away in an instant. That job with David doesn't seem safe, Luz. You shouldn't be working such long hours in a dangerous place. He's only using you, can't you see?" Avel stood then, placing the ring on Luz's left hand. "What do you say?"

She held her left hand in the sunlight, examining the way the gold shined across her skin. "All right," she said. "Okay. Yes." She kissed him quickly, feeling some level of fluttering in her bones.

Avel yipped and kissed her heartily on the mouth.

"Let's keep it between us," said Luz. "Like you said. Just for now?"

Avel agreed, his smile trembling some.

As they made their way through the meadow, Luz spotted Lizette bent through the window of Alfonso's Chevy. She was shaking her head. Alfonso was inside at the driver's seat, the radio up loud. He seemed stunned, rubbing the top of his chest with an open palm.

"Come here," Lizette shouted, frantically waving. "They've got 'em. Shot 'em dead."

"Who?" Luz asked, running now.

They were listening to a news program, the special alert wavering in signal strength.

The death car is riddled with holes, every one made by steel-jacketed bullets from the high-powered rifles in the hands of the officers. Many of these bullets passed entirely through the door on Clyde's side, through his body, struck Bonnie, passed through her body, and then out through the door on her side of the car. Any one of these bullets would have been fatal to both, but after having killed fourteen people, most of whom were officers of the law, and having come safely through so many gun battles, it didn't seem advisable to fire just one bullet.

Luz listened intently as she slid her left hand into her dress pocket, concealing her new gold-plated engagement ring.

The death car and its bodies were later towed to a morgue, where a crowd of onlookers pushed through the windows and with white handkerchiefs attempted to soak up some of Bonnie's blood, a keepsake of sorts.

TWENTY-EIGHT

Where the World Registers

"Cover more of her arms," Lizette said to Natalya, who examined Luz on a Thursday evening before the shop mirrors. She had walked over first thing after leaving the office. The sun wouldn't set for several hours, and light poured into the dressmaker's. "Something draped around her collarbones and chest. And where's the hat?"

"I don't think bonnet will look good but you're the boss," Natalya said as she held a string to Luz's wingspan.

The women held different pieces of fabric to Luz's body, turning their faces from side to side, examining Luz's hips and bust, her skin tone, wrist size, the way her toes crunched into satin heels. Her body had changed so quickly from several years before. In some ways, Luz still thought of herself as the girl she was before her breasts and hips emerged, as if some eternal self was buried inside her ever-changing flesh. The fitting was exhausting and Luz couldn't imagine that, soon enough, she would have to do it all over again, but this time for her own wedding. She had told only Lizette about Avel's proposal, unsure about the idea of such pervasive change.

Natalya told them she'd get to work on modifying a simple lace dress, fitting it with netted sleeves. Of course, Lizette didn't take into consideration that Luz would nearly die of heatstroke in the middle of summer wearing such a concealing dress. There were certain battles Luz knew not to pick, and which dress she wore to her cousin's wedding didn't seem like a place to wage war.

"What's wrong with you?" Lizette asked. They had left the dressmaker's and were on their way to the streetcar. The city was ripe with heat, pulsating with the stench of grease and rotten fruit. "Do you hate the dress? I mean, you don't need to be completely covered, but the church demands it and you know how strict those old priests can be. And don't get me started on the nuns. I won't even look their way."

"No," Luz said, "I'm just nervous."

"About what?" said Lizette, yanking gently on Luz's hair.

In the shadow of a shoemaker's shop, they walked past a group of children who were hunched together in a circle blasting marbles. One of the boys, a pudgy kid with dark skin and freckles, flicked his ball bearing and howled like a little coyote. At their streetcar stop, Luz positioned herself against a brick wall, facing traffic.

Lizette stood before her, both hands on her hips. "Tell me what's wrong."

"I know I'm supposed to feel happy," said Luz, "being engaged now, but I don't feel any way. I haven't even told anyone else."

Lizette shook her head. "Luz, you got to tell Maria Josie."

Luz looked away, ashamed. "How did you know? How could you tell Alfonso was the right one?"

"He's good to me. He's kind. He makes me laugh. He has a job." Lizette stepped beside Luz in the shadows and reached for her left hand. "That's all you need, really."

"But what about true love?" asked Luz.

Lizette scanned the crowded summer streets. "True love isn't real, not for girls like us at least. You know who the world treats worse than girls like us? Girls who are alone."

After getting off alone at her streetcar stop, Luz strolled the city, taking note of the red geraniums hanging in clay pots from balcony windows. There were the chorus sounds of patio parties, a dog's distant bark. Luz eyed those on evening walks, young couples holding hands, a little boy with a yo-yo, an old woman pushing a cart filled with rusted cans. Luz crossed Eighteenth and headed for Hornet Moon, but she took a long way home, running her fingers through yellow wheat growing in a neighborhood lot. A moment of rest, time with the quiet of the world.

As she continued walking, Luz remembered one morning when her father had woken her up before his shift in the mines. Normally, she had to share his affection with her mother and Diego, but on this morning no one else was awake. *Good morning, beautiful girl,* her father had said in English and then changed into a song in French. Luz didn't know his language. He didn't share it enough for his children to learn. He took her hands and held them to his chest. Luz could feel the way his body trembled with each note, the long tenor in his lungs, the sonorous tremor of his ribs. *What does it mean, Papa?* she had asked. *It means, you are my light, my world,* he said. And in that moment of early morning, their household asleep, Luz felt like the most important girl in the world, and she wondered if someday when she found her one true love, would he make her feel that way, too. But the feeling was fleeting, and soon her father was gone.

Luz blinked into the fading sunlight of Denver's evening. She glimpsed David's Chevy slowly parking in front of Hornet Moon. He did not see her and ran from the car after slamming his door. She approached him from behind, studied the way he sprinted toward the front entrance.

"David," she said, as he was searching the ground, presumably for pebbles to toss at her window.

He turned around at once, and stood there, silent and looming, their eyes locked in some kind of embrace. He snapped into motion, held the newspaper high. Luz didn't need to search the page very long because there, as the evening headline in bold, was the news: DENVER TO OPEN GRAND JURY INVESTIGATION INTO ESTEVAN RUIZ'S DEATH.

"Put on something nice," David said. "I'm taking you to dinner."

The Brown Palace's grandeur was a shock. The triangular stone building was nine stories high, ending in a ceiling that dazzled in shards of glass. Black onyx filigree railings lined center balconies. Lilies rested in waterfall vases. A white man played a grand piano before a massive fireplace. Wealthy Anglo guests carried on in expensive suits and elegant summer dresses. In red velvet uniforms, bellhops bowed and thanked and bowed some more.

"Where the World Registers," David said, pointing to the lobby's sign. He then motioned for Luz to follow him as a young Filipino waiter showed them to their seats in the dining room—a far corner, as requested.

After they were seated and had ordered their meal, Luz was embarrassed that she was sweating with nervousness. She sniffed the air, making sure she couldn't detect her own odor. *Roses,* she thought, and found flowers behind her on a mantel. "I've never seen anything like this," she said.

"I figured you hadn't been inside before," David said. "It's the most magnificent hotel in the West. Every president since Teddy has stayed here. Actresses. Politicians." David leaned across the table, lowering his voice. "They say there are tunnels beneath it."

"For what?"

"What else? Women and booze." He laughed and reached for a cigarette from his breast pocket. He struck the match on the inside of his watchband. "You know, I've never stayed here before. I'd love to see what the rooms are like inside. Wouldn't you?"

Luz was still trying decipher what David meant when the waiter returned with a three-tiered tray of cheeses and meats and a steaming porcelain kettle. "What will happen now?" Luz asked. "Now that they're investigating the murder?"

David blinked, a long while. "I wish I could tell you. It could be the officer is indicted for murder. Or nothing could come of it at all, but I'd rather not think about that. Today is a triumph—let's focus on that."

Luz had requested her tea leaves and the strainer on the side. She pointed to the teacup and saucer before David. "I could read for you," she suggested.

"My tea leaves?" he said, dismissively.

Luz nodded. "You could be prepared." She paused a moment, searched the expansive dining room. "For what will come."

David gazed into his cup. He spun it by its handle. "Sure, what the hell?"

"Really?" Luz asked.

"Yeah," he said. "If anything, could be fun." David winked.

Luz motioned for him to scoop the leaves into his cup. She instructed him to focus on his question, the case, what was at stake for him and everyone involved. "Move away," she said, "from all other thoughts."

"Like a prayer?" he said.

Luz told him that was true, though he didn't seem like the praying type.

David laughed. "You," he said, "have no idea what I've asked for." He then blinked several times. "All clear, boss."

Luz poured hot water over David's leaves and whispered for him to keep holding his question while his tea steeped. For a moment, they sat together in silence, Luz leaning into the velvet cushion of her chair as she watched David's eyes move over her face until he grinned.

"Ready?" Luz asked, and David nodded.

"Now," she said, "drink and keep holding your question."

David brought the teacup to his shiny lips and blew across the steam. He gazed downward as he drank, eyes hidden, mouth wet. After several minutes, he looked up and passed the cup to Luz.

"Let's see," she said, turning the teacup counterclockwise on the table. Luz normally would feel something at first glance, but the cup felt cold and empty.

"What do you see?" David asked optimistically.

"Still looking," she said and brought the cup closer to her face, where an image came into focus. What at first appeared to be a black bird shifted into a bear.

"It's easy," said Luz with relief. "That's an easy one. A bear. It means something from your past is hanging over you. Does that sound like something you might know?"

But when Luz gazed at David, he was speaking to the waiter,

asking about something she couldn't hear over the piano music, which had risen above their conversation, louder than anything else in the room.

"David," Luz called out, unable to hear her own voice. He continued speaking to the waiter, oblivious to Luz shouting his name. The piercing piano music grew louder until Luz worried the sounds would damage her ears. Frightened, she stood from the table. She yelled *David* once more, but was forced into her seat by an invisible weight. The music stopped. The hotel went black. Luz waved her hands in the air, frantically fumbling for the table, but it was gone. The hotel was no longer there. Everything had vanished.

She heard it before she saw it, and smelled it, too.

A crowd. Jeers. Gunpowder. The ruffled snout of an angry animal, a stench like rotten glands.

And then Luz saw.

Through a murky day, high on wooden bleachers, featureless faces blurred in a circled audience. Luz inhaled and examined herself in a fringe gown with white suede boots. She held a rifle, surprised by its dead weight. Several yards ahead, an elegant white man in an old-fashioned suit stood with some playing cards in his hands and others balanced atop his head. He stared into Luz's eyes and mouthed something that she was certain was love. Luz felt his affection travel inside her, sliding down her throat, and settling behind her breasts. The man smiled. Kindness seeped from his blue eyes. Luz raised her rifle, aiming to shoot his cards, but from the sidelines of her vision came a black fog. The crowd screamed.

A bear running, full speed, its body colliding into Luz and knocking her to the ground. The rifle fired.

The sounds grew deafening—shrieks, labored breathing, the

death-stench of the bear's wet mouth, teeth ripping fringe-covered thighs. The pain was so great that Luz feared she'd die of it, but through her agony, she maneuvered her rifle and shot her last bullet upward into the bear's barreled chest, the steaming warmth of the animal's blood pouring onto her like rain. As if on cue, the bear went lax, its impossible weight smashing Luz into the ground. She lay pinned to the sawdust-covered earth, her face turned to the right, her lungs flattened, unable to inflate. The world was muted as boots shuffled and between their mud-caked heels, Luz followed her line of sight into the crowd, where a cloaked figure stood in black, a woman making the sign of the cross.

That's when Luz saw the body of the man who loved her. How he had collapsed into the sawdust. His face was vacant, overflowing, pieces of whitish and pink inner self on the outside. His cards were speckled in blood—a red queen, a black spade, a red diamond seven. *This,* Luz thought, *is my last look at you?*

When she opened her eyes, Luz was in the Brown Palace, David at her side, fanning her with the newspaper. "I need to leave," she said, sputtering through tears. "Now, right now."

After David drove Luz home, she ran to her bedroom, opening the drawer with her stationery and pencils. In the main room where Diego and his snakes had once lived, Luz sat on the floorboards and began a letter to her brother.

Something very bad is going to happen . . . or maybe it already has.

PART 4

TWENTY-NINE

Simodecea's Final Shot

The Lost Territory, 1905

S he had warned him, told him they were losing the theater, but Pidre assured her that Mickey had taken care of it. *They're paying, it's a lease, don't worry.* Again and again her husband explained to Simodecea that no human being can possess land. Again and again that summer Simodecea watched as new tents went up throughout the property, the canvas shacks fluttering her eyesight like the blurred edges of reality just before a person faints. Lights out.

The tents soon gave way to permanent wooden structures, towers serving as platforms above newly dug portals into the earth's crust. The Anglos built smelters in a matter of weeks, and the landside erupted with the sounds of their gutting, the churning of machinery into the ground, the picks and axes of men beating weapons into rock. There were company guards, armed men who patrolled the grounds, their pitiful retired military rifles the same color as their hands smeared in gray dust. Simodecea never saw this new element, radium, the cause for this glowing rush. As the prospectors came nearer and nearer to the adobe home, the Lopez family began to suffer the sounds of white men pissing into sagebrush, the streams of their spit into tin pails, the grunts they made when relieving themselves anywhere they pleased in the clotted woods. Simodecea wondered about the lands where they had come from, and in what state of disregard they had left them.

There came a dusty, long-shadowed afternoon when Pidre returned from Animas with his cart empty, though he had intended to stockpile grains and rice for the coming theatrical season. From their porch, Simodecea watched him arrive, her hand held above her eyes, a shading protection. Pidre's lips were tight as he walked toward the house, his deep burgundy hat crinkled in his hands.

"They're saying we owe a balance," he told his wife.

Simodecea shook her head. She told him that couldn't be right.

"And when I paid it, they told me my money wasn't good."

"What do you mean?"

"They said Indian and Mexican money is no good here."

"Money is money," said Simodecea and squinted beyond her husband's shoulders.

"Not to them it isn't. Not anymore at least."

That afternoon, Simodecea walked into Mickey's office.

"Show me the deed," she said, and pointed a Smith & Wesson at his feet on the desk. She cocked the hammer, three clicks, a drumroll.

Mickey sipped bourbon from a clay mug, and with his sagging jowls he looked mildly inconvenienced. He shook his head and swiveled in his wheeled wooden chair. He stood slowly and went to the top drawer of a cherry-oak cabinet. He pulled the deed from its resting place, and flung the paper across his desk at Simodecea.

"It's no use, Simo. That son of a bitch fucked us."

She scanned the document, lowering her revolver and tucking it into its holster beneath the folds of her dress, warmly against her thigh. When she came back up, she gazed at Mickey with such contempt that she felt like smacking him in the face. "What's this about *mineral rights?*"

Mickey took a swig of his bourbon. He wiped his wet mouth on the back of his hand. He offered some to Simodecea. She refused. "I'm sorry, Simo. I didn't know then. All the silver had run dry."

"What're you saying, Mickey?"

"Otto, he's sold everything beneath our feet. That mining company from out East is coming for all of it, the house, the theater, all of it until they squeeze every last drop of glowing rock from this land."

Simodecea peered through the grimy window above Mickey's desk. In the distance, across the sashaying sweetgrass, the company's wooden platforms were like a crown above his head. She swallowed and shot him a look, as if to say, *Fix it.* "I know you'll do what you can to save our theater."

"But you don't understand," he told her. "It's over. They're coming for more and more of it."

"Listen to me, you indolent Irishman," said Simodecea. "This is our life. This is my family, all we have. We are not just going to give up, and neither are you."

Through the dust-chuted office light, Mickey lowered his face in shame. He spoke as if watering the ground with his voice. "I never meant for this to happen. I didn't read closely enough."

Simodecea stepped around to his side of the desk. She gathered her dress in her hands, kneeling beside Mickey as if filled with piety instead of disappointment and rage. She reached for his hands, showing an unusual tenderness. "Start pushing back."

When she came home that warm-breeze evening, Pidre was with the girls, hauling firewood into the shed beside their adobe house. The sky was violet blue, and Venus was twinkling as if communicating with distant worlds. Mosquitoes and gnats soared, making the oncoming night denser with life. They were preparing for colder months, and the girls were capable of carrying armfuls of kindling while their father hoisted several logs. Pidre gave Simodecea a peculiar look as she appeared beside their porch, a fixed expression of worry pulling her lips and jaw downward. Pidre whispered for the girls to finish up helping and go on inside. They were so small but so tough, and Simodecea savored the strength they showed. It was important, she thought, especially for little girls.

When she approached him, Pidre held her firmly in his hands, pressing his face into the lace of her dress as he inhaled along her neck. "It's done," he said. "It was a mistake."

She pulled away, tears in her eyes. "How can you just accept this?" She flung her hands outward, pointed toward the theater, the red ridge, the winding creek and that landside now covered in the parasite of men.

"I don't accept it," said Pidre. "But I was told this would happen, and I worry it will bend into something worse."

They looked at each other. The air smelled of food smoke and wet fields, the comforts of night. Simodecea observed the purplish rings around Pidre's gray eyes, a color resembling stone, as if her love had been jostled from the earth. "Head inside," he said. "I'll finish out here, and we can start dinner."

That night as they made love beneath the vigas of their dirt-walled home, Simodecea lay with her face to the ceiling, gliding beneath Pidre's up and down movements, his rhythm singsong as a bird. The bedside table was illuminated in golden candlelight, coloring them as embers in a fire. Simodecea reached her arms behind Pidre's broad back, pulled him to her breasts and breathed, admiring the weight of his person, the sweet cave-like smell of his follicles, airways, and pores. His prominent nose knocked into her forehead by accident, and she chuckled. They both did, pleasurably in their dance, and as Simodecea laughed into the ceiling, her neck craned and eyes opened, she caught sight of a figure standing in the corner, a hooded face shielded by night. Simodecea shouted and collected the wayward sheet onto their bodies. It must be one of the girls sleepy-eyed from the other room, but as Simodecea eased into an upward position, searching the cool corner, the blank walls in tidal firelight, she whimpered at the emptiness, the cloaked figure gone.

They arrived in the morning. Simodecca was readying the girls for the day, frying eggs and pouring glasses of milk. Sara was in an odd mood, eating slowly with one hand beneath her chin, like an exhausted grown-up, a girl who had seen too much. Maria Josefina was on her belly in the parlor, searching beneath the wooden benches and rocking chair for her missing red boot. Pidre was in the yard before their adobe home. He was drawing water from the well, carrying it alongside the squash and corn Simodecea kept in rows before the porch. There was music from the birds, the under-water swilling sounds of robins and finches and mourning doves. Simodecea peered out the window, where several yards away Pidre was returning to the well for another pull.

It was three of them with Mickey trotting ahead of the line. They came over the hillside of red rock and sagebrush, some ways ahead of the colony of tents, their figures silhouetted against blue sky. Two appeared to be company guards. The third man wore an elegant ivory suit, and he was sweating under the brash sunlight, wiping glistening perspiration from his neck and puckered face with a hazy cloth. Mickey was shouting to Pidre, waving his arms while his beard refracted a ray of sunlight, as though he existed as a lit match. Simodecea turned around to the girls, and they were as they had been. Everything was as it had been.

The suited man presented Pidre with a kind of document, which he held for only a moment before handing it to Mickey. There was some commotion then. Mickey tossed the paper toward the men, and then pulled Pidre by the hem of his blowing tunic. The suited man directed the guards to scoop the paper from the dirt, treating the document as if it were a mandate from God. They raised it again, an oblong contract or a shield. The guards pointed to the house, where Simodecea hoped they could not see her face behind the shadows of the cotton drapery.

She saw the mirror-like flash of metal first, the way Mickey reached for his hip and brandished the pistol she had never seen but had more than once wondered about. She knew he kept one, and it worried her because a mind like Mickey's wasn't too steady. He tilted the pistol, and like that, the company guards pulled their rifles and in a ricochet of gun blasts sprayed bullets across the land.

The water bucket Pidre had been holding erupted from his

hands as he collapsed backward and down, heaping beside Mickey onto red dirt.

Simodecea lost the sounds of birds, her sense of the home's interior, her daughters eating breakfast. Time had collapsed, as if those bullets were fallen stars exploding through reality. She had become a divine reflex fueled only by fury and heartache. Simodecea snapped away from the window and fetched her Remington. She walked outside onto the porch. She lifted her gun, and before the company men could catch sight of her marking eye, Simodecea fired three shots, each bullet straight into a white man's heart. When she had finished, she screamed and fired again, but this time into the cloudless sky, as if to shoot into God.

She had never run like that before, barefoot over rocked earth, her left foot sliced on a knifing piece of quartz. She was bleeding by the time she arrived at Pidre's side, the bottom of her gown smearing in her own blood and soon mixing with that of her husband. Though she had seen the carnage of gunfire before, Simodecea still gasped with disbelief at the magnitude of human fragility.

The .44-caliber bullet had entered his neck and carved into his throat. Profuse sprays of blood had rained over his body and land. Simodecea put her hands to the gaping black hole, felt her husband's swampy shallows on her fingertips. She held them there, searching for a way to patch her love back together. She removed her shawl, forced the threads into Pidre's destroyed airway, but as she pushed harder and firmer, it was clear that his life force, his inner self, his soul, was gone. With no beating heart, his body was an emptied and desecrated house. Simodecea used the sleeve of her dress to wipe blood from Pidre's open eyes. She closed them and wailed, as if to destroy this reality with the force of her emotions. She screamed and rocked and looked to Mickey, where she saw that some of his skull and much of his brain were scattered about the dirt. She could not bring herself to look at the others, their legal document among the massacred.

In her confusion and grief, she stood from the ground and dragged her husband's body toward the porch by the roots of his arms. Glancing behind her to make sure the path was clear of large rocks, Simodecea spotted the crying faces of Sara and Maria Josefina in the window, serving as a type of center, a reminder that she existed in this plane. Simodecea turned her neck and continued to pull. Beyond Pidre's boots were the tops of those white tents like the peaks of shuddering, false mountains.

They'll kill us, she thought, and pulled with the strength of several men, carting the body of her beloved into their home.

The first thing she had them do was clear the table. Simodecea placed a white sheet across the pine with the help of her girls, who trembled as they all flopped their father's body onto the surface. Sara said she could not breathe because she was crying with such force, and Maria Josefina was holding her big sister, as if to keep her from falling over. Simodecea pulled their marital blanket from the bedroom and draped it over her husband's body. Pidre's blood had leaked a glinting trail from the yard, up the porch steps, and into the house, now pooling on their floor.

Had Simodecea stopped to take stock of the gory, blood-soaked woman she had become, she would have seen that she was a bright, glowing red. But instead, she was frantically planning, calculating distances and train fares, their ability to escape the company guards, the Animas sheriff, the hateful lying world in which their lives had been dropped. She turned to her girls, and told them to put on their good shoes. *In Saguarita you have a distant cousin, Angelica Vigil. Say this name, remember how it sounds.* She searched the house for her pistols and a map, marked Saguarita with black ink, and stuffed these things into a kidney-colored satchel, which she draped over Maria Josefina's right shoulder. "Can you carry it?" she asked, and Maria Josefina nodded through her agony.

They set out on foot. It was midday, skies ablaze. Simodecea had changed out of her soiled dress and was now hidden in a pair of Pidre's trousers and an unseasonably warm deerskin jacket. The girls had howled at leaving their father's body on the table, and Simodecea did not scold them or ask them to quiet. She felt release each time they wailed, the duty of motherhood keeping her from revealing her own pain. They walked for several miles through desert and heat until the beginnings of town seemed like an endless dream. Horses and carriages, law offices, and saloons. Simodecea kept her face downcast as she traversed the townscape with her daughters. They had made it, reached the train station's ticket window, but in that long line of people like ants, Simodecea heard the click of a loaded pistol at her back. Before she turned to face her destiny, she leaned forward and gave each of her girls a squeeze of the hand, and from the depths of her soul, Simodecea shouted, "Run."

KILLER MEXICAN WOMAN CAUGHT, MIXED-BREED CHILDREN FLEE

DENVER, COLO., AUGUST 30, 1905. A rumor is circulating among railcar passengers arriving from the southern portion of the state that an armed unknown Mexican woman has been captured after shooting in cold blood two company guards and prominent mining superintendent Henry Sullivan of the Everson Luminous Corporation. There is no indication of motive. Townsfolk are demanding swift retribution against the murderous Mexican. It is said her mixed-breed children may have escaped on foot.

❧

THIRTY

The Split Sisters

The Lost Territory, 1912

Sara and Maria Josefina met several times a week to share a hand-rolled cigarette along the westerly facing adobe wall of Santa Isabel Catholic Church on the corner of Mariposa and First in downtown Saguarita. Despite the irritation of their employers, once the sisters had completed their seemingly endless chores of feeding chickens, corralling meandering cattle, and beating millipedes and scorpions and thick gobs of mosquitoes from the manta techo, the gauzy and filthy veil that hung below the vigas, the girls rushed from their separate households to be with each other as the afternoon bells of that old Spanish mission tolled.

Most of their conversations revolved around observations each sister had made of her employer. Maria Josefina was housed by a land-grant family named Trujillo who had laid claim to the land for nearly 150 years, some distant grandfather, a direct descent of Juan de Oñate. Sara resided in the home of an Anglo family run by a decrepit patriarch named Carson Mears who had made his fortune in the gristmill and sawmill industries of the Lost Territory.

They were young women now, fifteen and fourteen. Sometimes Maria Josefina would inhale the redolent tobacco with a serious face and try to tell Sara of her bad dreams. The images she saw of her father's throat open like a gorge, her mother shackled and dragged away as the girls ran for their lives on that terrible day so many years ago. Whenever Maria Josefina spoke this way, Sara would turn and gaze into that wide and blue sky, the white peaks of the Sangre de Cristo Mountains. "Remember what I said," Sara would tell her little sister. "You have to stop thinking about it." But Sara did not follow her own advice, and since they had been in Saguarita, her own visions and dreams had intensified, coloring her entire existence an overpowering blood-soaked red. In the end, Sara would try almost anything to shut it off.

When they had first arrived by cattle car in Saguarita, the girls had walked to San Isabel Church, where they slept on the wooden floors between the pews and the kneelers. They did not trust anyone, and were fearful of hospitality. On that first night, Sara imagined a great fire overtaking their bodies in the church, the flames scorching the fat-fleshed bottoms of their feet as if they were held to the blaze by demon spirits. She woke screaming, alerting the nearby mayordomo to their existence. He was a kind man named Benjamín Jirón, and he looked upon the small girls as if he'd discovered rare and starved twin rabbits resting in his church. He was beside himself with sorrow as he lifted first Maria Josefina and then Sara, one over each of his shoulders, carting them to the home he shared with his wife, Eulogia, beside the little church. They fed them calabacitas and fresh tortillas and heated acequia water for washing. Sara pleaded to know the whereabouts of Angelica Vigil, that long-lost cousin their mother had so desperately remembered. They eventually discovered that Angelica Vigil had fallen ill several years earlier and gone to live farther south in the valley, but by all accounts, she was certainly deceased by now and had no family left to speak of. Benjamín and Eulogia would have kept the girls, raised them as their own, but they had so little to spare. In the end, the archdiocese offered to find the girls employment within the homes of the few wealthy families of Saguarita, who were always looking for poised domestics. Benjamín sobbed into his large fists as he told the little girls the news—they were to be separated, split sisters between households.

On their last night together in the mayordomo's home, Maria Josefina looked over at her sister from the hay-filled bed on the dirt floor. She clutched a corn-husk doll given to her by Eulogia. "Hermana," she said. "I don't want to be without you. I'm afraid."

Sara slowly swiveled her dark eyes toward Maria Josefina. "I know," she said, trying to sound strong.

"We can run away again. We don't have to be apart."

Sara looked into the room's darkness. A crucifix on the wall appeared to tilt. "We can't," she said. "We are too little to run again."

Several hours later, Sara woke to the sounds of Maria Josefina sobbing in her sleep. Like a dog kicking through her dreams, her arms crawled in the air.

"What is it?" Sara asked breathlessly.

Maria Josefina told her that she had seen their mother standing against a brick wall. There was the crack of gunpowder and her mother quickly turned, facing the firing squad as the bullet entered her skull, tore through her head, driving in from her right temple, erupting like shattered glass behind her eyes. The outside world seeped in, her mind flooding with light.

"Push it away," Sara had said. "When the bad dreams and pictures come up, push them down, as far away as you can."

Maria Josefina was shaking with fear, but she tried as her big sister suggested, placing the dream of her mother in a deep and hidden box within a room of her mind, a place she'd swear never to go.

And in this way the girls began to forget their mother and father.

Sara was the first to hear of the dances. Several of the domestics from other families had been attending them on Friday nights.

"They're coal miners," she told her sister, as they stood outside the church that afternoon, passing between them the last of their cigarette. "Alicia from Antonito says some of these guys have a lot of money to throw around, and some of them she claimed will get rich."

Maria Josefina, who by now went by what her employer called her, *Maria Josie,* stammered as she blew the last of the cigarette smoke from her poised mouth. "And what's it to us?"

"That's how we can leave Saguarita," Sara said imploringly. "Get out of these wretched houses, these horrible chores for no pay and nothing but moldy beds and stale tortillas."

Maria Josie scrunched her face with what Sara suspected was skepticism. Above them, the sun was a thick sphere of heat in the last days of summer—the air smelled of roasting corn and the wetness of hay.

"Suit yourself, hermana," Sara said, peering into the mountains. "But I'm getting out."

They went together the following Friday. Maria Josie agreed reluctantly. Each sister crept from her back-house bedroom and sprinted across pastures of moonlit grass, the dirt soggy beneath their feet. The night shined silver on their black hair and the cows mooed bombastically as the girls rushed to the glowing cinderblock dance hall on the edge of town. The gray structure was illuminated in an empty field—gated by red willows and a burned-out barn. The music could be heard from several yards away, something stringed and bouncing, buried lyrics of French or perhaps something else. Sara was never too sure when it wasn't English or Spanish or Tiwa, the languages of her childhood, the sounds of her parents.

There were far more men in the concrete dance hall than neither Sara nor Maria Josie were used to being around at once. Their gamy and smoky stench rose from thick-shouldered bodies in faded denim and leather suspenders and earth-worn hats. These men of varying heights and weights, facial features, some bearded and some not, they swarmed the rectangular building with an elevated stage, sidelong mantels, and an overhanging white scaffolding. The pine floor vibrated with the stomps and twists of dancing men, those few women from Saguarita and the nearby villages moist-faced with perspiration, the air humid with human sweat and fogged breath. The band rumbled onstage, music heavy with mandolin and fiddle. Sara laughed at the giddiness of their world.

They hadn't been there fifteen minutes when several of the men approached the sisters. Sara welcomed their attention while Maria Josie brushed them away. These men were Mexican and Welsh, Irish and Black American, Austrian and German, Polish and Belgian and more. They approached the sisters speaking accented English or Spanish and complimented them with alcohol-laden whispers, how pretty their skin and eyes, their mixed-breed features, their abundant curves. At this Sara grimaced, but one of the miners, a man named Benny, told her the others meant no harm.

He asked Sara if she'd like a drink of his cup. At first, she shook her head and remembered that her mother had once told them that they ought never drink liquor. *Your ancestors were not built for alcohol. It will poison your body and ruin your minds.* But as Sara recalled her mother's warning, she turned her nose up and pushed the memory away. She told Benny, *Why, sure, I'd love a sip.*

One drink turned into three or four and then it was five or six, and Sara drank like she'd never thirsted so deeply in her life. The more she drank, the more her body felt lithe, lifted from the pine floor. She laughed and felt beautiful and gazed past Maria Josie, who looked on with terror in her wide brown eyes. As the dance hall thrummed with exuberance, Sara wondered how she could have gone so many years without this liquid that spilled down her throat. Benny then picked up Sara like she was nothing more than a rag doll and placed her along the mantel, seating her upon a throne. She giggled and shocked Maria Josie as she leaned into that Belgian man for a kiss again and again.

As they walked home late that night, Sara felt the world falling away, piece by piece, rock by rock, mountain by mountain. She felt cleared of the responsibility of grief—only laughed and smirked, telling Maria Josie in high hiccupping sounds how wonderful this man's mouth was, the bulges of his veins along his hands and fore-arms, the way he danced her into the night and did not turn away as she removed her shoes, barefoot with dirty soles on that pine floor.

"I don't like this," Maria Josie said, as she delivered her sister to her back-house door. "You're not being yourself. It's like someone else is inside of you."

Sara could not see straight and for a moment she imagined Maria Josie was two women, as if her sister carried within her the light of someone else. "You just hate men, don't you?" She fell then, slamming her hands into the dirt outside her door, ripping a fingernail from her left hand. She was too drunk to feel the pain, and she marveled at this with delight.

"Those men will only take advantage of you," Maria Josie said.

"What're you gonna do?" Sara slurred. "Live alone in a back-house your whole life?"

"I'm going to do great things," Maria Josie cried. "I am, and you can, too."

But it was no use. Sara had stopped listening, felt herself falling asleep where she stood.

It was two months later when Sara told Maria Josie the news. She was moving with Benny north—the coal mines he had been working outside of Saguarita had run dry.

"He's needed in Huerfano," Sara said with a practiced expressionless voice.

"He's needed nowhere," said Maria Josie.

It would be several years before Maria Josie left Saguarita herself, several years before she would learn that Sara had given birth to two of Benny's children, a little boy named Diego and a precocious little girl named Luz.

THIRTY-ONE

An Animal Named Night

The Lost Territory, 1922

M aria Josie noticed the white automobile as she marched forward in a floppy hat and a flowered cotton dress. The car peeked over a faraway hill and for a long time seemed stationary on the red ridge. She walked a dirt road walled in evergreen and blue spruce. Smoke Rock stuck out like a skeletal thumb against her right-side mountains. The springtime air was cluttered with pollen and the sting of new snow. Maria Josie had started the night before, and now it was dusk. Her shoulders ached from trading her satchel's thick strap from one side of her body to the other. Her feet were wet with blisters and her wool socks were stained with pus. Her womb was sore, of course, and she bled like it was her period, though it hadn't come for almost eight months. Maria Josie listened to her heartbeat like a muffled ceremony drum, the dull implosion inside her chest keeping time along with the sun and very soon the stars.

Along the way, Maria Josie had passed several ranches with resting farm trucks and curlicue iron fences. She had walked

slower than she anticipated, or the distance was farther than predicted. She had taken few breaks, changed her soiled rags in the
woods, drank from small streams. In the beginning, she imagined
she'd only have to walk a short way before an old man farmer
would stop his truck, pile her into the back with the chickens and
hay, and transport Maria Josie on a bed of blankets all the way to
the city. Away from Saguarita. The baby she had been forced to
bury beside the river. The man who never loved her. The loss of her
father and mother and sister, all that tied her family like a rope.
But that old man farmer never came, and now it was almost full
dark. The temperature dropping.

The white automobile inched along, until it accelerated in her
direction. A car like this was exquisite, out of place, a Pierce-
Arrow, they were called. Maria Josie had seen them in magazines
at the general store on Mariposa Street. The coffin-shaped hood
curled with golden headlights. *Just my luck,* Maria Josie said, and
stepped into the road, praying for the car to stop. When it did, the
driver didn't roll down the window, but fully swung open the door.
A white woman with deer-brown hair. She looked like a doll in a
sailor's dress with red lips and white teeth. She wore a bonnet, and
she glanced at Maria Josie's middle section for longer than was
polite.

"Are you headed somewhere nearby?"

Maria Josie didn't know any women who drove, and besides
that, the people of Saguarita still rode wagons pulled by tired
mules. "I'm headed to Denver, señora."

The woman laughed, and even through twilight, lipstick was
visibly smeared over her teeth. "You're not getting to Denver tonight, or tomorrow night, or probably the night after that. Not
walking at least."

"Figured I'd get a ride from someone going that way."

"Haven't run into any?"

Maria Josie pushed her hat higher on her head and turned her shoulder to the rising moon. She noted that the woman spoke with a strange and quick cadence. Her clothes were finer versions of the dresses modeled in *The Saturday Evening Post.* "Time has gotten away from me."

"Haven't you got a family?"

"No."

"A husband, anyone?"

"Pardon me. I need to keep walking."

"You're liable to be killed by a bear out here. Why don't we give you a lift?"

Maria Josie was startled to see a narrow black German shepherd sitting tall in the back seat. "Is your dog nice?"

"Nice enough."

They drove in silence for several miles, leaning into the road's forested walls. There were the engine's breathing sounds, and the black dog panting behind Maria Josie's neck. The woman seemed preoccupied, asking few questions. She looked small behind the steering wheel, and her eyes focused on every stray animal streaking silver across the road. Smart. She was a smart woman. She said her name was Millicent. Her husband was away with their son on a hunting trip and did she ever feel more free? No. She did not. "You're an Indian, correct?"

"My father was," said Maria Josie.

Millicent shifted in her seat. She gripped the steering wheel tighter. "I'm somewhat of a collector. I have several pieces from this area. Hopi?"

Maria Josie told her no. She peered out the window.

"I'm going to my father's ranch. You can stay with me tonight. There's plenty of room."

Maria Josie thanked Millicent for her kindness, but said that she'd hate to put her and her father out.

"He won't be there. It'll just be you, me, and Noche." She said this without gesturing toward the dog. It was understood she had an animal named night.

Millicent turned down a dirt road that was almost invisible in the dark. She drove for several minutes, the car hopping over gravel, the sounds of spitting rocks whipping the bottom of the Pierce-Arrow like hail in reverse. There was no fancy iron gate to welcome them to the ranch. The wooden home stood in the dark with a single light glowing from a window. It was enormous and appeared vacant. Millicent stopped the car in a paved lot.

"Is this a cattle ranch?" asked Maria Josie.

"My father is in the oil business. This is more of a vacation home than a ranch."

"My father was in the theater business," said Maria Josie, with a certain amount of bite.

"I thought you didn't have a family." Millicent laughed. She whistled for Noche as she stepped out of the car. "Come on, Maria Josefina, you'll catch cold."

The home was a cavernous space with levels and staircases and echoes of emptiness. Noche trailed Millicent as she walked a hallway in her high-heeled shoes, lighting the lamps and opening doors. At each stop, the house revealed itself to be more grand. Maria Josie now understood what she meant by *collector*. There were Diné squash blossom necklaces in glass cases, Zuni pottery on high shelves, beaded Ute wedding dresses pinned to the walls as if an invisible and crucified bride watched them as they walked. Where did it all come from? Were the makers all dead? Maria

Josie moved toward a mask of the Talking God. The mask was larger than half her torso and hawk feathers poked down a long trail from the skull, while the eyes were black slits in a square leather face. Turquoise dripped from the side panels, and the center, where humans have their mouths, was a familiar circular hole. The rabbit fur was tattered, and the spruce branches lining the neck were disintegrated.

"It's one of my father's favorites. Navajo, I believe."

"Pretty." She didn't tell Millicent that masks are their own spirit. She wondered if it had been fed recently, or if it was angry or sad. When she was a child, there was a hoop dancer in her father's show who kept a mask. He fed it cornmeal, cared for the spirit as if it were alive.

Millicent had started a fire in the main room. Noche stood beside her like a statue come to life. Through the massive windows, the sky was a dazzling lid, turned and tightened above them. The rocks and pines were moon blanched. There were dark pillars of smoke across the mountainside. *Someday, and someday soon,* Maria Josie thought, *these sights will be gone from my life.* Millicent stood at a cart with glasses and crystal bottles. She poured something brown and offered it to Maria Josie. They were both young, though Millicent was maybe a decade older. She had crow's-feet around each eye.

Maria Josie said, "Señora, I'm very tired. Could I have some water?"

"For heaven's sake. How rude of me. You must have walked all day." She snapped her fingers, leading Maria Josie into the washroom. "I'll heat water for a bath and fix you some tea."

It wasn't long after Maria Josie began to bathe herself that she felt like weeping into the reddish water. She couldn't go back now. She had made her choice. It struck her then that this night was the beginning of her new life, one without anyone else. She worked the sides of her belly with Ivory soap. She listened to the dings and tics of the house sighing beneath the water. When she sat up again, Millicent and Noche stood in the doorway, a cold breeze pushing into the washroom. She held a towel. "You're not carrying anymore, are you?"

Maria Josie dropped her hands from her breasts to her belly.

"The father?"

Maria Josie watched the black dog, how its tail coiled like a snail's shell. "Hauenstein. He's a German man, a doctor."

"These things can be so complicated." Millicent then did something peculiar. She leaned over the tub, wrapped Maria Josie in the towel, and kissed her hair.

Before dawn, Maria Josie dressed herself in a change of clothes she carried in her satchel and walked several miles in the dark. As she approached the main road, the sky purple with dawn, a brown pickup truck slowed its crawl over the mountains. A white-haired farmer carrying a load of chickens said in Spanish, "Where to?"

"Denver," said Maria Josie, and hobbled into the truck bed, where she found a pile of wool blankets surrounded by feathers.

THIRTY-TWO

To the Wedding

Denver, 1934

On the Sunday afternoon of Lizette's wedding, Luz sat with her in the stone-walled bridal chamber of Saint Cajetan's Catholic Parish and watched as her cousin stepped into her gown as if dropped into a pail of cream. Teresita was there, too, a relative's baby affixed to her hip in her mother-of-the-bride silver gown. Maria Josie stood nearby dressed in her finest pin-striped suit, a red rose clipped to her hair. Girl cousins in lilac dresses moved in and out of the chamber, women convening in an underground tunnel.

There was a knock on the door, and Lizette turned in her billowing dress. "Who is it?"

"Your papa," said Eduardo, croaking as if he were choking on tears. "I've brought a visitor."

"It better not be Al," said Lizette. "He ain't allowed to see me till the big show."

"Pete's come to offer his well-wishes, mija."

Lizette motioned for her mother to open the door.

Eduardo stood there teary-eyed.

"So emotional," Teresita said to her husband, ushering him inside. "Come on, you still have to walk her down the aisle."

Papa Tikas trailed Eduardo into the chambers. He wore a white tuxedo and smiled under his mustache as he carried an enormous bouquet of peonies, roses, and carnations. It must have cost a fortune.

"My my," said Lizette. "Christmas came early—thank you, Papa Tikas."

"What a beautiful bride you make," he said, handing the flowers to Teresita, who placed them on a side table. The petals absorbed light, as if competing with Lizette to be the center of attention.

"Lizette," said Papa Tikas, taking her hands in his. "You've grown into the most exquisite woman. Our community is proud. And I wasn't always so sure that'd be the case."

She opened her mouth in mock anger.

"And, Luz," said Papa Tikas, glancing her way, "how lovely you are, as well. I can't stay long, and I'll miss the party, but here—" He pulled from his coat pocket a white envelope, handing it to Lizette. "That should cover all of the meats. My treat for my beautiful girls."

"Wow," Lizette said. "Thank you so much, Papa Tikas." She handed her mother the envelope and Teresita tucked it safely into her handbag. Papa Tikas leaned over and kissed Lizette on the cheek. She studied him for a short while. "I wouldn't say *your* girls," she said playfully, and then with some measure of thought: "I'm Alfonso's now. But really," she said, eyeing herself in the chamber mirror, "I'm no one's. I am my own."

The men laughed, and Eduardo edged Papa Tikas toward the door. Before they left the chamber, Lizette's father turned around. "You belong to me and your mama. You'll always be ours, mija."

Luz smiled. She admired the closeness of family, how deeply they loved.

After the men had left, Lizette fanned her face with a printed homily, groaning about the heat causing her eye makeup to run. Luz laughed, imagining Lizette with smeared mascara looking like some enchanted clown. She stood, adjusting her underpants beneath her bridesmaid's dress, then the lace collar covering her shoulders and chest, and finally the small bonnet affixed to her hair. She glanced at herself in the solemn mirror hanging in the corner.

"Someone get water in here, will ya?" Lizette rattled the homily in her hands. "This heat!" She lifted her arm, revealing sweat marks, and made a face.

"Right away," Luz said, dutifully. All morning she had run errands for Lizette, waking up at four-thirty to prepare the pig for roasting. She had decorated the Fox Street home with a cedar arch, red and gold ribbons, white streamers like fringe. She had checked with Avel that his mariachi band could play well into the night. She had organized the younger cousins in teams, assigning tasks, finding chairs, filling jars with walnuts, stuffing paper bags with tea candles. The next morning, she was expected to return to the Fox Street home by eight o'clock to help tear down party decorations, but David had said he needed her in the office first thing. Lizette was irritated by this, and if there was one thing Luz knew that her cousin wanted to get right, it was her wedding.

Luz walked the innards of the church, past the old library, near the children's room, beneath an archway of roses dedicated to La Virgen. When she finally arrived in the church's kitchen, she

filled a tin pitcher with water from the rusty pipes and made her
way through the lobby toward the stairwell. She stopped in the
doorway of the sanctuary, peering at the few seats already taken
by elderly relatives. The altar was set with lilies and lavender
drapes, reminding Luz of Easter Mass. Incense curled in the air
and somewhere, from a distant pew, a wet cough echoed over
wooden floors. Avel was also seated, his hair obediently parted to
one side. At the sight of him, Luz felt happiness, a kind of ease.
He turned then, and the lovers shared a look of admiration. Luz
stuck her left hand into the holy water beside the door and
blessed herself.

"Wow. You look . . . very covered." It was David. He grinned
and held his hat in his hands, dressed finely in a black suit, his
cologne mixing with the musk of his skin.

Luz smiled. "It's the rules, David. You should be used to that, at
your churches."

"If it wasn't an ordinance of God, I might think that someone
was afraid you'd overshadow them."

Luz held up the pitcher. "I'm on way to deliver water. Do you
need help finding your seats? I assume your date hasn't arrived
yet."

David was quiet for a beat. He licked the edge of his right
thumb as if about to turn the page of a book. "Going stag for this
one. Most beautiful girls in town are already here."

"Oh," said Luz. "Well, please excuse me. Today, I am a servant
of the bride."

Lizette stood in the hallway outside the chamber with several
cousins fanning her while Teresita and Maria Josie adjusted her
veil.

"Where," Lizette said to Luz, "were you?"

Luz held up the pitcher and was quickly dismissed.

Teresita let out a yelp. "You have to stand still," she said to Lizette. "One of your pins got me."

The women affixed the mantilla to Lizette's hair, Maria Josie patting her head a little too hard as some kind of joke. What a sight she was. Lizette inhaled, her wedding gown tightening across her chest. She was beautiful, her hair and makeup impeccable, the scent of jasmine drifting from her body. She was joyous—it spilled from her eyes, her smile, her touch on the back of Luz's hand. The cousins and aunties had gathered around her, as if Lizette were now a mother hen, leading her own flock. One of the madrinas appeared in the hallway, letting the bridal party know it was time to enter the church.

They marched into the sanctuary in pairs. Luz scanned the craned-necked crowd of Westside Mexicanos and Park Lane Filipinos and some Greeks and a few Italians and a full pew of Natalya's family—how they all whispered and aahed at the sight of the wedding party. The men were dressed in gossamer barongs that Alfonso had special-ordered from California, the women were brilliant in lilac sheaths. Luz had linked arms with the best man, a cousin of Alfonso's named Remilio from San Francisco. He had a skimpy mustache over shapely lips, a perpetual smile across his fetching face. As she walked the aisle to the altar, Luz remembered flashes of her childhood—she and Lizette dressed in pillowcases and sheets, young girls in the backyard beneath a peach tree, mimicking a groom's kiss on their small hands. Now Lizette was a real bride, her father's property to give away. Luz stood with the wedding party, gazing down the long aisle, awaiting her cousin.

Eduardo appeared first and the entire church seemed to watch as one penetrating eye. Then it was Lizette, her face hidden beneath the intricacies of her mantilla, lace dotting her vision, as if she had been fished from the Platte River and placed in a net. Luz stared at her cousin with wonderment. Was she prepared for what was to come? Were she and Alfonso to live in happiness? Would their friendship diminish? But in some horrible way, Luz knew that it already had. Their lives were diverging.

Lizette stepped forward over waxed floors, prismatic sunlight filtered through a stained glass crucifixion. She seemed to drift rather than walk, as if carried by the invisibility of fate. The crowd gasped in delight. But a peculiar thing happened midway to the altar. Lizette's veil slipped from her head and rode the length of her curled black hair before falling to the ground. The edge of the mantilla was stuck in the door, and several back-pew guests stood in an instant, attempting to free the flimsy fabric from the clutches of the lock. It was no use, as if someone had tied it there in impossible knots. When Lizette reached the altar, she winked at Luz with a snicker.

That's my cousin, Luz thought with pride.

They went through the motions of mass, standing and kneeling and standing some more. The priest was a young bald man who had recently left a post at a mission church in the Lost Territory. He spoke of God's dominion over the universe, the animals, the rivers, the mountains and lakes. He explained that Lizette and Alfonso were coming together in Christ through the act of his death. And as he spoke, Luz tried not to focus on the pain from her heels and instead stared into the pews, briefly watching Avel as he prayed. But Luz was startled. There, beneath the seventh Station of the Cross, Jesus Falls for the Second Time, Luz imagined she saw Diego. She steadied herself and looked again. Her brother was gone.

"What God joins together," the priest finally said, "let no one pull apart."

Alfonso and Lizette exchanged rings and then kissed for several heartbeats, their throats pulsing with the movements of their tongues. They soon rushed into the optimistic sunlight of day as their loved ones showered them in rice, hard kernels pelting them in white.

At dusk the wedding party snaked to the Fox Street home, following the path of paper lanterns through the backyard. The grass was textured blue, the sky a whisper of day. Alfonso and Lizette entered the celebration, blushing as the crowd cheered them over to the head table. Luz was seated to the right of Lizette, high on a makeshift stage. The yard was set with round tables covered in white cloths, unmarked bottles of tequila near pine-cone centerpieces. In time, the backyard warmed with dancing bodies, the humidity of human existence.

Cousins of cousins had arrived from as far away as Alamosa to cook the marital meal, a roast pig, heaping piles of calabacitas, loads of thick tortillas, beans and tamales, and Filipino dishes, too—chicken adobo, pancit and lumpia, and leche flan. The guests lined up for dinner while Luz and the rest of the wedding party obediently stayed in their seats. They were to greet the guests who approached Lizette and Alfonso at the high table as if paying homage to a new king and queen.

Lizette was extravagant beside Luz, leaning across the table, her smile and arms and breasts abundant against her visitors as she embraced them with enthusiastic *Thank you*s and *I hope you enjoy yourselves*. Alfonso shared in his bride's excitement, lounging in his chair, relishing the sight. After the guests greeted the married couple, they parted like a sea.

There were speeches and applause, laughter and tears. The sun set behind the mountains, spilling golden rays across the yard's white streamers, as if the world was streaked in paint. The mood shifted from boisterous dinner conversation to a deeper, sensuous feeling that Luz somehow attributed to nostalgia, some sadness for an earlier time. She excused herself from the table, and walked toward the bathroom. She was stopped by several guests before she could slide through the back door and into the crowded kitchen, the dominion of older aunts. It was heavy with food smoke, the smells of pork and cinnamon, sweet cream and coconut. Luz was annoyed upon finding a line to the upstairs toilet, which contorted down the stairs and around the hallway like an eel. She sighed and had prepared herself for the wait when she felt a tug on her left wrist. It was Avel, pulling her into the laundry closet underneath the staircase.

Luz laughed in the dark and Avel moved his fingers through her hair, along her lips. "Hi, baby," he said.

And, quietly, Luz said, "Hello."

"I've been dying to be near you all night," Avel whispered.

"Me too," said Luz. "The bride's working me to the bone."

There were the sounds of Avel fumbling, searching for the light's dangling cord, but he gave up and swatted toward Luz's face. They fell into each other, kissing in the darkness. "I can't wait until our day, our wedding," he said between kisses.

Luz pressed her face into the nook between Avel's chin and chest. She listened to his heartbeat through his bolero jacket, beneath his silver bolo tie, the muted sounds of the party on the other end of the door like far-off echoes in a cave. She elevated herself on tippy toes and moved her lips toward Avel's mouth.

Then the laundry closet flooded with light.

Lizette stood before them in her wedding dress, hands on her hips, a look of angry amusement across her married face. She opened her mouth and licked her lips. "Okay, lovebirds," she said. "We need Avel for the money dance. You're keeping me from my bucks."

Luz and Avel fixed their clothes, wiped their mouths. He waited as she finally got a chance to use the upstairs bathroom and then they headed outside into the party, giggling with bowed heads.

By now, night had fallen.

The backyard was a vision of lanterns and electric lights strung between the peach tree and slender aspens. A wooden dance floor had been unfolded across the coarse grass. Luz hurriedly took her seat as Avel and his band ascended the stage. They cleared spit from their horns, plucked strings for tuning. The night sky was a backdrop of stars, erupting in mariachi. Lizette and Alfonso danced as guests showered them in coins and bills, the flicker of silver dollars careening across their arms, pelting their skin and hair at an alarming rate. Luz watched Avel onstage with a kind of gracious respect. She imagined their own wedding, but despite how hard she searched within herself for pictures of their life, Luz arrived at nothing, an ending path.

"I need to talk to you." It was Maria Josie, standing behind Luz.

"If it's about the laundry closet, I didn't mean anything by it. He just pulled me in."

"I heard from Teresita that you and Avel are planning to be wed." Maria Josie reached for Luz's hand and asked where exactly had she kept the ring.

"I was going to tell you," Luz said, sheepishly, revealing the ring on a fake gold chain about her neck. "We both were."

"But you didn't," said Maria Josie, her eyes defiant in their judgment.

Luz went to say more but as she spoke the sounds of her voice etched into her own ears, a static thrust like a crackling radio. She shook her head. She stood from her chair. Eye level now, she peered into Maria Josie's face. Her auntie was older than she'd ever been, but with rich skin, darkened eyes, pupils like comets.

"I don't want to hear nothing about it," Luz said in anger. "What am I going to do with you my whole life? Live in Hornet Moon, beg for heat and full meals?"

Maria Josie's eyes widened. She looked upon her niece with an expression that Luz knew was the ugliness of pity. A wind gust carried over from the roadside, flung gravel into the air. The lights and paper lanterns shivered and the trees jittered, as if afraid. Avel's music blared onstage. The dancing continued.

Maria Josie spoke through contorted lips. "You have no idea what kinds of sacrifices I've made for you and your brother. What I've done in order to be here for you, and still, there is a reason you didn't tell me, Little Light."

"You weren't here for Diego," said Luz. "You sent him off like a stray dog."

Maria Josie blinked. Luz thought she could hear her auntie's eye ducts pressurize with tears. "I will not explain myself."

"Neither will I," said Luz, and sat down, turning her back to her auntie, who staggered away with the heaviness of an injured hawk.

What does she know? Luz thought. *Nothing.* But the moment she thought this, she felt ashamed.

Lizette and Alfonso had finished the dance and collected their loot in a wicker basket, stepping away from the dance floor as the band moved into a waltz. Remilio stepped before Luz. He was handsome, and while Luz was seated he was taller, towering over her with an outstretched hand.

"Your fiancé asked that I dance with you. Shouldn't have you sitting here all alone."

Luz looked at Avel, who watched them intently as he blew into his trumpet. When his part came to a rest, he placed the horn at his side, giving them each a smile and a wave.

"Sure," said Luz, standing from her seat. "I'd love to."

The dance floor was crowded by guests with a drunken sheen. There was laughter and conversation beneath the music and children darting between couples, chasing one another with white-gloved hands. Remilio was a sophisticated dancer, holding the line of his shoulders and swaying Luz delicately from side to side, her lilac dress blooming above her feet. She focused on the beat, the music vibrating throughout her ankles and heels. As they twirled beneath twinkling lights, onstage Avel breathed into his horn, and in the distance, far above the city, the moon was nearly full, cloaked in hazy clouds. When the song crashed to a close, Remilio kissed Luz's cheek, thanking her for the company. In the shuffle of bodies ushering away from the dance floor, Luz felt a tug on the backside of her dress, then her hand in another's.

It was David, pulling Luz across the party, as if running in the rain for cover.

"Where are we going?" Luz asked, breathless.

David shushed her as he guided them into the house, through the back door, and into the laundry closet, the same room where Luz and Avel had just been. Luz felt a strange sensation, obvious déjà vu, but something more, a vision of herself and David from above, recognition of an event before the final act.

"What is it, David?" Luz whispered.

David didn't search for the drawstring light. He kept their bodies slightly apart, his breath warm on Luz's face. A faucet dripped behind them. The voices of partygoers growled on the other side of the door. David's smell was thick, sweet, soil and oranges. Something good.

"I want to know more," David said low. "About what you saw at the Brown Palace."

Luz could feel her own breathing surge, her heartbeat in her fingertips and neck. "Right now? I'm supposed to be outside with the guests."

"No one will notice. Promise."

"David . . ." Luz said in a honeyed way.

She turned to leave, moving toward the door, but was drawn back by both wrists. David had pushed Luz to the wall, where he kissed her on the mouth. Luz was surprised at the fervor with which she moved her tongue inside his lips. He tasted of salt and faintly of liquor. He pulled the light string, and the room came alive with white walls and a washbasin, cabinetry, rows of folded towels. They stared at each other, as if understanding for the first time a message written between them. David kissed her again and Luz saw that his mouth had become swollen with wear. She was surprised at her focus, her hunger, as if she were gorging herself on some part of David that existed where only she could go. Luz didn't have normal control of her thoughts—her body and her mind had become want.

Though Luz was nervous, afraid of the parts of David she'd never seen, the places no one else had felt on her own body, she gripped his hands and guided them beneath her bridesmaid dress and cried out, softly, into the scoop of his ear. When she moved her face away and their eyes met, Luz made a choice. She wanted David. She wanted him more than anything.

"I want to be with you," she said.

David picked her up with both hands, resting her small body on the edge of the sink. He unzipped her lilac dress, revealing her warm breasts, gripping them firmly. David lifted Luz and held her body against his, wrapping her legs around his torso until she felt him moving aside the folds of her dress and the thin fabric of her underclothes, guiding himself inside her body, entering her with a deep and fulfilling pain.

"I'm in love with you," Luz said through staccato breaths, trying to make herself believe so.

David reached up from her hips and with his left hand, shoved his damp fingers into Luz's mouth, keeping them steady, telling her to bite down, and Luz did, worried the entire time this is how it all worked.

And then the door was kicked in and this time it wasn't Lizette. Avel stood before them and the room filled with shock, as if the walls wanted to gag, expelling what was inside. Luz froze in horror, then dropped her legs from their position around David. Avel's eyes moved to her breasts and Luz was ashamed, for he hadn't seen her nakedness before. She pulled her gown upward as David adjusted himself and reached for his waistband. He kept his eyes low, not sharing a single glance with Luz.

"Avel," Luz said, slinking off the metal sink.

David straightened his tie with deft hands. He reached for a folded towel from the rack above Luz. He wiped his hands on it and flung the white cloth over his shoulder. Without acknowledging Avel or Luz, David twisted around, moving through the doorway, walking out to the party, as if he had only been in the laundry closet cleaning up a spill.

Luz looked to Avel. She fixed her hair, holding her hands over her face. Through clenched teeth, she cried out, "Forgive me."

Avel shook his head with a sadness so thick it felt like a wall. He reached for Luz's throat and, with a gentle tug, snapped the golden chain around her neck, placing the engagement ring securely in his breast pocket. He said, "I really loved you." He then left, darting into the party, his shoulders low.

Luz cried in small, climbing moans. But she soon heaved tears so uncontrollably that she wasn't sure how a soul could feel such humiliation, such loss, all this pain wrapped together in one. She sobbed then, thinking of Diego, her father, every man who had ever hurt her. Someone must have called Lizette to the house, because she soon arrived at the laundry closet and screamed in terror at the sight of her disheveled cousin, weeping against the sink.

"What has happened? Who has done this to you?"

Lizette's shrieks rose around them like a shelter, and Luz imagined the sounds of the cousins drifting high into the night sky, an eye looking down at the party on Fox Street, all the sparkling lights and dancing bodies, the children rushing from room to room, the steel pots steaming on the stove, the house a theater of life.

"Luz," Lizette pleaded. "Who did this to you? Tell me."

But all Luz could do was weep, shaking her head a violent no. "It was only me," she cried. "There's no one else. It was just me."

THIRTY-THREE

El Mariachi

Avel stood across the street from the Law Office of David Tikas with a cigarette in his lips, the lighter clinking in his left hand and his gaze locked on that defiant-looking building. He thought of the first time he had laid eyes on Luz Lopez, before he knew her name, how she ran down Colfax Avenue with a red wagon filled with laundry sacks, the stone buildings closing around her like a tomb. Her eyes were feral but she carried herself with the same elegance as a wolf. She looked bright, like a girl who joked. Later, huddled outside, stealing swigs from a basement bottle of mezcal in broad daylight, Avel had stood with his new neighbor, a man named Santiago, who played mandolin. Avel swallowed three long pulls of Santi's mezcal and said, *I just saw this broad on a job. I've seen her before, out on the street. I'd like to know her.* Santi had wagged his left leg, laughed. *Have her fall right into your lap, if you know what I mean.* Avel shook his head. *Not this one,* he'd said. *She reminds me of them church girls, the ones from back home.* Santi had tossed the empty bottle into the street and it shattered. *Those girls,* he explained, *don't exist.*

Avel stood outside the law office and cursed the now starless sky. A dry wind blew from the east and ruffled the few high birch trees along Seventeenth Street. It was late now, and the city was silent. No traffic whined in the distance, no horns honked, no streetcars rattled. Avel pulled Luz's office key from his pocket. She always kept it in the same spot, affixed to the metal ring with her keys to Hornet Moon.

He entered the office slowly. He considered Luz's empty chair, the magnitude of her desk, the walls aching with their own kind of sadness. He hated to think of her in that chair being watched through the windows. The office sighed in its own blank darkness and, though not a soul was present, Avel could feel the echo of Luz's movements through the space—her repetitive walk from the desk to the filing cabinet, her bending and turning her neck, the clink of her key in the door, and every single time she was summoned to his office, where she stood dutifully before David's desk, asking in her sweet and devoted tone what it was he needed.

"That's enough of that," Avel said aloud. He forced his elbow through the plate glass between David's office and Luz's lobby. The crash matched the intensity of pain surging through Avel's arm, and oddly in his chest. Blood appeared on his sleeve, blooming over his shirt cuff. He stepped into David's office. He knocked furniture to the ground—the cabinets, their files, all the work Luz had done to order and preserve, now scattered about the floor. The bulletin board behind David's desk caught Avel's attention and he stepped closer, flicking his lighter to examine the webbed display of photographs, newspaper articles, and maps. Pinned nonchalantly among the scraps of information was an article from the

Rocky Mountain News, YOUNG DENVER ATTORNEY MAKES A NAME, SEEKS JUSTICE.

Avel flicked his lighter near the article's bottom edge, watched the flame swallow the yellow page. He then took the lighter to several maps, and moved on to the photographs, which burned in a curdling, wax-like way. The entire bulletin board went up in flames. Avel used the lighter on the files next, then the wastebaskets, bookshelves. What at first happened slowly then happened all at once. The curtains burned. Black smoke billowed and collected, eclipsing the already darkened tin ceiling. The walls showed the skeletal lines of the underlying lath. Avel coughed and squinted through smoke, his body covered in sweat. Heat pressed upon his back, pushing him outward as he turned around and stepped through the ghost of Luz's path, exiting the Law Office of David Tikas as it burned on that summer night, so near to the full moon.

THIRTY-FOUR

Portal

Denver, 1926

Papa Tikas had thrown David's twentieth birthday party in a friend's vacant house. The celebration had gone into the night. The home was three stories, and there were statues of lions all around the perimeter. It was lighted with lampposts, and the summer night was comfortably warm. Luz and Lizette were playing with chalk outside beside a stone carport with a great wooden door. Luz called it the Magic Arch. Her mother used to talk about sacred archways in the Lost Territory, a portal that could carry her from one world to another.

"We'll draw the hopscotch squares into the Magic Arch," Lizette said. "That way, you only win if you make it back out."

They had just one piece of chalk between them, and it wasn't even sidewalk chalk. Lizette and Luz had stopped Eduardo in the billiards room, and lingered before him as men smoked cigars and swilled tumblers of mezcal and whiskey. While the men talked, Lizette swiped the blue cue chalk from a mantel. Her father had caught her. He chuckled and said she was an ornery little cat, but he also said she had hung the moon and stars.

Whenever Papa Tikas threw one of his parties, the grown-ups drank like they'd never tasted anything so sweet. They danced and played pool, hardly noticing the mischief of their children.

"What're you girls doing?" It was David, who had exited the Victorian house through the deliveries door. He stepped down from the rock porch and walked toward Lizette and Luz with his summer jacket flung over his shoulder. David was a decade older than the girls—Luz and Lizette were both ten years old. He was smoking a cigarette and hovered over them as they drew numbers across the pavement. They had barely made it under the Magic Arch and were still mostly along the sidewalk.

"Nothing," said Lizette, hiding the blue chalk behind her back.

"I already saw it. Just don't let anyone else catch you out here." David inhaled his cigarette. He sighed, as if exhausted by his own party. Luz didn't see him often. He was usually away at school, and whenever he was home in Denver, he worked in the market with a surly attitude. Luz had heard him arguing once with his father. He said he didn't want to return to Colorado after his schooling. He wanted to stay in New York. *But your family is here*, Papa Tikas had said. *Don't be so selfish, David.*

"Happy birthday, David," said Luz, smiling but looking down.

David thanked her and winked. He kneeled where she was seated on the pavement. He pointed to the number Luz had just drawn. There was blue chalk on her green dress. She had a matching bow in her hair. Diego had helped her tie it before they left the apartment.

"What's this supposed to be?" David said.

Luz didn't know if he was teasing her. "You can't tell?"

"I mean, it sort of looks like a sickly four." He cocked his head. "I don't know, Lucy Luz. Your numbers might need some work."

She felt embarrassed, and her face reddened. She examined her number, trying to understand what was wrong.

"Come on," said Lizette. "It's a nine, David. So, you gonna play hopscotch with us or what?"

David laughed at Lizette. "Since when do you have so much attitude?"

Lizette stuck out her tongue.

"All right," David said after a pause. "I'll play." He sprang up and checked around the ground. "We need something to throw— what do they call it?"

"A shooter," said Luz.

"That's it," David said, and lifted a bottle cap from the ground.

"You go first," said Lizette, who seemed bored with the entire thing.

David had put out his cigarette in a sandy pit at the side door. He stepped beside Luz and tossed his shooter. It landed far beyond the first square.

Lizette said, "That's not even how you play."

At that moment, the carport's magnificent door swung open and out came Papa Tikas and his younger brother Dominic, ushering an Anglo girl with flapper hair into the underside of the Magic Arch. She had an angry-narrow expression and her stance was wobbly. Papa Tikas was placing her summer shawl over her shoulders and sliding the gold chain of her purse onto her skinny arm. He was piling her things upon her as if she were a cart he was pushing into the alley, something you'd see beside a sign labeled FREE.

"What did I tell you?" he said. "You were not to come here."

They overheard Dominic say something in Greek before placing his hands around the girl's wrists and yanking her away from the house, as if she were nothing more than a doll in a box. She was crying now, her bottom lip drooping.

"You can't even face me?" she cried, but Dominic struck her in the face with his open palm, and she turned around abruptly as a black Ford drove under the Magic Arch.

Papa Tikas opened the car's passenger door, and before the young girl ducked inside, he handed her a fistful of dollars.

Dominic scoffed. The girl leaned forward and, with a great whimper, told Papa Tikas, "Thank you." She then kissed Dominic on the mouth for a long while.

Luz was astonished. Dominic's wife was inside the party just beyond the door. Once Papa Tikas had ushered the girl into the car, he turned away, but Dominic watched as it drove off. He then spat onto the ground, very near to their hopscotch squares. He looked blankly at his nephew and headed inside. Luz peered at David, whose face twitched.

"She's pretty, huh?" said Lizette, who had stood from the ground.

"Who?" David said, as if oblivious.

"That girl. Your uncle's new girlfriend."

"What're you talking about, Lizette?"

Lizette smiled roguishly and made eyes at David. Luz kept quiet, tucking away the image of the girl being shoved into the car.

"I'm going back inside, girls. Clean up your mess when you're done."

When the cousins were alone again, Lizette gracefully threw the shooter and went through the squares, switching turns with Luz.

They were both careful not to scuff their booties, as each had been warned they'd be in big trouble if they harmed their church clothes. As they hopped and skipped in and out of the archway lights, Luz imagined she was jumping between times. She saw herself as a little girl in the Lost Territory with her mother and father walking through snow fields, carrying fresh laundry to the company cabin. Then she saw herself in Hornet Moon with Maria Josie, beside the window to her new city, those few photographs of her parents scattered about the floor, the only remnants of them she had left. She saw herself eating Cream of Wheat for breakfast with Diego in the white-walled kitchen. They were listening to the radio, the summertime heat blowing in from the windows, the mountains far away behind the screen.

After some time, Luz and Lizette had grown bored of their "baby game," as Lizette started calling it. She sighed and took a seat on the sidewalk. "That was wrong of Papa Tikas's brother, by the way. My papa would never do that to my mama. He loves her a lot. He's always kissing on her."

Luz nodded. She said she could see that.

"I just want you to know, when we grow up and find our true loves, they better treat us good. Otherwise people fight and hurt each other. Men especially. Like our neighbors in the back. They're always screaming—their papa takes the belt to everybody, even his wife."

Luz felt scared. She said, "What if we don't want to find true loves? Can't we just be by ourselves?"

"I never seen nothing about that. Just nuns." Lizette made a sour face. "But you know what? Even they have each other and God."

"Well, we have each other, too," said Luz, knowingly. "And you have your mama and papa and all your brothers."

Lizette looked off into the archway, as if considering something of great magnitude. She looked and looked, and when she rotated her eyes to Luz, she said, "Yeah, that's true."

"Let's go back inside now," said Luz. "I'm tired of this Magic Arch."

THIRTY-FIVE

Woman of Light

Denver, 1934

In the morning, Luz dressed herself in her gray work dress and sat on her bed. She hadn't slept, and Maria Josie snored softly on the other side of the hanging sheet. The apartment smelled of day-old perfume and alcohol rising from human pores. She listened to the beginning notes of songbirds. Luz pulled her bruised knees to her chest, held herself with both arms. She was sore, her mouth, her breasts, between her thighs. As soon as she woke up, she had placed flowers from the wedding at her altar and lit a candle, not really knowing why. She watched it snuff out—a single line of smoke rising from the wick.

Luz's eyes felt tender as the window glowed with sunrise. She turned her face into the light, dimly bathing her skin. The rosary from Simodecea was draped over her left wrist. She thought of saying a Hail Mary, but as she heard Maria Josie stirring awake on the other side of the room, she decided to get out of the house. Luz stood, quietly disappearing from the bed. She headed for work.

She took the long way through the city. Steam billowed between office buildings and tenements, churches and mills. The air was crisp, pleasant. But nothing could move her thoughts away from herself. Ashamed. Luz was shamed. She felt it all night long. The longer she walked, the more this feeling burrowed into her mind. But wasn't this moment in her life supposed to be joyous? Wasn't it supposed to be about love? With every step, she grew angrier at her body, at her emotions, at her inability to be loved by David, or to let herself be loved by Avel. Did this mean David would be with her, marry her like Avel had wanted to? But Luz didn't even want that for herself. She laughed a clipped laugh. *Stupid,* she thought. *I'm being stupid.* Luz wondered about Avel then, knowing full well that she'd never see him again. She could feel his leaving in the tepid breeze, the way river water slushes over lumped rocks, moving only forward not back. She lifted her face to the sky, felt her naked throat, her skin where Avel's ring had once dangled around her neck. She was suddenly very afraid. She knew it could have happened to her, a pregnancy, and with every certainty she'd ever know, Luz did not want that with anyone right now, and with David, not at all.

She cried a little then, wiping her eyes as she turned onto Seventeenth Street, the banks and other office buildings optimistic in red stone. She didn't want to go to work. She didn't want to see David at all. But she had to, and as she walked, Luz imagined herself disappearing, her body lapsing into invisibility, one limb at a time. The sky was layered in morning brilliance rising from the prairie and lapping against the Rocky Mountains. The entire city, Luz's whole world, seemed to awaken as one.

When she arrived on the office's block, a searing smell clung to the air. A crowd had gathered, fifty or more men and women of all ages from the different neighborhoods. They held signs with Es-

tevan's name, they carried flags with the words LIBERTY and JUS-
TICE, an old woman prayed the rosary on her knees. There was a
truck parked nearby and two men stood on the bed, shouting into
white megaphones with the name of a radio station printed on the
side. Luz stood mesmerized, listening to their chanting. *We won't
be intimidated. We won't give up.*

She stepped deeper into the crowd, wading through the thicket
of shoulders. There was the biting stench of charred metal. The
sounds of crackling wood. Luz cleared the grouping, the sight
jolting her heart.

The law office, burned.

Blackened ceiling beams. Light fixtures among the havoc,
pieces of glass, ribs of a steel radiator. A brass drawer handle, the
hollow shell of a teakettle. The office remnants had melted and
molded into one another, silvery and dark. In some ways, the piles
looked sodden, as if joining the dirt. The buildings on either side
and above the law office were miraculously still standing. But everything she and David had worked for was in ashes. Luz stood
there dazed until someone pushed into her. At that moment she
caught sight of something on the ground, a red handkerchief from
the remains. She placed it in her pocket.

And where's that silver-spoon attorney? someone shouted from
the crowd, and soon they were chanting, demanding that David
explain what would come next.

Luz turned, scanning the dozens of sorrowful faces. She spotted David standing away from the protesters. He was speaking to
police officers, who vacantly looked past him. David had taken off
his jacket. In his shirtsleeves, he argued with the cops. One of
them laughed. Luz wondered if she should rush to David's side,
ask how she could help. But as she watched him walk the line of
his burned office, running his hands through ash, she realized that

she didn't want to be seen by David anymore. In fact, she hoped he'd never see her again. Luz slowly backed away then, covering herself in the shadows of people.

From behind her, someone shouted to look to the truck, and through waves of protest signs, Luz glimpsed a woman climbing onto the pickup, her black hair unraveling down her shoulders. She took the megaphone with a terrified shyness. She clutched a piece of paper in her hands.

Since my brother's life was so viciously taken, Mama does nothing but sleep. Our father is gone and has been for many years—killed in a mining explosion where they only recovered his left hand, the simple wedding ring intact.

Celia, Estevan's sister. Luz listened and watched as she read her own words in her own voice. First in Spanish and then in English. The crowd moved with each syllable, cries of anguish. *A lamp unto my feet,* a woman yelled behind Luz. *A light unto my path.*

This could be your family, Celia shouted in the megaphone. *Your bother, your son, your father. This could be your loss. But it's not. It's mine, and you might think you're lucky, but for every lucky person, unluckiness arrives. Our existence shouldn't depend on luck. It should depend on justice, what is good, what is right.*

As Celia finished speaking and stepped down from the truck, her face and hair caught the sun in such a way that she appeared electric. The bolt was profuse and spread around her, an aura of light. Luz followed that glimmering line until she saw the light pulsating throughout the people, in and out of their lungs as they breathed, anchoring them to the earth and flaring into the sky. Luz peered at her own palms. She marveled at the way she shined. It was as if she were dipped in light, humming like the stars. At that, she smiled some and crossed the street, walking in the direction of her family.

—

The Fox Street home was lively with cleanup. Teresita was in the front yard picking cigarette butts from the bushes, tossing them into a rusty bucket. Her boys were scattered about the stoop, cleaning the concrete with vinegar and rags. They didn't acknowledge Luz's arrival, keeping to their tasks, their eyes occupied with work.

The house still smelled of party foods, though the scent of lemon floor cleaner lingered. Parts of the stairs were still wet from mopping. Through the small window at the turn in the steps, Eduardo was visible in the backyard, sitting alone, his hat in his lap, his face calm and still. Luz wondered if he had taken a break from tearing down the cedar arch, but the longer she looked at him, the more she wondered if he was all right. He seemed out of sorts, holding his hands to his mouth, running his fingers through his hair. *Of course,* Luz thought as she continued upstairs. His only daughter, the person who hung his moon and stars, was leaving their house, and probably forever.

When Luz opened her cousin's bedroom door, Lizette was seated on the wooden floor before a travel trunk with brass buckles and leather straps. She was glowing in a sunbeam, her movements slow as she folded a yellow dress, neatly tucking the sleeves and wrapping it in tissue paper. She spoke without looking at Luz. "Nice of you to show up."

Luz stepped inside the bedroom. She closed the door. "Wouldn't miss it for the world. What're you bringing with you?"

Lizette pointed to the bed. It was piled with dresses and cowboy boots, her new-used fur coat, her red party dress, piles of books. Beside it all was her wedding dress hanging from a hook on the wall. "I'm trying to fit everything, but the house has no closets."

"That won't do. Make the living room your closet then."

She laughed. "You're right," Lizette said, her voice lower than usual. "I didn't expect this."

"Expect what?"

"I thought today would feel different. But I'm still just me. I mean, now I'm going to have my own life, my own little family someday. I thought it would take longer. When I was a little girl, it seemed so far away. Everything seemed so far away. And now we're here, and that's all behind us."

Luz thought on this. She said, "Sometimes when I'm reading tea leaves or daydreaming, I see things so clearly, from anywhere in time. It's like we aren't far away from anything at all."

Lizette looked up. Her eyes were puffy, her skin smooth.

"I think everything that's ever happened or going to happen to us and the people we love is around," said Luz. "All we have to do is reach for it."

Lizette laughed and got up from the floor. She pretended to reach for Luz.

I'm right here, Luz thought. *I'll always be right here.*

"Why were you crying last night?" Lizette asked. "Tell me what happened."

Luz dropped her gaze. She nodded a little at first, and then with certainty she said, "Okay."

Luz went to Maria Josie later. She was at the mirror factory with a flaming torch at her station. When Luz stepped through the garage door, Maria Josie removed her goggles, stopped her work, and quieted her torch. She waved for Luz to come near. Luz rushed across the factory floor. She was crying by the time she held her auntie, her large form encompassing her niece in warmth.

It felt like hugging Diego, Lizette, her mother, and her father—anyone she'd ever loved was present in that embrace, and Luz cried, telling her auntie that something had happened to her, something that made her feel very bad about herself, about everything.

"What's wrong?" Maria Josie asked, running her fingers through Luz's hair. "Tell me, what has happened?"

And through the crackling of her voice, Luz pushed closer and told her auntie about it all, but first she began with an apology. She had been right—Luz had no idea what Maria Josie had been through to protect her family.

Luz was only beginning to understand how they had gotten to this part in their story.

HERO SNAKE STRIKES AGAIN, STOPS BANK BANDITS

Denver, Colo., July 23, 1934. Two men at noon entered the South Broadway Daniels Bank and with revolvers ordered Cashier Jones to hand over $2,000 cash. The bandits were halted when a female rattlesnake emerged from the vault, striking one of the bandits and startling the other into paralysis. The snake slithered toward the business part of the city. There is no clew to the snake.

THIRTY-SIX

Diego's Return

When Diego received Luz's letter demanding that he come home, he was living in a migrant camp outside of Provo, Utah. He had walked in the morning to the post office, a triangular slant building on the edge of a dirt road. The mountains in Provo were nestled against the city, and after reading Luz's letter, Diego gazed upward at the massive, jutting mounds as if they, too, spoke to him. The answer was clear.

He gathered the few possessions he had collected on his travels, mostly religious emblems, little cards with Our Lady of Guadalupe, San Miguel, vials of holy water. He packed his new snake. By now not so new. With Sirena in a wicker basket, and everything Diego owned slung over his shoulder in the leather satchel, he set out for Denver just before the morning shift. There were no goodbyes. In the fields, every hello possessed within itself a farewell. People were as transient as the crops, picked and packaged, shipped afar, feeding the mouths of families Diego would never see.

He set out walking until a family of farmers picked him up from the side of a county road and offered him a lift to the town of Vernal. He stayed one night and met a young Mexicana widow in a saloon called Athens. Her name was Miranda. She had a strong nose and a missing tooth, making her smile seem mysterious, ethereal. He stayed with her for two nights. They made love outside her wooden cabin on grass shining with moonlight. After he kissed her goodbye on the second morning, Miranda rolled over in bed and unlaced the front of her cotton nightdress. Diego held her left breast with cold hands, and Miranda winced with a delicate grin.

Over the next few days, Diego walked. The landscape shifted from the lush greens of valleyed farmland into a rising mountain terrain. He drank from streams, leaning over the rushing coolness, cupping his hands into snowmelt. At least once a day, Diego removed Sirena from her basket and allowed the snake to slither over rocks or dirt, anything to keep her outercoat healthy, breathing in the land. Diego spent much of the time on his walk thinking of nothing, his mind a calmness saturated with the views of jagged red stone, ancient and bruised.

Shortly after he crossed the state line into Colorado, a farm truck filled with chickens slowed to a stop. The driver was an old woman, Anglo with silver hair and tiny blue eyes. "In back," she said. Diego took off his hat, saluting her with appreciation. He rode with the chickens for half a day, feathers fluttering across his vision, smearing sections of white across the land. They stopped for a little while in a mining town called Somerset, where the old woman unloaded half her chickens, sold for a bag of shearling and several crates of large tomatoes. They had a lunch of those tomatoes on stale bread high on a cemetery hillside, surrounded by emptied coal mines. Diego walked the graves, noting surnames from all over the world, until he came upon a man named Benny Dumont, same name and birth year as his father. The man had died three years earlier, and from the looks of other gravestones with that exact death date, it seemed to be some kind of explosion. Diego stood silently as he imagined his father trapped underground, swallowed by rock and flames. *Guess it wasn't better out there without us, was it?* When the old woman called out for Diego to return to the truck, she motioned for him to sit up front. They drove in silence as Diego quietly cried.

They soon said goodbye in Glenwood Springs, a large redbrick town with healing baths. Diego camped for a night on the banks of a canyon river and cleaned himself in the morning in the rushing waters, but the cold ached his body to the core. He then walked to the center of town and found himself at the public pools with a front entrance like a grand hotel. The clerk, an Anglo girl with strawberry hair, smiled at Diego but then nonchalantly shrugged and pointed to the sign NO MEXICANS, BLACKS, OR GOOKS. "Company policy," the girl said. Later, that night, he met her outside the Baptist church on Main, where they made love quickly in the shadow of fragrant alleyway pines.

By the time he reached Georgetown, Diego needed to earn some money. He stopped outside a miners' saloon with Sirena. They performed several tricks, nothing too complicated, Sirena rising to the sounds of his voice, head nodding, tongue flicking. Miners soon tossed coins into the open basket. The day shift in the coal shafts had just ended, and now the crowds widened. Diego felt uneasy but kept performing—money was money. But it was only a matter of time before one of the miners pushed forward from the depths of the crowd. His face was smeared in soot, a narrow jaw. He spoke with a kind of European accent as he called Diego the devil, first spitting on him and then gathering phlegm from his throat and launching it across Sirena. Diego lost his temper, lunged forward, and swung at the man. In Georgetown, he spent the night in jail, a brick cell with a barred window, a view of the stars.

He arrived in Denver by train through the city's western entrance. It was dark morning, a glowing violet line pushing over the plains. Diego's eyes were burning with coal soot as he hopped from the lumber train, landing in the rail yard with a gritty crash. He stood, dusted himself off, and heard a man's voice yelling for him to stop. Diego ran from the yard cops, snagging his leg on a switcher and drawing blood before he found himself crawling under a chain-link fence leading into the Westside. He first ran and then walked swiftly over red sidewalks. Near an alley on the edge of downtown, Diego heard the grunt and tug of a small animal from a dilapidated bush. Jorge, Blind Dog, his tongue flashing from his pink lip. Diego laughed. "I don't got nothing for you," he said, and Jorge momentarily growled before yawning and coughing as he hobbled away.

By now, it was blue dawn.

When Diego first saw downtown, the factories, the brick businesses, the South Platte River and Cherry Creek, he felt as if he were embracing an old friend. "Look at you," he said, and pulled Sirena from her basket to see. They walked, starting from the low numbered streets and moving toward Hornet Moon. Diego cut across Seventeenth Street and noticed a black cavity, a burned-out hole, where the saddlemaker and several other businesses once were. There was a newspaperman behind Diego, readying a stack of papers to sell for the day. Diego turned to the man. He asked what had happened.

"You don't know?" he said, shaking his head. "They burned that young attorney's business to the ground."

"Which lawyer?"

The man said, "Dave Tikas. Too bad, they say he was gonna help a lot of us. Now, it's all gone, and his daddy's place, too, started some damn war."

Diego asked more questions, but the man waved him on and told him that if he wanted to know so much, he ought to buy a newspaper. Diego obliged. With the paper in hand, he set out for home.

Maria Josie and a woman Diego had never met before were at the kitchen table. When he saw his auntie, she stood in astonishment. They didn't speak for several moments, only embraced. Maria Josie explained that Ethel was her friend, and Diego shook the woman's hand. "Where's Luz?" he asked, and Maria Josie pointed down the hall. "In bed."

Diego first knocked and then opened the door, spotting Luz with her face turned to the wall. He stepped through the room, its uneasiness a bleach-like sadness. Across Luz's altar were photos— Mama, their father, and himself.

"Luz," Diego said gently, and, when she didn't turn around, he said, "Little Light."

Luz turned her body in bed, and her eyes fell upon her brother as if she were seeing a spirit. She hobbled upward on her elbows. She looked into his eyes. "Are you real?"

Diego laughed. He kneeled at her bedside. He held his sister's face with both hands. "Yeah, I'm real."

Luz cried into his arms until parts of his white shirt were see-through with tears.

———

In time, Luz told Diego some of what had happened while he was gone. She spoke of the law office, the corruption in the city, Estevan's murder, her times with Lizette and Alfonso. The more she spoke, the more Diego said he felt guilt, helplessness. He told his sister that it was his fault.

"No," said Luz. "It's the choices we make."

She never told Diego about Avel and the missing office keys, or how not too long after David's law office burned, someone else torched Papa Tikas's grocery store to the ground. David left Denver after that. But she did tell Diego what she had seen. Her visions, she explained, had grown and kept growing. "I can see things about our people. I know our stories."

The family of four now—Diego, Luz, Maria Josie, and Ethel—drove the next morning to Saint Agnes Home for Children. Just as Luz had described, the lawn rolled out in lush greenery behind high stone walls. Along the driveway to the front entrance, speckled birds landed on the grass, pecking and prying insects from the lawn. The clouds beyond the home were low and off-white. The others waited in Ethel's car as Diego stepped out and approached the building.

He returned after a long while. The birds across the grass lifted into flight as he stepped over the stone steps, carrying a white bundle in his arms. She was a baby girl, and her eyes were a dazzling green while her skin and hair were lavish and brown. Diego kissed his daughter and handed the baby to Luz in the back seat.

"We'll call her Lucille," he said to his sister. "Now, go on, tell her our stories."

Luz nodded and began to think of what she would tell her niece. She would start, she decided, with a woman she had seen in her dreams, a sleepy prophet.

ACKNOWLEDGMENTS

A thank-you is in order for those who helped me with the process of writing this book over the last decade.

To my mother, Renee Fajardo, my grandfather John Fajardo, my godmother Joanna Lucero, and to my elders in the spirit world who protected and taught me with their stories and whose reverberations will live on until the end of time. To my father, Glen Anstine, for being one of my first readers and biggest supporters. To Julia Masnik, who helped birth the earliest chapters and assisted me in finding the story of Luz. To Nicole Counts for seeing my characters for who they are and guiding with her light. To my six siblings and their children who keep the stories alive. To my publisher, One World, for believing in this book. To my team: Rachel Rokicki, Andrea Pura, Oma Beharry, and Carla Bruce-Eddings, and, of course, to Chris Jackson.

Thank you to the historians, archivists, and educators across the Southwest who fielded my research questions: To my long-lost cousin whom I've since found, Dr. Estevan Rael-Gálvez. To the brilliant and kind Dr. Karen Roybal of Colorado College. To Charlene Garcia Simms at the Pueblo County Library. To Trent Segura for countless resources and conversations. To my brother Tim for his legal expertise. To Connor Novotny for his overwhelming support. To the wise Melinna Bobadilla. To Dr. Yvette DeChavez who spoke truths beside the fire. To Brian Trembath of the Denver Public Library's Western History Collection. To Patricia Sigala who hosted me in New Mexico as a teenager. To Phil Goodstein for expanding, keeping, and sharing knowledge of Denver's past. To Terri Gentry of the Black American West Museum. To Lois Harvey of West Side Books for providing me research materials for over half my life. To Mat Johnson, whose teaching has given me so much. To the late Daniel Menaker. To Joy Williams for her mentorship and light. To Sandra Cisneros, whose work showed me how to dream. To Julia Alvarez for her madrina support. And to Ivelisse Rodriguez, who has always been there for me.

Thank you to the institutions that provided me with space and support to complete this novel. To M12 Studio for concentrated time in Antonito, Colorado. To Yaddo, MacDowell, History Colorado, and the American Academy of Arts and Letters.

And to all descendants of the Manito diaspora.

WOMAN
OF
LIGHT

A Novel

Kali Fajardo-Anstine

Random
House
Book Club

Because
Stories Are
Better Shared ™

A BOOK CLUB GUIDE

Dear Reader,

I grew up in Denver, the Rocky Mountains to the west and the sunrise prairie to the east. My world was steeped in family, heritage, and a deep reverence for the storytelling of my ancestors who had migrated from Southern Colorado to Denver during the Great Depression.

There was my glamorous Auntie Lucy, gifted with the sight; a snake-charming great-uncle; and my great-grandparents, Alfonso, from the Philippines, and Grandma Esther, from southern Colorado, who taught me her remedios in her white-walled kitchen.

I heard tales of their labor in the sugar beet fields, of the gowns they handmade for the dance halls, and more sinister stories, too. My Auntie Lucy spoke of the Ku Klux Klan's massive influence in Denver, and how, as a small girl, she would lie against the floorboards of her tenement, hiding from their sight for her safety.

I've always known my heritage to be a nuanced blending of Pueblo Native American, Mexican, Filipino, and European ancestors who came together in what is now known as Colorado. For many years, I thought my family story was a rare occurrence in an American society that often demands a people choose one identity, ostensibly erasing so much of our history.

Years ago, while I was writing the first drafts of *Woman of Light*, I visited my great-grandparents' grave on the outskirts of Denver. The cemetery's rows were covered in snow, and crisp air kicked down from the mountains against my back. "Grandma Esther," I said, "I am writing a book about us, and I hope to make you proud."

I've always known it would be part of my life's work to tell the story of my ancestors, a book that would illuminate the historical tragedies and triumphs of my community. I wanted to subvert the Western genre and to provide a space for Indigenous, Latinx, and multicultural characters based on my own ancestors to thrive in literature.

I am so excited for you to meet Luz, Diego, Maria Josie, and Lizette, and I hope you feel transported through space and time to the 1930s and beyond. I wrote these characters, and their stories, with immense love.

Warmly,

Kali Fajardo-Anstine

DISCUSSION QUESTIONS

1. Discuss the significance of the novel's title, *Woman of Light*. What role does light play in the book?

2. Which character was your favorite, and why?

3. How does the novel address the importance of storytelling? How do you think we inherit the stories of our ancestors, and what power do these stories they hold over us? If you are comfortable with it, share a story about one of your ancestors, and discuss the ways it influenced your life.

4. Kali Fajardo-Anstine writes, "Sometimes men were like that, treating a girl's voice as if it had slipped from her mouth and fallen directly into a pit" (page 33). How does the author give the women of this novel their voices?

5. Discuss the novel's visual imagery, from the landscape to the characters' clothing. How does the author bring the setting to life?

6. How is *Woman of Light* a new narrative of the American West? How does it compare to older, more textbook literature in this canon?

7. Fajardo-Anstine writes of Pidre, "He couldn't help but think that Anglos were perhaps the most dangerous storytellers of all—for they believed only their own words, and they allowed their stories to trample the truths of nearly every other man on Earth" (page 73). How does *Woman of Light* recenter Indigenous Chicano storytelling? Why do you think that's important? Did reading this novel make you want to seek out other voices that have been sidelined throughout history—and literary history? Explain.

8. There are fantastic elements to the novel, such as the clairvoyant tea-leaf reader. Why do you think the author decided to include these elements, and how did they enhance the story?

9. "'School doesn't make you smart, Luz,'" Ethel tells her. "'It's just a type of training. Real intelligence—that comes from our grit, our ability to read the world around us'" (page 230). Do you agree? Why or why not?

10. The novel's timeline shifts as Luz has visions about her ancestors, and as Fajardo-Anstine reveals more to the reader about the past. How did these shifts affect your reading experience? What does *Woman of Light* have to say about the passing of time, and how things do and do not change?

11. "Luz felt partly made of mountains," Fajardo-Anstine writes, "as if the land was family" (page 149). Discuss this quotation, and the role that land—and ownership—play in the novel. Consider things like the names of towns, and both official and unofficial claims of ownership.

12. What messages do you think Fajardo-Anstine was sending about the themes of family, legacy, and land? How did you feel when you finished the book?

REFERENCE GUIDE

C heck out the links below to learn more about the historical events that inspired *Woman of Light*.

1. America's forgotten history of Mexican-American "repatriation": npr.org/2015/09/10/439114563 /americas-forgotten-history-of-mexican-american -repatriation

2. The San Luis Valley, Spanish and Indigenous influence on Colorado: fs.usda.gov/main/riogrande/learning/history -culture

3. The Treaty of Guadalupe Hidalgo: cpr.org/2018/06/13 /treaty-of-guadalupe-hidalgo-has-lasting-effects-on -southern-colorado/

4. The rise of the Ku Klux Klan in Denver: denverpost
   .com/2021/06/06/denver-kkk-history/

5. The Colorado lynching of Preston John Porter, Jr.: eji.org
   /news/historical-marker-in-denver-memorializes-racial
   -terror-lynching-of-15-year-old-boy/

6. Redlining and Denver housing: history.denverlibrary.org
   /news/new-whg-redlining-maps-denver

7. The Maestas case and desegregation in Colorado schools,
   1914: nbcnews.com/news/latino/latino-history-buried
   -colorado-marks-forgotten-fight-school-equity-rcna21207

8. Dearfield, Colorado, an all-Black settlement founded in
   1910: nbcnews.com/news/nbcblk/inside-dearfield
   -colorado-ghost-town-was-once-bustling-all-black
   -n975716

9. Chicanx history and Denver's Westside: chicanomurals
   ofcolorado.com/mural-maps

10. The Colorado radium boom: montrosecounty.granicus.com
    /DocumentViewer.php?file=montrosecounty_dcf9b210d5d6
    dea4285065174e9affa6.pdf

11. The Sand Creek massacre: smithsonianmag.com/history
    /horrific-sand-creek-massacre-will-be-forgotten-no
    -more-180953403/

12. The Colorado Coalfield War: guides.loc.gov/chronicling
    -america-colorado-coalfield-war

13. The Ludlow Massacre: newyorker.com/magazine/2009
    /01/19/there-was-blood

PHOTO: © ESTEVAN RUIZ

KALI FAJARDO-ANSTINE is the nationally bestselling author of the novel *Woman of Light* and the story collection *Sabrina & Corina*, a finalist for the National Book Award and winner of an American Book Award. She is the 2021 recipient of the Addison M. Metcalf Award from the American Academy of Arts and Letters and is the 2022–2024 Endowed Chair in Creative Writing at Texas State University. She is from Denver, Colorado.

kalifajardoanstine.com
Instagram: @kalimaja

To inquire about booking Kali Fajardo-Anstine for a speaking engagement, please contact the Penguin Random House Speakers Bureau at speakers@penguinrandomhouse.com.